PLANTED
WITH
HOPE

Tricia Goyer AND Sherry Gore

HARVEST HOUSE PUBLISHERS
EUGENE, OREGON

All Scripture quotations are taken from the King James Version of the Bible.

Cover by Garborg Design Works

Cover photos © neirfy, Loraliu, llaszlo, SCPhotog, Elysium Multimedia / Bigstock

Published in association with Books & Such Management, 52 Mission Circle, Suite 122, PMB 170, Santa Rosa, CA 95409-5370, www.booksandsuch.com

Published in association with the Steve Laube Agency, LLC, 5025 N. Central Ave., #635, Phoenix, Arizona, 85012.

This is a work of fiction. Names, characters, places, and incidents are products of the authors' imagination or are used fictitiously. Any resemblance to actual persons, living or dead, is entirely coincidental.

PLANTED WITH HOPE
Copyright © 2016 Tricia Goyer and Sherry Gore
Published by Harvest House Publishers
Eugene, Oregon 97402
www.harvesthousepublishers.com

Library of Congress Cataloging-in-Publication Data
    Names: Goyer, Tricia, author. | Gore, Sherry, 1965- author.
    Title: Planted with hope / Tricia Goyer and Sherry Gore.
    Description: Eugene, Oregon : Harvest House Publishers, [2016]
        Series: Pinecraft Pie Shop ; 2
    Identifiers: LCCN 2015038965 | ISBN 9780736961318 (pbk.) | ISBN 9780736961325 (eBook)
    Subjects: | GSAFD: Love stories. | Christian fiction.
    Classification: LCC PS3607.O94 P58 2016 | DDC 813/.6—dc23 LC record available at
    http://lccn.loc.gov/2015038965

Printed in the United States of America

16 17 18 19 20 21 22 23 24 / LB-CD / 10 9 8 7 6 5 4 3 2 1

Gardening is a way of showing that
you believe in tomorrow.

Amish Proverb

Verily, verily, I say unto you, Except a corn of
wheat fall into the ground and die, it abideth
alone: but if it die, it bringeth forth much fruit.

John 12:24

I needed the quiet so He drew me aside,
Into the shadows where we could confide
Away from the bustle where all the day long
I hurried and worried when active and strong.
I needed the quiet though at first I rebelled,
But gently, so gently, my cross He upheld,
And whispered so sweetly of spiritual things.
Though weakened in body, my spirit took wings
To heights never dreamed of when active and gay.
He loved me so greatly He drew me away.
I needed the quiet. No prison my bed,
But a beautiful valley of blessings instead—
A place to grow richer in Jesus to hide.
I needed the quiet so He drew me aside.

Alice Hansche Mortenson

Prologue

Emma Sutter lifted the ice cream cone to her lips, took another lick, and licked her fingers too. It was chocolate, her favorite, and she wondered if *Aenti* Ruth Ann would let her have it every day. Sometimes things like that happened, mostly because she'd lost her momma. Even though it had been two years, Emma still got two scoops of ice cream when most other kids just got one. Two scoops was a lot for her only being eight years old, and sometimes her stomach hurt when she was through, but she didn't want to tell *Aenti* Ruth Ann that.

Dat said that people wanted her to feel happy again, and sometimes she was. Sometimes ice cream did help…just not deep down where it hurt the most. Not in the hole inside that she was saving for a mother.

Emma took another lick and then glanced up at *Aenti* Ruth Ann to see if she noticed the drips trailing down her fingers. Thankfully, her aunt was too busy chatting with her friend near the front door of the pie shop. Too busy to notice how sticky Emma had become.

The sun was warm overhead—much hotter than it had been in Kentucky. She'd asked for ice cream instead of pie. She'd promised to eat it all, but now it was melting faster than she could lick.

Footsteps sounded behind her, and Emma turned. A pretty woman approached, tall and thin, with red hair. Not a bright orange-red, but a light red that looked almost golden in the sun. The woman had a nice smile too. She paused, pulled a wipe from a plastic package, and handed it to Emma. "I thought you could use this."

"*Danke*." Emma nodded and then quickly wiped her hand, glancing at her aunt from the corner of her eye. When she finished wiping, the woman took it back, holding it by the corner. It hung limply in her hand.

She handed Emma another clean wipe and pointed to her lips, making a wiping motion. "I always get two scoops at Big Olaf's too, but I've learned to get them in a cup so I don't end up with drippy hands and an ice cream mustache." The woman laughed, and her eyes twinkled. "This Florida sun is twice as warm as the sun up north, don't you think?"

Emma wiped her mouth, and then she handed the wipe back. "*Ja*. Hotter than the hot side of a wood burning stove." The woman smiled. Then, looking around, Emma saw the large pots of flowers near the front door of Me, Myself, and Pie. "Are you the gardener? What is your name?"

The woman tucked a strand of hair that had slipped from her *kapp* behind her ear.

"My name is Hope, and I guess you can call me a gardener, but I've personally given up my title." Hope sighed, placed a hand on her hip, and looked at Emma. Hope didn't have the sympathy in her eyes that Emma usually saw when people looked at her, and she liked that.

Emma took three quick licks. "Did you used to be a gardener?"

"*Ja*, I guess you can say that."

"Do you wish you could be a gardener again?"

"I do. Very much." Hope cocked an eyebrow. "You sure ask a lot of questions."

Emma took another lick of her ice cream, but it was impossible to keep up. "If I had a garden I'd let you come and pull *my* weeds."

Laughter spilled from the woman's mouth, and Emma smiled. Seeing smiles was better than seeing tears.

"You would, would you?" Hope shook her head. "I'm not sure if I'd pull someone else's weeds—it wouldn't be fair to them. That's part of the joy of gardening—seeing your hard work pay off in your own space. Standing back and noticing that what you did really mattered."

Emma nodded, even though she didn't understand what Hope was talking about. "My dat likes to work in the garden too. My *mem* used to…" Emma let her voice trail off, remembering the she was in Pinecraft now. Remembering that people didn't know her mother here. Remembering that she didn't want to tell Hope what had happened to her mem, otherwise she'd look at her with sadness too.

The woman moved a few steps closer to the large pot of flowers. Two large, empty buckets sat there. Hope turned them over. She sat on one, and then she patted the other, motioning for Emma to join her. Emma looked to her aunt, took a few steps, and then did just that.

Hope reached into the pot and used two fingers to pull a small weed. "What does your dat like to plant?"

"Oh, just 'bout everything. Except beets. Says he hasn't much use for those."

The woman wrinkled her nose, and then she leaned close. "Don't tell anyone, but I tend to agree." She shrugged. "I'd still plant beets, though, if I had a garden again. It wouldn't seem right if I didn't. What good is a garden without beets, carrots, potatoes, corn, cabbage…" Hope's voice trailed off. She swallowed hard, as if something was stuck in there. Hope reached down and pulled up another weed, harder this time.

Emma leaned forward and looked more closely at Hope's face. The twinkle in her eyes was gone. Hope still smiled, but her eyes weren't smiling. It reminded Emma of all those days when Dat took her fishing or for a pony ride back on their farm. Even though he smiled she could tell he was really thinking about *Mem*. He still got that sad look, but not as much. And Emma wondered if this woman had lost someone too. She also decided she liked this woman. Liked her very much. Maybe this woman could be Dat's friend since they had both lost someone.

"What is your last name?"

"Miller." The woman turned to her, meeting her gaze. "Hope Miller."

"I'm Emma. Emma Sutter."

"And where do you live, Emma Sutter?"

Emma shrugged. "Here in Pinecraft now. My dat's—"

"Emma, time to get going." Her aunt's voice interrupted. "I promised Hannah I'd make her lunch, and I'm afraid I've been chatting far too long." *Aenti* Ruth Ann approached. She smiled at Emma, then tilted her head and looked at Hope. She also leaned forward a little, as if taking a closer look.

"Are you one of the Miller girls? One of the younger four?" *Aenti* Ruth Ann asked, obviously forgetting she'd just told Emma they had to leave.

"*Ja*, I'm Hope, the second oldest. My older sister Lovina opened the pie shop here." Hope pointed. "And my younger sisters are Joy, Faith, and Grace. Grace is one of the new scribes in Pinecraft. Maybe—"

Aenti Ruth Ann cut off Hope's words. "And Lovina will be married soon from what I hear?"

Hope pressed her lips together, and her eyes darted from the front door of the pie shop back to Emma's aunt. "Well, nothing's been published yet…"

Aenti Ruth Ann fiddled with her kapp string, twisting it around her finger. It was what Emma's aunt always did when she was thinking hard.

"And the rest of you are single?"

There was something in her aunt's eyes that Emma hadn't seen before. Interest? Curiosity? No, something different. It was the same look that her dat got when he was baiting his fishing hook. It was excitement over what he expected to come.

"Aenti Ruth Ann, Hope is a gardener. Hope likes ice cream too." Emma lifted her cone. Her fingers were once again covered with drips.

"My, you have a big mess there." *Aenti* Ruth Ann pointed at her cone. "Why don't we throw the rest of that cone away and wash up, and I'll share my pie after lunch?"

Emma nodded excitedly. Ice cream, pie, and a new friend all in the same day. A new friend Dat just had to meet. He needed someone to look at him, too, with eyes not filled with sadness.

Butter Pecan Ice Cream

2 envelopes Knox gelatin

½ cup cold water

4 cups whole milk

2 cups granulated sugar

2 tsp. vanilla extract

1 tsp. salt

3 cups heavy cream

1½ cups pecans, pieces or whole

1 cup butter

1 cup brown sugar

Soak gelatin in cold water. Heat milk till just before boiling. Remove from heat. Add gelatin, sugar, vanilla extract, and salt. Let cool. When cooled, stir in cream. Place in freezer.

In a saucepan, melt butter and heat nuts until crisp. Stir in brown sugar. Mix well. Add to ice cream once mixture has partially frozen.

Chapter One

When the outlook is not good, try the uplook.

AMISH PROVERB

〜

H ope, can you scoot down a bit more? Faith has yet to find a
place to sit," Mem called to her.

Hope Miller forced a smile and scooted farther down the picnic table's bench. Ten people were squeezed around the table
already, and even though a cool breeze ruffled her *kapp* strings,
the press of bodies nearly suffocated her.

She picked up her fork and attempted to scoop up another
bite of sausage, sauerkraut, and creamy potatoes.

She'd heard the murmurs around the park that it was Becky
Fisher's sauerkraut recipe. The older woman had passed away,
but thankfully her recipe continued. The food smelled good, but
Lovina pressed so closely against Hope that she had no room to
extend her elbow to get a scoop of food. Hope tried to adjust herself—lifting her arm a little—but it did no good. The people were
too tightly packed around her.

Take a breath. Take a breath. You're all right, she told herself.

The words did no good. The jumble of voices and press of bodies overwhelmed her. She put down the fork and placed her hand

13

to her chest. Beneath her hand her heartbeat pounded through the thin cotton fabric of her dress and apron. From the corner of her eye she glimpsed Mose Yoder eyeing their table as if preparing to ask to squeeze in. *Please no.*

Even though she'd just started on her meal, Hope pushed her plate away. She needed space. She needed quiet. The hundreds of voices of Plain people attending the New Year's fund-raising Supper at the Park swirled around her head. She didn't have a garden to escape to—not here in Pinecraft—but she did have the park. Pinecraft Park was packed with people near the pavilion, but beyond that the green grass and canopy of lush trees beckoned her.

Hope straightened in her seat. "Excuse me, Lovina. Can I get out?"

Lovina turned to her and her dark eyes widened, filling with questions. "Is everything all right? You're not coming down with something, are you?"

Hope forced her lips into a smile. "Me? *Ne.* I shouldn't have eaten that piece of pie so close to the meal."

Lovina cocked one eyebrow, and Hope knew her sister wasn't buying it. The taste-testing of Lovina's newest pie had been three hours ago, and Hope hadn't eaten more than a sliver.

"Really now. It's the pie that stole your appetite?"

"*Ne.*" Hope leaned close to Lovina's ear, and then she lowered her voice. "It's just that there are so many people. Everyone is talking at once. I just need some fresh air for a moment. I promise to be right back."

Lovina nodded, and she then whispered something in Noah Yoder's ear. The two had been inseparable ever since they'd worked together to remodel the old warehouse into a pie shop. Me, Myself, and Pie had been up and running nearly two months already, and it was doing better than anyone had expected.

Whatever Lovina said caused Noah to glance over and look at Hope with concern, but he didn't say a word. Instead, he slid off the end of the picnic table bench, making room for Lovina and Hope to stand.

"*Danke.*" Hope took a step back. "I'll be right back, I promise. I'm just going to stroll down to the creek."

Noah sidled up to Lovina, as close as they could be without touching. "Watch out for gators." He grinned.

Hope nodded. "I will. Don't worry now." And without hesitation she moved away from the table.

No one else seemed to notice her leaving. *Mem* was busy in conversation, talking to her friend Regina who was still in town for the season. As they talked, they also eyed a group of bachelors who'd just arrived last week—no doubt attempting to choose ones for the remainder of Mem's single daughters. Thankfully, Mem now approved of Noah Yoder. No, more than that, she acted as if he'd been her choice all along. But Mem still had four more daughters to worry about. She acted as if getting her daughters married was her only purpose in life.

Hope had heard Mem and Regina chatting over coffee this morning. They'd been talking about one of their neighbors, Hannah Wise. Not only had Hannah just been married eight months ago, but she was already expecting twins. As she spoke, Hope noted the longing in Mem's voice. After all, most of her friends were grandmothers many times over now.

Just as long as Mem and Regina didn't concern themselves with *her* love life next. With each passing day, Hope had a growing desire to leave Pinecraft, return up north, and find a job that could support her. Mostly, she just wanted to find a garden to tend.

Since it was only January, she still had four months to find such a garden. Even though the sun shone brightly in Pinecraft, most of Ohio and Indiana was still covered in snow. And hopefully by the time the ground thawed she'd know just where to go. Did God have a good place for her? She'd been thankful to be here for her family, especially during Dat's illness, but with each passing day Hope longed for a farm with squealing baby pigs, black-and-white dappled calves, and a large garden in need of a gardener.

With quickened steps, Hope moved away from the table, and instead she fixed her eyes on the creekside trees in the distance. Heavy, dark moss hung from the limbs, and she smiled, remembering something she'd overheard last week from a young boy new to Pinecraft. "Look Dat, even the trees have beards down here."

Maybe those weren't true beards, but Hope knew one bachelor who'd no doubt be growing one soon, just like all married Amish men. In the dark of the night, in the quiet of their bedroom, Lovina had shared that she and Noah were discussing wedding dates. They'd wait until after the busy winter season, when things at the pie shop slowed down, but it brought joy to Hope's heart that one of the sisters had found love.

Hope was also excited to hear that Hannah would be a mother of not only one, but two babies, but those things just added to the list of all the ways she fell short. She wanted all that, but she also wanted space—space Pinecraft couldn't offer her.

As Hope left the crowds behind, her heartbeat slowed to its normal pace, and a memory filled her mind. Just before she'd sat down with her plate, her youngest sister, Grace, had told Hope that she wanted to introduce her to someone—the new schoolteacher. A male schoolteacher by the name of Jonas Sutter. Hope had nodded, and then she'd quickly forgotten about it. Her guess was that Grace had been simply trying to pull her into the conversation—since she'd never met the man before. No one seemed to understand that Hope rather enjoyed listening without having to insert her opinion. She just hoped that Grace hadn't seen her leave and planned to track her down.

"Five minutes' peace, please." Her words escaped in a whisper. And then she quickly said louder than she should. "And if you try to follow, Grace, I can run faster than you!"

As if on cue, laughter filled the air behind her, and she paused and turned back. There wasn't an inch of space left in the steel pavilion, and even the volleyball bleachers were filled with teens sitting and eating with plates on their laps. Mostly there were families clustered together, enjoying the sun, the event, and just being together. Being part of a family like that was something she wanted…but as Mem had told her it was something she'd never find if she kept hiding away.

Hope clenched her fists at her side as she walked on. *What's wrong with me? Why do I always run? Hide?*

From the time she was a child she wanted to find a good man to love and become a wife and a mother. Yet even as she yearned for those things, she yearned for them from afar. As much as she longed for a family of her own, it was the noise and the busyness of her own family that pushed her from their midst. Being one of five girls, there was always movement, always noise, and always conversation in their home. As a child she'd run to the barn to watch the quiet cats or to the cool well house where she kept a few *lumba babba*, or rag babies, to tend to in the quiet.

But then, at the age of eight, she discovered the garden. Weeding the garden had become her chore that summer, and it was one she never gave back. The next year Dat had given her a plot of ground to call her own, and each year her plot had grown bigger. By age fourteen she'd taken on the complete garden as her own.

Not only did she enjoy the straight, neat rows and the peace and quiet, but she also soon came to appreciate the harvest and the satisfaction of a job well done.

As Hope continued on through Pinecraft Park, the aroma of sausage faded away and the musky scents of the grass, trees, moss, and brackish water filled its place. Hope still could hear voices behind her, but they were quieter now. Hope released the breath she'd been holding. At least out here she had the ability to think.

"Emma!"

From the edges of the gathering a tall man with a dark beard cupped his hands and called into the woods. He wore an Amish hat, and his voice called out as if trying to chase Emma down.

Hope smirked. "Good luck trying to find her."

There had to be no less than fifty Amish children in the park today. Each of the young girls wore similar dresses and *kapps*. It was like trying to find the right bobbing head in a sea of others just the same.

Hope scanned the area near her, just to make sure there was no little girl, and then she continued on. She walked parallel to the creek, taking in the shimmer of sunlight on the greenish-blue water.

It was then that Hope noticed something out of place—noticed *her*. Down at the bottom of the concrete boat ramp a small girl was climbing into a canoe. Hope gasped as it swayed with the movement of the water. The girl had somehow untied the rope and was swinging it above her as she fearlessly climbed in.

"No, no. Stop!" Hope rushed to the edge of the river's bank and peered down. "You'd better not do that. Those canoes aren't so sturdy, and look, there's a current. It could sweep you away."

The girl froze and turned. She shielded her eyes, trying to make out Hope's face. "I'm just looking," she said. "I'll get off."

Hope recognized the girl. It was the same child she'd talked to in front of the pie shop a few days ago. The girl couldn't be more than seven or eight. Emma, yes, that was her name.

"Emma, I heard your dat. He's calling for you."

Hearing that, Emma froze. Then her whole body seemed to move at once. With a jerky motion she turned, trying to scramble to dry ground before she was caught.

"Emma, wait!"

The girl scurried faster. The canoe rocked and swayed. Emma reached out, grasping for something to hold on to, but there was only air. She cried out and her eyes widened. She took another step toward the bank, but the movement caused the canoe to shift. Then, in one smooth motion, the canoe turned.

"Emma!" Hope's voice rose and then caught in her throat as the young girl slipped into the dark brackish water, kapp and all.

Becky Fisher's Sauerkraut

Cabbage
1 Tbsp salt

Shred cabbage and pack in quart jars, not very tight. Make a hole through the middle with a wooden spoon. Put one Tbsp of salt into each jar. Fill jars with boiling water and seal jars real tight. It will be ready to eat in 6 weeks. More salt may be added if desired. The cabbage is delicious served hot over mashed potatoes with cooked sausage.

Chapter Two

Trying times are times for trying.

AMISH PROVERB

ⴲ

Hope darted down the grassy bank toward the water. She rushed toward the canoe—toward the ripples where Emma had disappeared. The canoe righted itself and rocked gently, but there was no sign of the girl.

Hope half ran, half dove into the water. She reached out her arms, searching, grasping for the small body. The water rushed up to her waist, and she struggled to find her footing on the slimy bottom. Hope searched, and her hands found nothing. Then, to her right, she spotted the white of Emma's *kapp*.

She lunged for it, reaching down at the exact moment Emma's face emerged. The girl's eyes were wide and filled with fear. She gasped for air, choking. Hope grabbed Emma's arm first. Then, with all the strength she could muster, she grabbed under her armpits, hoisting her up.

Emma gagged and coughed, reaching for Hope. Wet arms stretched around her shoulders. Emma's hands found each other behind Hope's neck and intertwined. Her legs wrapped around Hope's waist. Hope cocked her face to the sky, trying to breathe.

But the tightness of the girl's hold and the fear that still coursed through her at the sight of Emma going into the water made it difficult to catch a breath. The girl clung to her, and again Hope struggled to keep her balance. *Dear Lord, help.*

Hope kicked off her flip-flops, using her toes to grasp for footing. Then, with as much balance as she could muster, Hope struggled back to shore.

Emma's vise grip tightened, and a small sob emerged.

"Shh, I've got you. I've got you." Hope's arms circled the girl's body as she slogged to the boat ramp. Relief flooded over her as her feet found the concrete. She released a breath, the salty taste of the creek on her lips. "See, we're okay. Almost to shore…"

Another small whimper emerged from Emma. Hope continued up the ramp, finally leaving the water behind.

The girl's weight pulled on Hope. Water poured off of them both. A trembling started in Hope's knees and moved up her legs, and she took a few more steps.

Feeling as if all the energy had just been drained from her, Hope turned and sank down on the concrete. Emma was soaked, and Hope was too except for her *kapp*. Somehow she'd managed to rescue the girl and keep her head above the water.

The girl's whimpering turned into a soft cry.

"It's okay, I've got you. I've got you."

Hope pulled the small girl tight to her chest, cradling her like a mother would comfort an infant. Emma's legs hung down and her soggy tennis shoes rested on the concrete. Emma's whole body trembled—more from fear than cold, Hope thought.

"It's okay, Emma. You're all right now. There is nothing to be upset about. You're going to be all right."

"I—I almost drowned." Emma's chin quivered. "I was just looking—"

"I know you didn't mean for that to happen, and now you know it's not safe. I'm sure you won't do it again."

Emma shook her head. "*Ne.*" Then she looked at Hope with large, brown eyes, appearing so frail and small. "I won't…"

"Emma!" A man's voice called again, and Hope jumped.

"Is that your dat?" Hope asked in a low whisper.

Emma nodded.

Then a woman's voice joined in. "Emma!" *Her mem?*

"Over her! She's over here!" Hope called, and then immediately regretted it. Her wet dress clung to her, and she pulled Emma closer, hoping to hide her form. How inappropriate to be seen like this, and by a married man. Thankfully, Emma snuggled in.

The man approached the boat dock and looked down. "Emma!" Relief flooded his voice, and he hurried to where they sat. "What happened?"

Instead of answering, Emma buried her face under Hope's chin and tightened her fingers around the back of her neck.

Hope swallowed hard, wishing the man would step back. Wishing he'd give them space. The shape of her legs was clear under her dress, and she'd never felt so exposed. Still, she had to explain.

"I was taking a walk, and I saw her." Hope pointed to the upturned canoe. "She was exploring."

"What on earth, Emma?" It was a woman's voice this time. "Whatever did you do that for? Don't you know how dangerous that is?" The older woman hurried toward them. It was the same woman who'd been at the pie shop. The woman scowled and stopped at Hope's bare feet. Emma's dat stepped back, as if almost afraid to hear about what had transpired. Or maybe because Hope's clothes clung to her.

"It's as much my fault as hers," Hope quickly explained. "Emma was on the canoe, and I startled her. I told her that you were looking for her, and I urged her to get off. My words frightened her and…well, she tried to hurry…" Hope couldn't look at the man, so she turned to the woman. "Don't be too upset."

"She fell in the water? All the way in?" The woman's tone was sharp. "Emma Sutter, don't you know there are sharks in there? Come here. We need to get you home. Need to get you cleaned up."

Emma still clung to Hope, and Hope wasn't sure what to do next. The girl had to go with her dat, but prying the girl off would leave her completely exposed.

"Thank you for saving her. I'll wait over the hill." The man backed away, refusing to meet Hope's gaze. "Emma, thank the lady and then come. We must get you home."

Emma whimpered and pressed her cheek against Hope's chest. Hope gave her a quick squeeze. "Go on now. Your dat is waiting."

The woman—her Aenti Ruth Ann, wasn't it?—cleared her throat. "Didn't your dat say to thank Hope?" Her voice was stern, and Hope had no doubt that young Emma would hear more from her aunt after she got home.

"Thank you, Hope." Emma pulled away. She struggled to stand, and Hope helped her to right herself.

As Hope stood, she looked down at herself and heat rose to her cheeks. She was thankful that the boat ramp sloped downward so no one could see her from the park.

She was a dripping mess. Her dress and apron clung to her. She crossed her arms over her chest, unsure of what to do. Unsure of how she was going to get home. The park was full of people, and she'd have to walk right through the middle of them to get out of the park.

Ruth Ann must have been wondering the same thing. She took Emma's hand and eyed Hope.

Then, just as Hope decided she would hide out and wait until the crowd left, a voice called out.

"Ruth Ann, can you come for a minute?" a man's voice called.

Hope couldn't see Emma's dat, but she could tell he was just over the hill.

"Just a minute, Jonas." Ruth Ann walked up the boat ramp and paused near the top. A smile filled her face. "What a good idea," she said. "Emma, go with your dat, and I'll help Hope."

Ruth Ann disappeared for a moment and returned with a thin quilt.

Relief poured through Hope, and she gladly accepted it. "Thank you so much. Where did he get this?"

"Jonas said that Elizabeth Bieler from the fabric store brought it with her. She said there's always more people than seats, and she thought someone might be able to use it."

Hope took the blanket from Ruth Ann's hands, unfolded it, and then wrapped it around herself. "I'm so thankful that she did." It was a light quilt that had seen many years, many picnics. Thankfully there was enough room for her to wrap it around herself and hold it tight in front. Hope let out a soft sigh, feeling hidden once again.

"Would you like me to walk with you—at least out of the park?" Ruth Ann said.

"*Ja, danke*, but let's walk around the edges. I want as few people seeing me as possible. I don't want to make a big deal out of this."

"No, of course not. I'll try to keep you out of view. I'm sure that everyone will be so busy socializing and talking that they won't even notice."

Hope breathed out a sigh of relief. "I hope so." She stepped forward, her bare feet on the rough concrete. Her flip-flops were somewhere in the creek, but thankfully it wasn't much of a walk to get home.

She moved from the boat ramp into the grass, and it felt cool under her feet. The quilt around her shoulders smelled of spring and sunshine, but Hope also could still smell the fishy, salty odor from the brackish water. A shiver ran down her spine when she replayed Ruth Ann's words in her mind. Nearly as soon as a visitor got off the bus in Pinecraft they'd hear about Phillippi Creek, especially the sharks or alligators that were spotted every now and then in the murky waters.

As she continued forward, water dripped from her dress and squished between her toes, yet a prayer of thanksgiving rose in her heart. *Thank You, Lord, for protecting Emma and protecting me. Thank You for leading me to the creek at the right time.* A shudder moved up her spine. *I hate to think of what could have happened if I wasn't there.*

They neared the park, and Hope attempted to steer as far away from the crowd as possible, but it wasn't to be. As she neared the gathering, most of the eyes were on her. In the middle of them stood Jonas with Emma on his hip.

"There she is. There is my Hope." Emma's voice rose above the din of voices. She pointed. "She saved me from sinking!"

Grace pushed through the crowd and rushed forward. Mem and Dat followed, and soon Faith, Lovina, and Noah rushed up, circling around her. The only one who was missing was her sister Joy. Joy was working at the quilt shop, filling in for Elizabeth Bieler so the older woman could be at the gathering at the park. Hope's shoulders straightened as she tucked the quilt tighter under her chin. The muscles in her neck tightened, and she wished she could disappear into the blanket's folds.

Grace stopped in front of her, grasping her shoulders. "Are you all right?"

"*Ja*, I'm fine." She forced a smile, wishing she were anywhere but there.

"That little girl said that you saved her. She said she fell into the creek and you dove in and pulled her out."

"*Ja*, I did...Well, it was more wading than diving." Hope took a step back. The press of people caused her chest to tighten, and their stares nearly stole her breath. "It really was not a big deal. I'm just thankful I was there. I should get home..."

"I'm thankful too." Jonas stepped forward. "I still don't know how to thank you."

She dared to look at him now. He wore a beard, evidence of being a married man, and she wondered where his wife was. Maybe she'd stayed home today? If she were here she could have done a better job watching the young girl than he had.

Anger mixed with embarrassment, and it was directed at him. If this man, Jonas, had been paying better attention to his daughter none of this would have happened. She wouldn't be standing in the midst of this gathering, a dripping mess, hiding under a quilt.

Hope shot him what she hoped was an angry glance, but the emotions in his gaze caught her by surprise. Appreciation filled his gaze, but there was something more. Hope sucked in a breath and took another step back. She'd only seen that look in a man's eyes a few times before, but never so intense. And from a married man of all things. Jonas Sutter should be ashamed of himself!

Hope turned toward Grace and fixed her eyes on her sister. "Would you walk home with me? I don't want to walk by myself."

Grace wrapped an arm around her shoulders. "*Ja*. Of course."

Hope leaned forward and whispered in her sister's ear. "I—I just want to be alone. Get me out of here."

Even though Grace was the youngest, she had a boldness the other sisters didn't have. With Grace by Hope's side, no one would get to her.

Grace waved her hand in the direction of the crowd. "Please let us by. My sister is shaken up. I'm sure you understand."

"Hope, we can walk with you too." Mem's voice behind them held a note of concern.

Hope paused and looked over her shoulders. "*Ne*, Mem. Please stay. Please enjoy yourself."

Mem nodded, but she didn't seem happy. They continued on, Grace leading the way, motioning people to give them room. Before them the crowd moved to both sides, just like the parting of the Red Sea.

When they were nearly out of the park, a hand touched her arm. Hope paused and glanced over her shoulder to see the young girl.

Emma's lower lip quivered. "Dat told me to say that I'm sorry. I didn't mean to cause so much trouble."

Hope leaned down so her face was close to the girl's. "I know you didn't mean to, but please be careful from now on. I don't want to see you hurt."

Emma nodded, and then gave Hope a quick squeeze, which was gladly accepted.

"Dat also said we can stop by later to see if you are all right."

Even though she did not look back, Hope could feel Jonas's presence behind her. "Well, please tell your dat that isn't necessary. I am fine."

Emma jutted out her chin. Determination narrowed her gaze. "But I caused trouble. I need to make sure…"

Hope sighed. How could she make the girl understand? The real trouble was the way Emma's dat had looked at her—in a way no married man should. That wasn't anything she wanted to be a part of.

"I'm sure I'll see you around town. Maybe we'll run into each other at the pie shop. I can show you the new flowers I planted. Will that work?"

Emma nodded, but her lips curled downward in a frown. She clung to Hope's arm as if Hope was her mother and she didn't want to let go. Compassion filled Hope's heart. *Poor thing, she must not get much attention from her parents.*

Hope supposed not every young girl had what she had growing up—lots of love, lots of attention. Hope made a mental note to offer the young girl all the attention and affection that she could…just as long as her father wasn't around. The type of look he'd given her would not get past her *mem*, Regina, or any of the other women. And then they'd try to solve the problem by finding Hope a suitable husband.

The whole community prying into the matters of her heart was the last thing she wanted. Hope was someone who wanted to be left alone in the quiet of a garden. Someone who would rather be hidden than seen. Someone who felt perfectly happy with her own thoughts, her own plans.

Hope walked home with determined steps, happy to never talk to Jonas Sutter again.

Sunshine Pie

A pound of patience you must find
Mixed well with loving words, so kind
Drop in two pounds of helpful deeds
and thought of other people's needs

A pack of smiles, to make the crust
then stir and bake it well you must,
And now, I ask you must try,
the recipe of this Sunshine Pie.*

* "Sunshine Pie." *California Cultivator and Livestock and Dairy Journal* 20 (January 16, 1903):45.

Chapter Three

There are three kinds of people: those who make
things happen, those who watch things happen,
and those who have no idea what happened.

AMISH PROVERB

⟋⟍

Hope sat down at the small desk in the bedroom that she shared with Lovina. Even though it was after six, the sun had not yet set. It just didn't seem right, and the day didn't feel like New Year's Day. Yes, they'd served sausage and sauerkraut at the park—the traditional New Year's meal among the Amish— but the day itself was all wrong. If she were in Walnut Creek right now there would be a fire in the woodstove. She and her sisters might be playing Chinese checkers—a favorite game since their childhood. Dat would be done with the chores in the barn, and there'd be the sound of buggy wheels traveling down the road in front of their house—evidence of young men going to call on their sweethearts.

Even though it didn't feel like New Years, Hope decided to spend time thinking about the year to come. One of the Englisch ladies she used to work for called her plans for the year her "New Year's resolutions," but Hope had decided to do something different. Instead of resolving to make lots of changes, she'd decided to pick one thing to change and then do it. Last year she had decided to read one chapter in her Bible every day, and it was something she'd stuck to. But this year the decision would take more work to see it through. Hope pulled out a new notebook and turned to the first page. Then she wrote her goal at the top.

"Find a job up north and a garden to tend." Seeing it on the page caused her heartbeat to quicken.

She threw a longing glance at the seed catalog at the top of a pile of mail on her desk, wishing she had a big order to put in. Wishing she had a plot to plan. She picked up her pen and wrote her first step on the next line: Write to cousins and friends and inquire about work as a maud and gardener.

Her eyes welled up at the thought of leaving her family, but it was the right step. She'd been watching Lovina over the last six months. She'd seen Lovina blossom when she was doing the *one thing* that God had called her to do. Lovina had dared to take a step of faith and put all her eggs in one basket, as her grandma used to say. She'd risked her money, her reputation, and her dreams in opening a pie shop, and because Lovina was willing to take that step of faith, God opened doors that no one could have anticipated.

Hope's dream of just having a quiet place to garden, and maybe a family in a few years, seemed small in comparison, but the more she prayed about it, the more she decided that God could orchestrate a way for her to see her small dream fulfilled too. She didn't need a bustling pie shop, just a small plot of land. Her dream was much simpler, but that didn't make it any less important. Just as God created a variety of plants to grow in a garden, God had a variety of dreams He planted in hearts. She had no doubt a loving God had good plans—a fruitful harvest—for each person, whether big or small.

Hope turned to the next page of the notebook and decided to

write her cousin Eleanor first. Eleanor was five years older than Hope, but she lived near their old home. Eleanor had three small children and a large home and garden to tend to. Maybe she could use help?

Dear Eleanor,

Greetings in the name of our Lord Jesus Christ. I pray the Lord is sending sunshine to your hearts even though I heard it is a hard winter in Ohio this time of year. I remember those days when it was below zero and howling around the corners of the house. I'd put on three layers of clothes just to go out in the buggy. Things aren't this way in Pinecraft. In fact, early today I took a dunk in the creek. I didn't mean to. A young girl was playing in a canoe and fell in. But I did jump in after her, and I did walk home dripping wet without so much as a shiver. The blanket a kind friend gave me to save me from embarrassment helped, but I still believe that the first day of the year isn't a good time for a swim!

Even though I enjoy the sun, I'm ready for a move. My dat is doing well, which I am thankful for. I'd love a chance to move back up north. I'm writing to see if you are in need of a maud. I do enjoy caring for children. I was caring for a young boy here for the last year until his family moved away. I also remember that you have a large garden plot. As you know, gardening is one of my favorite things. There is nothing more satisfying than harvesting a plot and then filling a basement with canned goods and winter vegetables: onions, potatoes, squash, carrots, and apples. There are other families I can contact, but since I always enjoy time with you I thought of you first. I was thinking of moving in May, just in time to prepare the ground and to plant.

Please write back and let me know if you could use my help. A small salary and room and board would be all I'd require.

Your loving cousin,
Hope

Hope leaned back in her chair. She expected to feel better after writing the letter, but even as she wrote the words something nagged at her heart. *Maybe God does have something for me in Pinecraft. Maybe His plans are different from mine.* But how could that be? Pinecraft had nothing to offer her—and definitely not a garden.

Even as she tore the letter from the notebook, folded it up, and placed it in an envelope, an unexplained ache touched her heart. It made all the sense in the world to return to Ohio. It just had to work. Even though she racked her mind, she couldn't think of anything working out better.

I'll just send the letter and see where it leads, Hope thought. At least it would get her started on her plan.

She sealed and addressed the letter and set it on the desk. She'd mail it Monday, and then she'd wait for Eleanor's response.

Hope heard the front door open and voices filled the living room. Her parents and sisters were finally returning from the New Year's fund-raiser at the park. Her stomach growled, and she realized she hadn't eaten much all day. After arriving home she'd changed and then taken a quick nap.

Hope stood and attempted to freshen up her hair and kapp, but her arms felt as if they were made of lead. The events at the creek had drained her. She couldn't get the image of Emma's wide eyes or the memory of her soft whimpering out of her mind.

Now, as she hurried to the kitchen, she hoped that no one would make a big deal out of what she'd done. Each of them would have done the same if they were in the same situation. Yet she didn't have to worry. As Hope paused at the threshold to the kitchen, her sisters barely even gave her a glance. Instead they continued, deep in conversation.

"It's just the saddest thing, don't you think?" Mem sat down at the kitchen table. A network of wrinkles crisscrossed her forehead and a heaviness seemed to weigh on her heart.

"I heard that no one guessed anything was wrong with her," Grace chimed in.

Grace was a fair-skinned beauty with a sprinkling of freckles over the rim of her nose. Hope always envied Grace's ease with people and the effortless way she connected with others. "They say she was just lovely, with a sweet spirit. She loved to sew, just like Joy, and she doted on her little girl."

Lovina pulled a cherry pie from the refrigerator and began slicing it. Her mournful look nearly brought Hope to tears. Hope wasn't sure who her sisters were talking about, but of course Lovina thought pie would solve everything.

Lovina sighed as she slid a piece of pie onto a plate. "I can't imagine the guilt. Regina said that he was away. He'd taken his little girl to an ice cream social. She lay on the ground nearly eight hours before he found her. I don't think finding her sooner would have changed anything, but still…"

Hope entered the room and walked to the table. She placed her hand on Grace's shoulder. "Who are you talking about? What happened?"

Grace's cheeks were pink from the walk in the heat. "Oh Hope, it's the most horrible story. Regina told us. She's friends with the Sutters, and she didn't realize that Jonas had come to Pinecraft. He's just been here two days."

Hope's brow furrowed. "Jonas Sutter?" She sat down in the chair in front of the window next to Mem. The sun poured through the glass, touching her neck, her shoulders. Anger warmed inside her, too, yet she shivered to consider how he'd looked at her.

"*Ja*, it was his little girl you saved from the creek today." Mem clicked her tongue. "Oh, I don't want to think what could have happened if you hadn't been there. Could you imagine the guilt if he'd lost her too?"

Lovina placed a piece of pie in front of each of them. Only Dat held up his hand, indicating that he didn't want one.

Hope picked up the fork and poked at the crust. "Oh, I know who Jonas is, but who was this woman you're talking about?"

Mem picked up her fork and put it down again. She reached over and took Hope's hand, squeezing, as if she had horrible news she needed to share. "It is Jonas's wife. Or rather it *was* Jonas's wife. Sarah Sutter passed away two years ago, but it was three years before that when she had her stroke."

"Stroke?" Hope's mouth dropped open, and her mind tried to wrap around what she was hearing. The room was quiet except for the scraping of forks on plates.

"*Ja*, they have no idea why," Lovina said. "She seemed so healthy before. It's just one of those things…I suppose we just have to learn to trust God in matters like this."

Hope placed her fork back on the plate, unsure of what to say. She'd been so judgmental with her thoughts earlier, wondering where the girl's mother was and why she wasn't being tended to.

"So—so Emma's father…"

"He's a widower." The words shot out of Mem's mouth. "And that little girl. She hasn't had a mother for the last two years. No wonder she was wandering the park today. Where would any of us be without our mothers keeping us on the straight and narrow?"

"She's actually been without a mother longer than that." Grace's chin dropped to her chest as if the story overwhelmed her. "Sarah was paralyzed on one side and unable to speak for three years. Jonas hired in help for both his wife and his daughter, but can you imagine the weight that must have put on a man while also tending his farm and being part of the community? No wonder he left Kentucky. I'm sure he needed a break."

Lovina cocked an eyebrow. "Are you calling teaching school a break? How would you like to be in the room with fifteen children? I'd rather be behind a pie display with a hundred hungry customers." She shook her head. "Everything about this breaks my heart."

Her mother and sisters' voices continued, and the words spun around the room. Hope resisted the urge to close her eyes and cover her ears to block out their voices. It had been like this since she was a small girl. All these conversations. All these opinions. It wasn't as if they were saying anything bad or wrong, it was just that they didn't stop talking. She wished they could slow their words and just give her time to think. She put her elbows to the table and pressed her fingertips into her temples, blocking out their words.

Jonas Sutter is a bachelor.

Little Emma doesn't have a mother.

Sadness crept over her like ivy vines, wrapping around her heart.

Then came curiosity.

He was looking at me today. With interest.

Why hadn't Jonas already remarried?

Growing up she'd seen how things typically worked. It was common for Amish men and women to marry quickly after losing a spouse, often before a year had passed. Amish couples had big families, and a second marriage often became a necessity. Women needed providers for themselves and their children. Men needed help with their home, and especially raising their little ones. Perhaps with just one daughter—instead of a houseful of children—Jonas's need hadn't been so urgent. Or maybe love for his first wife made the idea of marriage a second time difficult.

Or maybe he's trying to find another person he could love that way again.

A memory filtered through her mind from earlier today. Jonas Sutter had thought ahead to her need, and he'd gotten a blanket for her to cover herself with. Then he'd looked at her with…with such admiration. Heat rose to her cheeks even now as she remembered his eyes upon her. No man had really looked at her before like that—like she was beautiful. Or if they had, she hadn't paid attention. Yet the way Jonas had looked at her had been shocking. She'd been shocked because she'd believed him to be a married man. It only made sense with his beard. But now…her stomach flipped and flapped like laundry on a clothesline on a windy day. Knowing he was a widower changed everything.

Hope placed a hand over her stomach, telling herself that she was simply hungry, but deep down she knew that was a lie. Her stomach flipped around as she tried to make sense of all her emotions. In one day's time she'd been angry at Jonas for his bold look, and she'd been thankful for his thoughtfulness at finding her that quilt. Now sadness for the loss of his wife overshadowed both of those, and an interest in the handsome widower stirred her even more.

Her mem and sisters' voices continued to swirl around the room, and she blocked them out as she moved to the pantry. She pulled out a loaf of bread, put it on the bread board, and then moved to the closest drawer for a knife. Then, through the fog of voices, she heard his name again.

"Jonas Sutter," Mem was saying, yet her voice was lower this time, as if she wore a soft smile.

Without turning to discover the reason, Hope reached into the pantry and pulled a jar of peanut butter from the shelf. Let them talk about Jonas Sutter all they wanted. It didn't really concern her, although part of her felt it did. After all, what if she hadn't been there to pull Emma from the water? Should she feel responsible now to check in on Emma and her father?

"Hope!" At her mother's raised voice, Hope realized that the room had fallen silent. Then her mother's voice continued. "She must be lost in her thoughts. It's been an eventful day," Mem said.

A sinking feeling came over Hope, and the hair on the back of her neck stood on end. Without turning, she sensed who stood behind her. Hope's heart pounded against the walls of her chest and tremors danced through her stomach.

"It *has* been an eventful day," a man's voice broke through. "And that's why Emma and I came to see her, to thank her."

"I helped *Aenti* Ruth Ann make Peanut Better cookies. They're my favorite," Emma's small voice rang out.

Hope turned slowly, wondering how she'd missed the front door opening and their guests being welcomed in. In the midst of her tuning them out, her mem and sisters had gone from talking *about* Jonas and Emma Sutter to talking *to* them.

"Peanut *Better* cookies?" Grace giggled. "Don't you mean peanut butter?"

Emma held up a paper plate filled with cookies. "*Ne.* We call them Peanut Better because we put in chocolate chips…which makes them even better than peanut butter."

Laughter filled the room, and Hope forced a smile. Even though she'd yet to look his direction Hope sensed Jonas's gaze on her. Mem stood to his side, and her lips were tight as she attempted to hold back a smile. A knowing look danced in Mem's eyes.

"That's so kind of you, Emma." Hope approached the young girl and leaned down. Emma's large, brown eyes that had been filled with fear earlier today were now warm and happy. They were the color of the dimpled brown cowpea seeds Hope had ordered last year, hearing they grew well in the Southern states. But her results had been disappointing in the sandy soil of their backyard. The cowpeas had never flourished.

Hope smiled, holding up the jar of peanut butter in her hand. "I do like peanut butter, and I was just going to make myself a sandwich. Would you like one?"

Jonas cleared his throat. "That's nice of you, but we just had dinner—"

"I want one!" Emma stepped forward. "Dat, just a half a sandwich, ple-e-ease."

Hope smiled and turned back to the counter. "We can share one."

"Emma." Jonas sighed. "We came to bring Hope these cookies and thank her for today, not to cause more work for her."

"As if making a sandwich is a lot of work. It's no trouble at all," she shot back before remembering they had an audience. Mem, Dat, and her four sisters all sat in silence, watching the exchange. Feeling the tension of their presence, Hope sliced two pieces of bread and spread them with peanut butter.

Hope called over her shoulder. "Jonas, would you like some?"

Jonas cleared his throat again, and he took the plate of cookies from Emma's hands and placed it on the counter. "Actually, that does sound good. If it's not too much trouble."

"Of course it's not. I hope peanut butter and jelly is fine."

"My favorite!" Emma called out.

Jonas smiled. "*Ja*, that's fine."

"Why don't you three take it out back?" Mem bustled to the back door, opening it wide. "I bet Emma would love to see the flowers you've planted, Hope."

Heat rose up the back of Hope's neck again, only this time it wasn't from the sun. "Oh, they're really not much, Mem."

"I'd like to see them," Jonas's words came quick. She didn't turn to look, but she wondered if he was still watching her. Was the same glimmer of interest evident in his eyes as it had been earlier today?

Hope's heartbeat clattered. "If that's what you want." She smeared the jelly onto the bread and sliced the sandwiches into triangles.

"I should say...I'd like to see them if you don't mind." He stepped forward to help her with the sandwiches, placing them on a paper plate.

"Of course not."

Don't look at him. Don't look for the same look in his eyes that you saw earlier. The Sutters are just being neighborly—that's all.

Jonas moved toward the back door, and Emma skipped beside him as if being in the Miller's home was the most natural thing in the world. When Hope had been Emma's age, she'd been too timid to act natural around strangers. Then again, who was she fooling? She still was.

Thankfully, she'd found a few good friends in Pinecraft, and they liked to go to the beach together. They didn't have to talk much. Instead, they just enjoyed the simple pleasure of lifting up their skirts a bit and walking in the waves.

But she'd never had a male friend, or even a child as a real friend for that matter. But as she joined the young father on the back porch Hope couldn't help but be thankful that they'd stopped by.

They took a brief tour of Hope's flower garden before they took their plates over near the swing and chairs. Hope sat in the chair and motioned for them to take the swing, which could fit two people.

"Dat says he's going to teach me to swim when we get back to Kentucky," Emma said. She plopped onto the white porch swing that Dat had made for Mem as a Christmas gift.

"That's not for a few months yet." Jonas sat next to his daughter, and then he pulled a sandwich off the plate and took a big bite. "We're going to be in Pinecraft for a while, remember."

"You have to stay. You're the new schoolteacher." The words shot out of Hope's mouth before she realized what she was saying. "But, of course, you know that."

"*Ja.*" Jonas nodded. "It's not something I've ever done before, but I told my sister that if she was open to my unconventional ways I'd take her place."

"Take her place?"

"*Ja*, it's Ruth Ann's classroom that I'm taking over. Her daughter—my cousin Hannah—is pregnant with twins and there have been some complications. I've never really asked what's going on, and I don't really need to know. Since things are quiet on the farm until spring and the school year here is over at the end of April, I agreed to come and teach."

"I see," Hope said.

Emma peeled the crust off her sandwich. "Then we are going back to Kentucky. I have a horse named Rocky, and Dat says when we get back we can start our garden."

Hope's eyebrows peeked. "Oh, do you like to garden, Emma?"

Emma shrugged. "I like making mud pies best." Once the crust was off, she ate her sandwich with vigor, as if she hadn't eaten anything all day.

Jonas finished his sandwich and then rose. "We didn't mean to interrupt your evening. We—Emma— just wanted to stop by and thank you for rescuing her." He placed a hand on the girl's shoulder. "She knows now she's not going to go down to the creek unless she has an adult with her."

Emma set her empty paper plate on the swing's seat and stood. She clapped her hands together. "Oh, will you come with me sometime, Hope?" "

Now, Emma, I'm sure Hope has other things—"

"I'd love to," Hope answered, not letting him finish. "The park is one of my favorite places. It's so quiet and peaceful down there."

"And maybe Dat can come too!" Emma reached up and took his hand, smearing peanut butter on his fingers as she did. Jonas released the young girl's hand, licked off the peanut butter, and then returned his grasp without batting an eye. Hope's stomach did a little flip. It was clear he spent a lot of time with his daughter and they had a natural comfort when they were together.

"We can do it tomorrow. After church!" Emma's eyes danced as she looked from her father to Hope. Hope saw something there...anticipation? Excitement? Was it possible that an eight-year-old could be a matchmaker? If Emma was anything like Hope's mother she could.

Hope swallowed hard, and worry wreathed her heart. This little girl had gone through so much. She didn't want her to get her hopes up. Hope knew very little about Jonas Sutter, and she knew even less about being open to a new friendship when a child was involved.

"Maybe not tomorrow," Hope hurriedly said. "But sometime this week might be nice."

Emma's shoulders sunk, and she nodded. She looked to her dat. Her eyes widened as if she was waiting for him to make the next move.

"It'll be a busy week. School starts on Monday, but I'm sure we'll see you around town." His face was expressionless. Hope couldn't tell if, like Emma, he was disappointed that they wouldn't be seeing each other the next day. If so, he hid it well. But Emma's face…well, the disappointment was clear, and it broke Hope's heart.

"There's a gospel sing on Birky Street Thursday night," Hope hurriedly said. "You bring your own chairs, but if you'd like, uh, we can meet there."

The hint of a smile touched Jonas's lips. "We'd like that, wouldn't we Emma?"

He looked down at the girl, but instead of answering she slipped her hand from his and rushed to the side gate. "Look, Dat, a cat!"

"He's stray, and I don't think he'll let you get too close," Hope called after the young girl.

Emma rushed forward as if not hearing. Jonas cupped his hands to call to his daughter. "Emma, wait up! Stay on the side of the street. Don't go out into the road."

Emma nodded, but she didn't slow and didn't turn back.

"This one always keeps me busy," Jonas said to Hope apologetically.

He hurried away with a slight wave, and Hope watched as Emma chased the cat and Jonas chased Emma. Finally reaching her, Jonas scooped up the young girl and hoisted her onto his shoulder. Both of her legs dangled on his right side, and Emma's laughter filled the air, warming Hope's heart.

She hoped to see them at the gospel singing, if not sooner. Hope picked up the paper plates they'd left and realized she hadn't taken a bite of her own sandwich. She didn't feel like eating now. Instead her stomach balled in knots. Her gaze wandered back to watch Jonas and Emma disappearing down the street.

Oh Lord, she prayed. *May it not be too long before I see them returning that way again.*

Emma's Peanut *Better* Cookies

1 cup all-purpose flour
1 cup cake flour
1 tsp. baking soda
1 tsp. baking powder
¼ tsp. salt
¼ cup shortening
½ cup butter
½ cup granulated sugar
½ cup light brown sugar
2 eggs
½ cup creamy peanut butter
½ tsp. vanilla extract
10 oz. chocolate morsels

Preheat oven to 350°. Line baking sheets with parchment paper. In a medium bowl, sift flours, baking soda, baking powder, and salt; set aside. In a large bowl, cream shortening, butter, and sugars. Add eggs, peanut butter, and vanilla. Mix thoroughly. Add sifted dry ingredients; mix until thoroughly combined. Stir in chocolate morsels. Drop heaping Tbsp of dough onto parchment-lined sheets, 3 inches apart. Bake for 12 to 14 minutes. Makes approximately 3 dozen cookies.

Baking Tip: You can make your own cake flour. For every cup all-purpose flour, remove two Tbsp and replace with two Tbsp cornstarch. Sift.

Chapter Four

You will always leave something behind—your influence.

AMISH PROVERB

❧

Jonas Sutter rolled up his sleeves and walked to the chalkboard at the front of Golden Coast Amish School, wiping off the day's lesson and preparing to write up tomorrow's. His first day of teaching had gone well. The older students had been respectful and interested in this farmer from Kentucky. They'd listened and done their assignments, but that didn't stop him from thinking about his farm. Thinking about all he'd left behind in Guthrie.

"Four months," he muttered under his breath. "Just four months and I can get back to the farm."

He'd repeated that same thought on the ride to Pinecraft from Kentucky, sitting in the back of a full van driven by an Englisch driver. He'd repeated that thought as he'd chatted with friends, old and new, at the New Year's gathering at Pinecraft Park. But after Saturday evening—and the visit to the Miller's house—the idea didn't seem as urgent. Would the days go by fast? Would he have enough time to get to know Hope Miller before he left? For the first time since Sarah's passing, he'd found someone worth getting to know better.

Unlike most public schools that went until June, the Amish school in Pinecraft finished at the end of April. One reason was they didn't take as many holidays as public schools—for Columbus Day, President's Day, or Thanksgiving. They also took a shortened Christmas break. When other public school students were still finishing up testing and their studies in May, most Amish children were already helping around farms, which was exactly what he'd planned for Emma.

Last year, if someone would have told him that the beginning of the new year he'd be living in Florida and teaching school to two dozen children, he never would have believed it. It had been a hard two years since losing Sarah. And an even longer three years before that as he watched the illness strip his wife of her mobility, finally taking her life. He'd always imagined he'd stay in Kentucky his whole life, but his oldest sister's need had drawn him here.

Jonas had read Ruth Ann's note at least ten times when it first arrived, and he thought of it again now.

Jonas, you know I wouldn't ask unless it was urgent, but Hannah's pregnancy is delicate. She's moving into one of our extra rooms until the twins are born. I'd promised to teach school this year, until a new teacher can be found, but I'm needed by my daughter's side. I know you, out of anyone, will understand. Can you come? Emma will love it here.

Love, Ruth Ann

Six sentences jotted off on a piece of typing paper was all his oldest sister had written. Older by twenty years, Ruth Ann seemed just as much as a mother as his own Mem. Two sentences replayed in his mind again: "I know you, out of anyone, will understand" and "Emma will love it here." Both were true, but the latter sentence sealed his decision. Emma *would* love Pinecraft—the sunshine and the ability to play outside most days. His daughter needed that. She'd spent too much of her life inside with him as he'd cared for Sarah. Even though Jonas wasn't confident in his teaching, he was confident that he'd do what he could to help Emma return to the cheerful, carefree little girl she'd been before his wife's illness. He wanted that more than anything.

As if on cue, the schoolhouse door burst open and Emma rushed in. The warm afternoon breeze followed her in, and he could see Ruth Ann waiting by the gate to the school.

Emma was tall for eight, and thin like he'd been as a child. Strands of wispy, light brown hair—the same color as his—fell from her kapp and framed her face. She paused before him and her dark brown eyes sparkled, looking so much like her mother's. Jonas no longer had Sarah, but he had a glimpse of her every time he looked into his daughter's eyes.

"Dat? Can I go with Aenti Ruth Ann to Lapp's Bike Shop? She said we're going to find a bike just my size to rent."

"*Ja.* That'll be fine. Just be back in an hour or so. I'd like to spend some time with you this afternoon." Jonas kneeled before her. "I'm used to having my little sidekick by my side, *ja*?"

Emma nodded. She offered him a quick hug.

When she released her arms around his neck, he walked to the open door and waved to his sister. Then he turned back to Emma, placing a hand on her shoulder. Sarah had been the tender one, always hugging their daughter, always taking her hand or brushing her fingers on Emma's cheek. He'd tried to do his best to take over that role, but his attempts were stiff and awkward, or at least that's how they felt to him. Still, Emma didn't seem to mind. She smiled up at him and turned back to the door.

"And maybe later we can ride down to the park?" she called over her shoulder. It was half a question and half a statement.

"*Ja*, of course…" He was going to add *As long as your chores are done*, but changed his mind. Living in Ruth Ann's house for four months meant Emma wouldn't be able to get away with anything. Ruth Ann had raised seven children and believed that play only followed hard work. Hannah was four years younger than Jonas. She'd always had delicate health and being pregnant with twins was taking a toll on her body—but caring for her on top of everything else was nothing that Ruth Ann couldn't manage. If anything, his oldest sister was determined and capable. If Ruth Ann set her mind on something it would get done. And his hope was that Ruth Ann would be able to help him tame Emma's independent streak. The little girl had been left to her own devices more than he wanted to admit. That was why he couldn't blame her when she'd wandered down to Phillippi Creek. Jonas was just thankful that Hope Miller had been there.

He'd tried not to look at Hope too many times at church yesterday. She'd been sitting on the long wooden bench next to her sisters—just a row in front of where Emma had sat with Ruth Ann. Emma had given Hope a quick hug after service was over, and they'd been chatting about something. Jonas hadn't tried to interrupt. Instead, he'd sauntered outside with all the other men to talk about the weather, who was due to arrive on the Pioneer Trails bus, and any news that they'd heard about their friends and their family from back home.

He smiled and pushed thoughts of the pretty redhead out of his mind. First, he had to prepare tomorrow's lessons. Only after could he let his mind wander, thinking of her. He scanned the room. Work came first.

The classroom doors were opened, pressed against the walls.

The building was quiet, which hadn't been the case just a few hours before. The window shades had been lowered to block out the sun, but now Jonas moved to them and lifted them to the top. He'd no doubt regret it later when the room grew too warm from the heat of the sun, but for now he'd enjoy the golden, slanted rays. One only experienced sunshine like this during the summer months in Kentucky. He'd enjoy it while he could.

Jonas moved to the blackboard, rolled up his sleeves, and began erasing the day's math lesson. The swish of the eraser on the board reminded him of the swish of a tail on a barn wall, but he pushed those thoughts away. He'd first kissed Sarah in her dat's barn with such a sound in the background.

"Good day, Jonas!" The voice interrupted him.

His heart leaped, but he pasted a smile on his face as he turned.

"Good afternoon, Clyde."

His brother-in-law wandered in with a pleasant smile on his face. The older man was broad shouldered and extra wide around the waist. Clyde hadn't been that way when he and Ruth Ann had married, but her good cooking, matched with the years passing by, had increased his waist size.

Clyde's smile was just as wide, and he'd no doubt just spent the last hour meeting those who'd arrived on this afternoon's Pioneer Trails bus—welcoming the snowbirds and telling his fill of big fish or alligator stories.

Clyde pulled up a chair in the back of the classroom, and Jonas forced a smile. Clyde was a woodworker. He always had a project or two in his shop, but his greatest talent was his ability to strike up a conversation with anyone. Jonas just hoped that whatever Clyde had on his mind wouldn't take long. He had a classroom to ready for the next day and lessons to prepare, and he wanted time this afternoon with Emma.

"Ruth Ann came home a bit ago with a piece of pie from that pie shop. Orange pie. I never had that before, but it was good."

"Really? Orange Pie, you don't say." Jonas put down his eraser and then flipped through pages in the math book. "I might have to try it next time I go by."

"You'll have to do that. I like that place. It's really brought some fun to our village. I wouldn't want to guess how many pies they go through a day with all the customers—the Amish here, and all those Englischers who've been showing up in their fancy cars."

Jonas crossed his arms over his chest, knowing he'd never be able to write up math equations on the board and chat at the same time. He leaned against the wall. He eyed the winter mural on the wall behind Clyde's head, realizing he should have taken that down after the New Year. Then he smiled, deciding to leave it up. After all, that was the only "winter" these kids would experience.

"You know, they did a nice job with that pie shop, but it's just a shame that they haven't done much with the lot," Clyde continued. "Ruth Ann mentioned it to me the other day. There's a half acre in the back of the building, you know. Seems to be a shame that it's not being used. All that space is valuable. Especially since most folks around here have tiny yards. And that's another thing that's bothering Ruth Ann. These kids growing up in this area don't know what it's like to live on a farm or grow a garden. What if one of these young girls in our school grows up to marry an Amishman from up north? What will happen when she moves up there and doesn't know how to garden and such?"

Jonas nodded and rubbed his head, wondering if this was Clyde—or rather Ruth Ann's—way of hinting about Emma needing a good role model in her life. At least three times since they'd moved her here Ruth Ann had talked to him about opening his heart up to love again, about finding a wife. About finding a woman who could guide Emma into adulthood. Their conversation had been as recent as last night.

"A young girl needs a mother to teach her how to care for a garden, a family, a home," Ruth Ann had said.

Jonas had teased her. "That's what I have you for, Ruthie. And I believe you should start tonight. How about Emma begins by learning how to make peanut butter pie?"

Ruth Ann whopped him with her dishtowel, but she had the same determined look in her gaze as Clyde did now.

"*Ja*, I suppose you're right," Jonas said, taking the bait and wondering what Clyde was leading to.

"That's why I think you should talk to Lovina Miller who owns the pie shop. Maybe see if you can make a garden plot out back. Emma can't stop talking about starting a garden in May back home, but why wait? I bet you could help get one up and running. You always did a *gut* job with your garden back home after..." Clyde's voice trailed off, but Jonas knew what Clyde had been about to say: *after Sarah died.*

In Amish communities the garden was a woman's place, but after Sarah's stroke Jonas had stepped in. He had to. The food raised in a garden was necessary to make it through the long winters, but did he really need another job beyond teaching school and being the sole parent of a mischievous young girl?

Curiosity turned to frustration, and frustration tightened Jonas's throat. He balled his fists at his side and felt his shoulders tense. Wasn't he doing enough to help his sister by just being here? And now this? They wanted him to take on more?

"A garden plot? And when would I have time to tend to that? Did my sister forget that I'm teaching school full time? And that I have Emma." The words came out sharper than Jonas intended, and he pressed his lips together.

Clyde stroked his long beard that fell to his second button and chuckled. There were few things that fazed Clyde, and obviously Jonas's crisp tone wasn't one of them.

"That's the point. You make it part of school. Kids don't need to sit in a stuffy room all day. They can get out and get some fresh air and learn about gardening." Clyde pointed to the books in the bookcase closest to him. "I'd guess there're some good biology texts that you could tie in."

Seeing Clyde's smile, Jonas's shoulders relaxed. The idea did sound appealing, taking his students out into nature instead of sitting inside a stuffy classroom all day. Even though they had two electric fans to move the air he missed Kentucky's cool breezes. But would that just add to his work? He guessed it would. It'd take work, take planning.

"I'm sure there are some good lessons I could incorporate. It's something to think about. Nothing that needs to be decided today."

Clyde lifted one eyebrow that told Jonas he didn't agree. "Or if you'd like I can head over and talk to Lovina Miller. Or actually, Ruth Ann said she'd be happy to mention something—"

"No!" The word escaped Jonas's lips. "Just give me time to think about it."

"*Ja*, well, of course." But even as Clyde rose from his chair Jonas had no doubt that he wasn't going to let things lie. Word would get to Lovina somehow. And then he'd really be stuck having to do what Clyde planned. He had to act first, or Clyde and Ruth Ann would take over and volunteer him for who knows what.

"Listen…" Jonas followed Clyde to the door. "I was thinking about taking Emma by the shop for a piece of pie this afternoon. So why don't I just bring it up to Lovina?"

Clyde's eyebrows lifted. "Today?"

Jonas ushered Clyde out of the door. "Today, I promise." He then smiled, guessing Lovina's response. He would mention it, and then he could promptly forget it. With the pie shop barely getting on its feet, the owner of Me, Myself, and Pie would not be interested in her nice grass being dug up for a school project, especially by a schoolteacher who had no intention of staying beyond the school year. Yes, he'd mention it, point out all the reasons it wouldn't work, and then let Lovina decide. Then—with a clear conscience—he could let Clyde and Ruth Ann know that Emma would have to wait until May to garden. Somehow his daughter would survive.

Besides, when he got back to Kentucky he'd have plenty of time to ask one of his other sisters or older nieces to take Emma under their wing. It wasn't like she'd be grown overnight.

But would that be enough? A mentor for Emma?

Ruth Ann wanted more for him than that. She wanted Jonas to find love again, but was that possible?

Hope Miller's sweet face popped in his mind again, but he pushed it away. She was too young, too beautiful. She'd never want to be with someone like him, who came with so much baggage—a daughter, a sad history, a broken heart.

Besides, he'd never find a woman as sweet, loving, and gentle as Sarah. Yes, Emma needed someone to teach her what being an Amish woman was all about, but that didn't mean he needed to fall in love again. After losing Sarah, Jonas wasn't even sure that was even possible.

Peanut Butter Pie

One 9-inch baked pastry pie crust
2½ cups milk, divided
1 cup sugar
¼ cup cornstarch
dash of salt
3 large egg yolks
1½ cups powdered sugar
½ cup peanut butter
whipped topping

Bring two cups of milk to a boil in a saucepan over medium-high heat. In a bowl, mix sugar, cornstarch, and salt together. Stir in ½ cup milk, add egg yolks, and mix well. Stir cornstarch mixture into the boiling milk. Bring back to a boil, stirring constantly. Remove from heat and cool.

To make crumbs, mix together powdered sugar and peanut butter until crumbly. Reserve ⅓ of the crumbs for the top of the pie. Put remaining crumbs in the bottom of the baked pie crust. Pour the cooled filling on top of the crumbs. Cover with whipped topping. Sprinkle the remaining crumbs on top.

Chapter Five

Too many of us don't know what's
cooking until it boils over.

AMISH PROVERB

⤜∽⤛

Jonas's hand tightened around Emma's as they neared the pie shop. She glanced up at him and her brow furrowed. He noticed a spattering of freckles across her nose that he was sure he hadn't seen before. She was changing so quickly. Growing up.

"We're eating pie? Before dinner?"

"*Ja*, we'll get pie. We'll share a piece, so as not to spoil our appetite, but I need to talk to someone while we're here too."

They paused before the front door next to a large pot filled with flowers. Emma reached out her free hand and brushed it over the top of a cluster of violets. Violets had been Sarah's favorite.

"About what?" She bent down and sniffed a pink blossom that Jonas didn't know the name of. Then her eyes rolled back as if enamored with the aroma. Sarah had done that too. She'd walked through her flower beds, bending down to enjoy the aroma of each one.

"Talking about a garden here…well, not really." He shook his head, hoping not to get his daughter's hopes up. "I mean, I just need to talk to someone that Aenti Ruth Ann wants me to talk to." How could he explain to an eight-year-old that he needed to have the conversation to put a halt to Ruth Ann's idea *before* she talked to anyone about it? If Ruth Ann was anything, she was persuasive. And if she wanted something it usually happened.

"Do *you* want to have a garden here at the pie shop?" Emma eyed him curiously. Then she scratched her head, looking through the window at the display case. "Vegetable pie doesn't sound good."

"It was just an idea—that your aunt had. There's a nice piece of land in the back, but I'm sure that it'll be too much work to follow through with. Especially with us leaving."

"Hope is a gardener." Emma pointed to the flowers that filled the planter and spilled over. "She planted these."

"She did?" Jonas looked at the pot closer. It was a perfect mix of color and fragrance. There were no shriveled flowers or dry leaves. If Hope tended these flowers she clearly took pride in her work.

"*Ja*. Hope said she'd liked vegetables more than flowers, and she'd like to be a gardener again." Emma shrugged. "I think it's sad that she can't be."

"How do you know this? When did you talk to her?"

"Last week—the day we got to town." Emma swung against his arm, pulling gently from side to side as she talked. "Aenti Ruth Ann took me for pie, but I wanted ice cream. It was melted all over my hands, and Hope cleaned it off. She was taking care of her flowers."

"So when you were at the creek, that was the second time you saw Hope?"

Emma nodded. "*Ja*."

"And Hope told you the first time that she wished she had a garden?" Jonas pushed back his hat and rubbed his brow where the brim had rested. "Do you know if Aenti Ruth Ann heard her say that?"

Emma shrugged. "I don't know. I had two scoops and it was too big. And too sticky."

Jonas nodded, pretending to be interested in Emma's ice cream but mostly wondering if his sister had something up her sleeve with this garden idea. Was Ruth Ann trying to play matchmaker? He wouldn't put it past her. But the truth was, hearing that Hope wished for a garden made him reconsider his conversation with Lovina.

He'd planned on presenting the idea of a garden to Lovina, and then he'd back himself out of the commitment. After all, he was a busy man. But Emma's words made him wonder. If he did help start a garden, would Hope Miller want to get involved?

A garden was a lot of work, but it wouldn't be without benefits. He *could* use it for his classes, and if it helped him to get to know Hope Miller better, why, that would be a bonus. And there'd be produce for the community.

Something inside Jonas told him he had to try. It would be a good project for Emma to be involved in while she was in Pinecraft. And if nothing else came of it, he'd have some time with his daughter—time he never seemed to get while tending the farm back home.

Jonas walked into the pie shop and found a booth. When the waitress came by he ordered a slice of old-fashioned cream pie to split with Emma, and then he asked if it would be possible to talk to Lovina Miller.

The waitress smiled. "Lovina's busy but I'll see what I can do. Can I tell her what it's about?"

"It's about a garden!" Emma blurted out. "Dat wants to grow one here in the back."

The young waitress lifted an eyebrow. "A garden?"

She looks familiar, Jonas thought. *In fact, she looks a little like Hope.*

He squirmed in his seat, wondering if she was one of Hope's sisters. Worried that she was. Word spread quickly in Amish communities. Many times an idea became a solid plan when passed along by excited lips.

Just as they finished their last bite, the owner of the pie shop, Lovina Miller, walked over and scooted into the booth next to Emma. Jonas had seen her nearly every time he'd come into the pie shop. She was dark-haired and petite with a warm smile. From what he'd heard she was going to be a married woman in a few months, although she and Noah Yoder had yet to publish their wedding.

"My sister said you wanted to talk to me? She said something about a garden?"

Jonas opened his mouth, but Emma cut in. "Dat wants to have a garden out back. A real garden just like our one in Kentucky."

"A real garden? Is that right?" Lovina's inquisitive gaze looked first to Emma and then turned to him.

Emma leaned forward, resting her arms on the table. "Right, Dat? A big garden, right?"

Jonas reached across the table and ruffled her hair. "I don't know how big. It was just an idea. My sister Ruth Ann thought of it first—maybe something for the children? She seems to think that the Amish children here in Pinecraft are losing out on so much by not learning to care for a farm or garden."

Lovina looked at Emma thoughtfully, then back to him. "You know, I've never really considered that before. I love the idea of a garden. And it would be so good for the schoolchildren. I do have a large area in the back. It gets plenty of sun and there is a water source."

Jonas raised his eyebrows, surprised she jumped on the idea so quickly.

"I know that a few gardeners around here have already started planting. Do you know when you'd like to start?" Lovina asked.

"Start?" He shrugged. "I was just sharing the idea. I can't commit to overseeing a project like that. I wish I could, but with this being my first time teaching I don't think that I should take on too much. I couldn't take on *all* of it for certain…but if you knew a gardener, and he or she didn't mind the children getting involved…"

Lovina drew a breath. "Oh, I see. I thought you'd wanted to oversee it."

"I would if I could, but I'm leaving in May. I have a farm to return home to. And—"

Lovina raised a hand, cutting him off. "*Ja*, I understand. Do you think…" A smile filled her face. "Do you think if I found someone to organize the garden and plant it that the children would like to help?" Her eyes sparkled. They were so dark he was certain he'd never seen any darker, but he saw something else too—excitement. It was as if an idea was forming in her mind. Was Lovina thinking what he hoped she was? Was she considering roping in her sister Hope?

Jonas cleared his throat. "*If* it's not too much trouble. *If* you can find someone interested, then I thought it would be a good idea. There is so much I could teach." Then he released a big breath. "I'll leave it up to you."

A weight lifted from his shoulders and an unexpected lightness filled his chest. The idea was no longer in his hands. He'd offered the idea and would leave the rest to Lovina. Ruth Ann should be happy with that.

Lovina smiled, and she drummed her fingers on the table top, as if eager to get back to work. "*Gut.* I'll let you know. But even if we can make it happen it'll be a few weeks before we can get everything ready and…" She stopped her words and pressed her lips together. "Can you just keep this idea between you and me until I figure out if it will work?"

"*Ja*, of course." He picked up the fork and took another bite of pie.

"Lovina!" The front clerk called to her. A phone was pressed to her shoulder. "We have someone from Sarasota on the telephone. They want to place a big order. A *big* order…I told them they should talk to you."

"*Ja*, coming," Lovina called over her shoulder, and then she turned back to Jonas. "When I find *someone* I'll let you know. I have an idea, but…well, just know that it'll be worth the wait."

"I can be found at the school."

"At the school then. *Ja, danke*, Brother Sutter."

He cringed at the name. The students called him Brother Sutter, but he was happy to be called Jonas around town.

"Just call me Jonas," he called out to Lovina, but she had already hurried away.

Jonas looked back across the table. Emma was sitting there, perfectly still, and as quiet as a church mouse. It was a skill she'd developed over the last few years. With visiting doctors and nurses, Jonas often asked them to speak to him in private, as to not upset Emma. Yet the young girl figured out that if she sat perfectly quiet, perfectly still, her father often forgot she was there and continued with his adult conversations.

Emma removed her hands from her lap and placed them over her mouth. Her eyes widened, and then the smallest giggle released from behind her fingers.

Jonas steepled his fingers and leaned forward. He attempted a serious look, pretending to be stern. "Emma, what do you think is so funny?"

Emma giggled again, and Jonas had a hard time not smiling. His lip twitched, and Emma giggled more.

She lowered her hands. "Lovina said we have to keep a secret."

Jonas nodded and released a sigh. The bigger a secret Emma felt it was, the harder time she would have keeping it.

He cleared his throat. "Lovina said to just keep it to ourselves for a few weeks. She wants to talk to someone first." *She wants to talk to Hope first, I hope.*

Emma nodded, and her kapp strings bounced as she did. "That's a secret, and we can't tell." She shook her head from side to side.

"No we can't," Jonas said as she slid out of the booth. And deep down he was hoping that he'd have at least a few days before word got out. But with an eight-year-old girl involved, he guessed that would be an overwhelming challenge.

Old-Fashioned Cream Pie

⅓ cup all-purpose flour
½ cup butter
1 cup brown sugar
2 cups cream
1 unbaked 9-inch pastry pie shell

In a large bowl, blend flour into melted butter. Add brown sugar; mix thoroughly. Add cream and stir until well blended. Pour into pie shell. Bake at 350° for 50-55 minutes. Let cool before serving.

Chapter Six

Faith is the bridge over which we can cross
all the unknown waters of tomorrow.

AMISH PROVERB

⌒

Hope Miller sat at the kitchen table and flipped the calendar, looking at the white squares stretching from January to May, marking off the months in her mind—January, February, March, April, May...that was only five months until she could start gardening up north. Five months until she could return to the life— the lifestyle—she loved.

Earlier in the day, she'd walked to the small Pinecraft post office and mailed the letter to Eleanor, asking if she needed help with the kinder and garden. Eleanor had always been a favorite cousin and hopefully the response wouldn't take too long. Once she knew where she'd garden and the size of the plot, Hope could start flipping through the seed catalogs in earnest. Then maybe her life—her days—would feel more right. More meaningful.

The sound of a car idling outside their cottage told her that some women had stopped to chat on their bicycles. The driver was patiently waiting for them to finish their conversation so he could pass. She lifted the white shade and peeked outside, noticing three older women talking. From the looks of their kapps they appeared to be from Lancaster. Hope had seen them before, but she didn't know their names. During the season it was hard to keep track of who was coming and who was going. She let the white curtain drop.

The sound of hammering also thumped out loud and clear. Noah Yoder's nephew and friends were putting in a new shed, two doors down, but from the sound of it you'd think they were just outside her front door. Even after living in Pinecraft a year, she still wasn't used to so many people crammed into such a tight space. So much noise.

Hope attempted to ignore the sounds. She pushed the calendar to the side, wondering what else she could do to occupy her day. Without a job she filled her time helping Mem, but there was only so much she could do in this small place, especially something that didn't involve food.

She'd woken up to the spicy smell of apple carrot ginger muffins and devoured three. She never enjoyed baking herself, but she appreciated the treats her mem and sisters made.

She rose to wipe down the kitchen counter once again, considering what her friends back in Ohio were doing. They might be ice skating or having a sewing frolic. Or—like her—flipping through seed catalogs and thinking of a northern spring.

It wasn't that she disliked Florida. Hope liked the beach. She liked wearing flip-flops in December. It was just that she didn't know who she was here. In Walnut Creek she'd been known for her gardening skills. She'd spent seven months in her garden and the other months planning next year's crops. But here? She was simply one of the Miller girls.

The warm Florida breeze coming through the open kitchen window fluttered her kapp strings. She looked out at the hopeless garden plot. A few thin plants stretched their spindly leaves toward the sun, trying to live. Maybe her crime had been planting them in the first place.

She didn't know how to help them. Didn't know how to make vegetables grow in the sandy soil in their yard. In Ohio, she knew how to test the soil, fertilize it, and plant neat rows. Here, she didn't have the money to seek out good soil and create a better plot.

Hope crossed her arms over her chest and pulled them tight. For so many years her garden had felt like her true home. She closed her eyes, picturing herself stepping into a garden plot, rolling up her sleeves, and sinking down on her knees onto the rich black soil.

I'll be appreciated up north. My work will matter.

It was what she wanted more than anything, and she'd have to return to Walnut Creek, Sugarcreek, or a similar Amish community to find it. Until then she was simply an observer in the world around her. An observer of a world she didn't feel a part of. Out of pure boredom, she picked up another muffin and took a big bite.

From outside the front window came the voices and laughter of two younger women riding by on bicycles. Next door, the whir of a pressure washer mixed with the roar of the water hitting the cement driveway. She glanced at the clock. It was nearly five. She'd missed the gathering at three o'clock to meet the large bus bringing in a new group of snowbirds from up north. Not that she had anyone to greet. Not that she knew many people from Pinecraft to converse with while she waited.

When she first moved to Pinecraft, she used to join her sisters to meet the buses, but she'd given that up. The longing to hop on the bus and head back to Ohio was too great. And then she'd feel guilty—after all, Dat needed to be here. And her sisters seemed to enjoy the place too. They were thriving, especially now

that Me, Myself, and Pie was open and doing well. Only she felt
out of place and discontent—the opposite of how a *gut* Amish-
woman should be. So to fill time that seemed to stretch out end-
lessly, she'd go and check on her potted flowers in front of the pie
shop. It wasn't a vegetable garden, but at least it was something.

Hope poured herself a glass of milk and took a swallow. She
smiled, thinking of the first time she'd met Emma in front of the
pie shop. She'd been adorable with the ice cream dripping all over
her fingers and chin, yet the young girl's questions had been surprising. The girl seemed older than her age. As if she'd already
lived a long life in her few years. Now Hope knew why—Emma's
mother's illness and death had caused her to grow up quickly.
There was also a maturity in Jonas Sutter's eyes. He'd seen a lot,
she knew. But he seemed stronger for it.

A songbird beckoned her outside. Placing the glass of milk on
the counter she opened the kitchen door and strode out the back.
Emptiness filled her chest as she stared down at the small plot of
land that she'd tried to garden last year. It was one-sixteenth the
size of her garden in Ohio, but somehow it intimidated her even
more.

Hope squatted and took a handful of the freshly tilled dirt,
sifting it through her fingers. What would be the cost of bringing
in good soil? She had money saved up from nannying little Arnie,
but his family had moved away, and she no longer had that job.
Besides, if she wished to return to Walnut Creek she'd need every
penny to get reestablished. She couldn't waste it on good soil for
a small plot she'd be leaving soon.

"So, do you think we need better dirt?" Her dat's voice interrupted her thoughts. He'd gone for a short walk and must have
just gotten home. Hope rose and turned to him, brushing off her
hands.

"I *know* we need better soil, but I just don't think it's worth it. It's going to cost a lot, and I don't think we'd get a big enough harvest in this small space. Maybe I should forget the whole idea of gardening here in Pinecraft. We can buy vegetables at Yoder's for cheaper than we'll be able to grow them. It just doesn't make sense."

Dat offered her a sad smile, and she quickly looked away. It was almost as if he could look into her heart and read all the emotions hidden there.

"A garden isn't just about what it produces, Hope. It's about working in union with God and nurturing His creation. I'm your dat, remember? I know a garden is where you think your clearest thoughts and where you escape from the noise of the house— of the world."

Hope cocked her eyebrows and her jaw dropped slightly. "I—I didn't think that anyone knew that."

Her dat moved to the swing, and he held the side rail as he sat. He took a deep breath, and Hope watched as it expanded his lungs. He wasn't healthy yet, but he was better. And that made their move worth it.

"You live in a home with four sisters," he continued, "and they all like to talk. They are so similar to your mother in so many ways. Look at Lovina—she told us the pie shop was for other people to connect with one another, but she's the one always visiting and chatting with her customers. Seeing Lovina in the pie shop I see her truest self—how God made her to be. And Hope, your truest place is in the garden."

Tears pricked Hope's eyes, and she quickly turned away. "*Ja,* well, it seems that God has different plans for me at this time, doesn't He?" She looked at the sorry little plot of land and tried to hold back the tears. As she took in her own deep breath, the thick, muggy air pressed on her lungs.

"Maybe God does, or maybe He has a surprise for you yet," Dat said.

Hope glanced up. "What do you mean?"

A smile broke through, causing the corners of Dat's lips to rise. "I won't say just yet. I'll just say that I stopped by the pie shop a bit ago to drop off a sack dinner for Grace, and Lovina wants to talk to you. She asked me to bring you to the pie shop tonight." He turned to the back door. "Get on your flip-flops. There's a table waiting for us, and Lovina promised me a piece of coconut creme pie. And she asked for you to bring your seed catalog. She has an idea. One I think you'll want to hear."

- -

Vegetables in a California Garden, 1933

Someone has said that it takes a robin to make a spring, but to me the arrival of the first seed catalogue is the real harbinger of vernal dawn.

Works of homely interest, yet colorful and alluring, the catalogues of my favorite seedsmen have always been my spring season literature. They tell of old garden comrades, vegetable varieties tried and true, and bring news of promising youngsters, strains just making their bow to the garden world. Eagerly I thumb over each page, selecting the "guests" to be invited to my garden; and how difficult it is to limit the invitations!*

---

* Ross H. Gast, *Vegetables in the California Garden* (Stanford, CA: Stanford University Press, 1933), 17.

Chapter Seven

It is better to rejoice that our purse is half
full than to fret that it is half empty.

AMISH PROVERB

H ope mindlessly turned the pages of the seed catalog as she
sat at the small table at Me, Myself, and Pie. She and Dat
had gotten there thirty minutes ago. They'd both ordered pie.
Dat had finished his, and Hope had only eaten half of her piece
of cherry. The pie was delicious, as always, but she had too much
on her mind to think about eating.

Lovina had acknowledged them a few times with a wave and
with the mouthed words, "I'll be there in a minute." But every
time she tried to approach, someone had stopped her to ask for a
recipe or to gush about what a great asset the pie shop was to the
community. Finally, when the last rush of people left and only a
few still sat around the tables, Lovina approached.

There was a sparkle in Lovina's eyes as she sat across from them,
and Hope wondered how much of that was due to the pie shop
and how much was due to Lovina's growing relationship with
Noah Yoder. Hope and her sisters enjoyed taking turns guessing
how long it would be before Noah and Lovina's wedding would

be published. Faith guessed that it would be in November—the typical month for weddings in the Amish community—but both Grace and Hope believed it would be sooner. It seemed silly to wait so long to marry the one you loved, especially here in Pinecraft. It wasn't as if anyone needed to worry about getting the harvest in, or even about spring planting. Waiting until November was not important in her opinion.

Lovina sat in the chair next to Dat and turned her attention to Hope. "I've been thinking. Wouldn't it be wonderful to do something with the back plot?"

Hope poked her fork into a cherry and twirled it in a circle. "Are you thinking about putting in an outside patio? That would be nice during the season. I've rarely seen the store without a line—more seating would be welcome."

"Oh, that is an idea too, and maybe something to consider in the future, but what I was actually thinking about was a garden."

Hope's head lifted. She dropped her fork to her plate. "A garden?"

"*Ja*. It's a large space—much bigger than our backyard."

"It would be a lovely idea if we were in Ohio, but I don't think that's a great idea here." Hope sighed, and the ache in her chest grew. "You know what a miserable time I've had in that little bitty plot in the backyard."

"That's true, but I talked to Noah about it earlier today. There are some garden clubs around here, and they have to get their dirt from somewhere."

"You mean their *soil*." Hope sighed. "I can't imagine the cost of bringing it in."

Lovina reached over and patted Hope's hand. "There will be an expense, but Noah and I think it's a worthwhile investment. If we get in good soil, I have no doubt we can have a wonderful garden. Noah's very resourceful. He knows so many contractors in the area, and they're always helping each other out. He's already talking about building some raised boxes or beds to make it easier. We thought the boxes would be a perfect work project for Mose, Gerald, and Atlee."

Heat rose to Hope's cheeks. Her lips started to open in excitement. "Wait...you're serious?" Hope pointed her thumb behind her, toward the back of the building. "You want to grow a garden—a real garden out back?" She sucked in a breath, taking in the aroma of baking pies, cherries, and promise. "But why would you do that?"

Lovina's fingers drummed on the table, as if she couldn't hold in her excitement. "Personally, I love fresh vegetables, and we have all that space not being used. It'll be something that can be enjoyed by..." Lovina pressed her lips together, and she stopped there. Then she shrugged. "Enjoyed by so many in this area. Please say yes. I'm excited just thinking about it."

Hope tilted her head and studied her sister's face. Lovina's grin was large—almost too large. With Hope's perusal Lovina glanced to the ceiling, as if the network of the warehouse's ducts and beams was the most interesting thing she'd ever seen.

There had to be more than what Lovina was letting on about, but Hope wouldn't press. Unhindered joy—something she hadn't felt for months—surged up from her stomach and caught in her throat. It shocked and amazed her that Lovina would do this for her. It would be an expense. It would be a risk. But looking at the spark in Lovina's eyes Hope knew it wasn't about the vegetables. It was about giving Hope a precious gift.

Hope reached across the table and grasped her sister's hand. She squeezed tightly, and then she looked to her dat. He was sitting quietly, but she could tell he was excited too. Pride beamed from his eyes as he watched the interaction between his daughters.

Tears lined her lower eyelids, and the cover of the seed catalog blurred. She ran her hand over the glossy page.

Would it really be possible to have a garden in Pinecraft? And if it was, would it be enough? Would her heart long to stay? If she did get a garden started that didn't mean she couldn't leave, could it? Maybe it would be the perfect project for Dat too. He was feeling better, and he didn't have a farm to run. Maybe she could do it for *him* as much as herself.

"*Ja*, Lovina. I like the idea…if you can find good soil, and if it doesn't cost you too much to set up." She considered telling Lovina about her letter to their cousin Eleanor, too, but changed her mind. She'd wait to see if Eleanor wrote back.

"Don't worry about any of the cost, Hope. All you need to do is look through that catalog and decide what you'll need to get started. I'll put in the order of seeds for you. I'll also talk to Noah and he'll take care of everything else."

Hope's chest warmed. Was this really happening? She wanted to pinch herself to make sure she wasn't dreaming.

Lovina turned. A new surge of customers had entered. Instead of being overwhelmed by them, Lovina seemed pleased. "I have to get back to the kitchen, but let's talk tomorrow morning when you've had a chance to look at the catalog." Then Lovina smiled, and her nose wrinkled up as she did. "Take time to dream tonight, Hope. Don't let doubts or worries keep you from dreaming." She rose and hustled off with a simple parting wave.

Hope watched her walk away, and then unexpected laughter spilled out. She picked up her fork and took another bite of her cherry pie. "Tomorrow? Lovina isn't wasting any time, is she?"

Dat stroked his long white beard, looking pleased. "*Ne*. From the moment that she decided to open this pie shop she's been a different woman. It's as if your sister has gotten a taste of what God can do, and she can't wait to see Him show up more."

Hope tilted her head and looked to her father with curiosity. She'd grown up her whole life going to church. She'd heard more messages from their Amish preachers than she could count, and she'd seen her father and mother leading a simple faith, but she'd never heard him talk in such a way.

"*Ja*, I suppose that makes sense," she finally answered.

Hope wanted to ask her father about all the changes within him—with Lovina—but she held her words in. It seemed odd to talk to him about spiritual things. It was so much easier talking about gardening.

She opened the first page of the seed catalog. "So what do you think I should plant? Maybe I should start by seeing what grows well in this zone, *ja*? I'm sure the library has some books on gardening in Florida." She again thought about her letter to Eleanor. Should she write her cousin another letter, telling her she'd had a change of plans? *Ne.* If Hope did get a job and decide to move, she had no doubt that her dat would be happy to take over the back-lot garden.

"It would be good to check out some books, just as long as you add strawberries sometime this year. There's nothing as wonderful as plucking a fresh strawberry right off the vine. I'm looking forward to that."

"I have to admit that one of the things I'm most excited about is the peace and quiet." She sighed. "There aren't many places to find it around Pinecraft."

"*Ne.* That's the truth. But I doubt that even this big warehouse can block out all the noise."

"Still." She smiled. "It'll be a place just for me. When the people and the noise seem to press in I'll have a place to go." She clapped her hands together. "Oh, and I'd guess with the right soil we'll have a wonderful harvest."

Another large group of customers neared, and soon all the tables around them filled. The noise of their voices caused the hair on Hope's arms to stand. Hope pushed her pie plate back from her.

"Dat, you don't mind if I go around the back to take a look, do you?"

"*Ne*, not at all. I'll be back in a little while." He winked. "Maybe if I sit here longer Lovina will offer me another piece of pie."

Hope rose and hurried out. The air was warm and humid, but it was much quieter—even with the traffic noise. As she rounded the back of the building, her heartbeat slowed. She took in the large grassy area separated from the buildings behind it by a tall fence. It was peaceful and quiet. Hope closed her eyes and pictured a garden there. She took in a deep breath that smelled of sun and grass, picturing small sprouts of new life poking up. And for the first time since they'd moved to Pinecraft, Hope had a sense of lightness in her chest. More than that, she had a glimpse of being home.

- -

Cherry Pie

2 Tbsp tapioca
⅛ tsp. salt
1 cup sugar
3 cups drained sweet or sour cherries, juice reserved
½ cup cherry juice
¼ cup almond extract
1 Tbsp butter

Mix tapioca, salt, sugar, cherries, juice, and almond extract together
in a large bowl and let stand 15 minutes. Pour into 9-inch pie shell.
Dot with butter. Cover with top crust. Seal edges and slice hole
in top for venting. Place on baking sheet and bake at 350° for 50
minutes.

Chapter Eight

If you want children to keep their feet on the
ground, put responsibility on their shoulders.

AMISH PROVERB

◦⊙◦

In just two days Jonas Sutter went from hearing about an idea for a garden from Clyde to discovering that one was going in at the pie shop. Jonas rounded the side of the building. Rays of the new dawn stretched down over the large grassy area. One never knew what a week would hold, he supposed.

Last night, after he'd put Emma to bed, Jonas had heard his brother-in-law Clyde chatting with someone on the front porch. He'd planned on ignoring Clyde and instead finishing his lesson plans for the coming week, but then he heard his name mentioned not once or twice, but numerous times.

Jonas had opened the screen door and peeked out.

"There you are," Clyde had said. "I'd thought you'd gone to bed."

"Oh no, just put Emma down."

It was then that Clyde had introduced him to Noah Yoder, and within thirty minutes Jonas had found himself agreeing to meet the man before school, bright and early, to help plan the garden plot.

Now, as two birds chirped overhead and a yellow and white butterfly danced by on the warm breeze, Jonas stood and surveyed the area.

"I'm glad you want to help me figure this out." Noah removed his hat and brushed his blond hair back from his forehead. "But don't let anyone know you're involved in this—not yet. Lovina has some things planned for this project—some people who want to get involved—but…" Noah's voice trailed off.

"But just as too many cooks can spoil the pot, too many gardeners can spoil the soil."

Noah chuckled. "I've never heard truer words."

Jonas held an ordinary college-ruled notebook and pencil in his hand as he walked the length of the area and then walked back to Noah. "What do you think of three rows of three raised beds? They'd run from north to south to catch the best sun. I've heard of using cement blocks, too, instead of wood. They last longer and they're easy to set up."

Noah nodded. "I heard of a place where I could get good soil too. I know you have to get to school this morning, but if you have time this weekend I'd love for you to ride along with me to look at the dirt." Noah offered a shy smile. "I know my way around a junkyard, but I've never been one to have a green thumb."

Jonas crossed his hands over his chest and chuckled. "*Ja*, of course. I'll see if Ruth Ann can watch Emma."

"You can bring her if you'd like. I'm sure one little girl couldn't get in too much trouble."

Jonas narrowed his gaze. "I wish that were so, but my daughter's a little too much like me. You remember the incident at the

park, don't you? Poor Hope Miller. I'm sure she was simply trying to enjoy a quiet walk." He shook his head. "But even if Emma
were on her best behavior, I don't want her too involved, not yet.
It's going to be hard for her to keep a secret."

"*Ja*, Lovina feels the same. She told Hope—" Noah paused and
his eyes widened. "Uh, pretend I didn't just say that."

Jonas winked. "Say what?" He looked to Noah and tried to
hide his expression of joy, but inwardly his heart warmed. As he'd
talked to Lovina he'd wished that she was thinking of Hope as the
gardener to oversee this project.

He turned his back to Noah and looked to the rising sun. Tenderness washed over him at the remembrance of Emma in Hope's
protective arms. For so long he couldn't imagine another mother
for his little girl, yet now this young woman in Pinecraft had
stirred his thoughts in that direction. He felt both unworthy of
someone like her and hopeful at the same time. And, even if she
wasn't interested in more than a friendship, this garden would be
a gift. If Hope was a gardener, like Emma said she was, then he
was happy to help.

With thoughtful consideration, Jonas sketched out nine long
raised beds. Then he walked over to Noah and held out the sketch.
"There is so much space to use, but maybe this is enough to get
started? And together we can run some pipes from that spigot to
create a simple watering system. It shouldn't take more than a few
hours' work."

His words were interrupted by a soft clapping sound, and
Jonas's head jerked up. He expected to see Lovina, or maybe their
dat, but instead an older woman stood there.

She was Amish, and she wore a simple brown dress and white
kapp. Her white hair was combed neatly without a hair out of
place. The woman wore walking shoes and yet leaned heavily on

her cane. Jonas tilted his head, wondering what she was doing out this early. Wondering where she'd been walking to, and how she'd even found them back there.

"I thought I heard voices!" she called, answering his last question. She neared them with a quicker pace than he'd expected.

Noah approached her, his smile wide. "Can I help you?"

"Don't you remember me?" She lifted her chin and gazed directly at Noah. "I'm Elizabeth Bieler from the fabric shop. Faith—Hope's sister—works for me, and I'm the one who let you borrow my quilt at the park last Saturday."

Jonas cleared his throat. "I'm actually the one who borrowed the quilt. Hope took it home. I hope it was returned."

"Of course it was returned." She smiled. "I've just come to inspect."

Noah's hat was still in his hand and he scratched his head. "Inspect?"

"*Ja*, I've come to hear about your plans for the garden."

Jonas's heartbeat quickened. He glanced at Noah. "Did you tell her?"

Noah shook his head, and they both turned their attention to Elizabeth, waiting for an explanation.

"No one told me." Elizabeth leaned on her cane. "I've been praying about it. I've been praying about a garden that would bring the community together—just like our garden did in 1942." The older woman jutted out her chin, appearing pleased.

Noah nodded, but in a way that told Jonas he was simply trying to appease the woman.

"1942, that was during the war," Jonas said. "I know that many Englisch communities banded together during that time." Jonas didn't tell the woman that history was his favorite subject. He waited to see what she had to say instead.

"*Ja,* and sometimes we can learn a lot from those who've gone before us, Englisch or not." She lifted her cane and pointed it at Noah's chest. "As soon as those raised beds are in I'd like you to tell Hope to come see me. Tell her I have something for her." Elizabeth smiled. "A gift."

Noah nodded, and Jonas could again tell that he was puzzled by this woman. Noah returned his hat to his head. "*Ja,* of course."

The woman walked away, humming a tune as she did.

Jonas looked to Noah, and the man shrugged. "So maybe I'm not the only one who guessed that this garden is for Hope."

"*Ja,* someone must be talking, but I suppose that's not my concern. It's my job to make sure the beds are in and to get the soil." Noah pointed to Jonas. "And then it'll be your job to take care of the rest. You did promise to help, didn't you?"

Jonas nodded. He didn't want to seem too eager, but he had to admit that he was looking forward to spending more time with Hope and working with his students in the garden.

"Just as long as you don't forget to pass that woman's message to Hope…when the time is right, of course."

Noah nodded. "*Ja,* I have a feeling Elizabeth Bieler will search us out if we forget."

Jonas looked to where the woman had just left. "And I'm eager to hear what the woman was talking about too. It sounded like that garden in 1942 was pretty important." He shrugged. "I'd planned on tying in science and math to our lessons, but maybe there will be a chance to add in some history too."

Jonas looked down at his sketch, wondering how everything had changed. He'd gone from teaching school to now being part of this garden. And then there was his friendship with Hope. Tonight was the singing that he and Emma were going to attend with Hope. Jonas stroked his chin, wondering if they'd make it through the night without Emma speaking of the garden. He knew his little girl, how excited and eager she was. Then again, he knew how much she liked Hope, and maybe the idea of a surprise would seem like a special gift to their new friend. That was how it felt to Jonas, and as he walked to the school he had a hard time hiding the extra bounce to his step. Tonight he would see Hope, and in the next week or so he'd help to give her the ultimate gift.

- -

Lovina's Pie Crust

3 cups all-purpose flour
1 cup solid shortening, chilled
½ tsp. salt
1 egg
5 tsp. ice water
1 tsp. vinegar

Mix flour, shortening, and salt. Beat egg and add water and vinegar. Add to flour mixture to make a soft dough (do not over-handle or you'll end up with a chewy crust). Makes one double pie crust or enough for two single crust pies.

Chapter Nine

No joy is complete unless it is shared.
AMISH PROVERB

〜

Jonas carried three lawn chairs down to Birky Square. A crowd was already gathered on the street and milling around the open, grassy area. Amish and Mennonites of all ages were gathering for the gospel sing. Old Order Amish women wore black dresses. New Order Amish wore similar dresses, but in lighter colors. Almost every young woman wore flip-flops, and one could easily tell where everyone was from by the cut of the dresses and the style of their *kapps*. Men wore everything from homemade Amish clothing to jeans and short-sleeved dress shirts. Laughter rose up among the flowing streams of conversation, but Jonas knew as soon as the music started the noise would still. Musical events like this were not common in most Amish communities. This was a special treat to be enjoyed by those who'd come down to escape winter's harsh grasp.

Emma walked by his side, and Jonas scanned the crowds looking for Hope. He spotted her near the back of the sea of lawn chairs. She stood alone, tall and straight-backed. Her dress was light blue, just a shade lighter than the sky overhead. Her eyes lit up, and a smile filled her face when she spotted them approaching.

"Oh, *gut*, I was hoping you'd bring chairs. My mem, dat, and sisters are using ours." She pointed to the other side of the gathering. Seeing the back of her parents' heads, Jonas nodded.

"I'm so glad that you're joining me. It's always nice to share *gut* music with new friends," she added.

"Of course. Emma and I have been looking forward to it."

When he first came to town Ruth Ann had talked about the concerts. It seemed strange to him that the Amish—who believed playing instruments was too prideful—would find such joy in watching others play. Within the crowd there was also a smattering of Englischers. His guess was that they'd be quick to clap along, but he had no doubt that even the Old Order Amish would begin tapping their toes to the beat once the four-part music group started to sing.

"We'll have to come back in a few weeks too. The first week of February they have a bean soup dinner to go along with the music. A sweet couple hosts it in memory of a sister lost. They cook it in a large kettle over an open fire."

Jonas set up the lawn chairs. "It sounds like something we should return for."

He sat, but Emma completely ignored her chair. Instead, she stood next to Hope's chair, leaning close. After a few minutes of listening to the musicians Hope leaned close, speaking low into Emma's ear. "Would you like to sit on my lap?"

Emma grinned and climbed on. Both seemed content to listen to the music, and Jonas's stomach scrunched into a tangle of knots. His palms grew sweaty, and he wanted to look at Hope again, but he was afraid he'd stare too long. He hadn't felt this way since he'd first sat across a fire pit at a singing as a twenty-year-old man and watched Sarah in the glow of the fire. He never thought he'd ever feel this way again.

For all of his life Jonas had learned to follow God's Word and his heart. From a young age his dat had spoken of that very thing.

"Read God's Word and trust, Jonas," he'd said more than once. "Know that God wants to be involved in every part of your life. See Him in the world around you, and when there is a burning in your chest, follow it."

That burning in his chest had led him to the small farm in Kentucky. The move had been good for him, and it was in Kentucky that he'd met Sarah. Falling in love with her had been the greatest experience in life, followed by the birth of Emma. Even through Sarah's sickness and death he never regretting marrying her. He would do it all again if given the chance. Loving her had meant everything to him. She'd given him more love in their married years than most men received in a lifetime, he guessed. And now that burning feeling, deep in his chest, had come again.

It was as if the Florida sun was trapped in his chest every time he was around Hope Miller. He'd experienced it the first time at Phillippi Creek. He'd been so frightened when he heard the woman's voice screaming his daughter's name. And then he neared the boat ramp and found Hope soaking wet, holding his Emma cradled in her arms. Emma's arms had been tight around Hope's neck and the beautiful woman had clung to his daughter.

Emma's embrace was partly from fear. It was also of need. He'd done his best to be a *gut* father. He'd tried to treat Emma with tenderness, just as he thought a mother would. But when Jonas saw Emma in the woman's arms he knew the truth. *I'm failing. Ruth Ann is right.* Emma needed a mother. He needed a wife. Seeing Emma in Hope's embrace told him that she could be the one.

He sighed, hoping that this inner sense wasn't leading him astray. After all, Hope seemed far from interested in him.

And he guessed why. Hope Miller was young and beautiful.

She was at least eight years younger. He had to face the facts. Hope Miller probably had lots of other bachelors interested in her. Those who were younger. Those who lived in Pinecraft year-round. Those who didn't have a ready-made family.

They listened to the music for nearly an hour. Jonas hadn't seen Emma so peaceful for quite some time. When the music finished they decided to walk down to Pinecraft Park. They talked about winters in Kentucky and Ohio as they walked. They talked about what their homes were like. Hope talked about her garden.

"Emma, when I was your age I used to pick a tin pail full of cherry tomatoes, washing them off under the cool water from the spring pump and then sitting under the tall maple tree and eating them all. I kept the heirloom seeds from those tomatoes. They were as old as the tree itself. Maybe older."

Emma wrinkled her nose and skipped ahead. "Yuck, who wants to eat old tomatoes?"

Jonas chuckled and shook his head, but he didn't explain. They seemed so content walking along like that.

"My grandfather once told me that our garden had been tended in the same plot since before the Civil War." Hope sighed as her arms swung at her sides. "I felt part of something there—part of history, part of the heritage. And I sensed I was meant to tend that garden."

Hope went on to share about her dat's illness and their move.

"And here?" Jonas dared to ask. "You don't feel the same about gardening?"

At the word *gardening* Emma reached up and took his hand, squeezing it. She glanced up at him and winked. Jonas smiled back, knowing their secret was safe.

Hope lifted her hands in the air in defeat. "Here, for so long, I felt like an imposter. The soil is an enemy. The sun a weapon."

"Those are strong words."

Hope cocked an eyebrow. "Have you tried to plant anything here?"

"No." Jonas shrugged. "But I have a feeling, Hope, that under the right conditions you'd be able to get a garden to grow…no, make that *flourish*."

She tilted her head and looked at him. She opened her mouth to say something, but then closed it again. Had she been about to tell him about the garden behind Me, Myself, and Pie? And if so, what stopped her from saying anything?

Give it time. Give her *time.* The words blew into Jonas's mind like a soft ocean breeze. Time? He didn't have much of it. As soon as the school year was finished in Pinecraft he'd be heading home.

The music played, and Emma started clapping along, but Jonas's mind wandered. Would there be enough time to see if anything special was growing between them?

Bean Soup

½ pound dried white beans
1 onion, chopped
1 tsp. vegetable oil
5 cups water
one ham hock
½ cup mashed potatoes (optional)
½ tsp. salt
¼ tsp. dried thyme
½ tsp. black pepper
½ pound bacon, cut into small pieces

Place beans in a Dutch oven; add water to cover. Bring to a boil; boil 2 minutes and reduce heat. Simmer on low until beans are softened. Drain and rinse beans, discarding liquid. Sauté onions in oil until soft. Stir in the beans, water, ham, potatoes, salt, thyme, and pepper. Add bacon pieces. Bring to a boil. Reduce heat; cover and simmer 1½ hours. Makes 7 servings.

Chapter Ten

Greet the dawn with enthusiasm, and you
may expect satisfaction at sunset.

AMISH PROVERB

⁓

Hope couldn't believe the difference that a week could make. She stood by Lovina's side and her mind couldn't take it all in. Nine raised garden beds had been built, and they were filled with rich, dark soil.

"Did Noah do all this?" The raised beds were two feet high and made with concrete bricks. They were perfect. The soil was perfect. The warm breeze carrying on it the aroma of salty sea air even seemed perfect today.

"Noah, Gerald, Mose, and Atlee…and a few other men from the community helped too." Lovina swept her hand toward the pipes leading away from the raised beds. "The best part is they put in an irrigation system. One of the local fellows made it so it'll be easy to water the vegetables. All of the beds will get at least six hours of sunlight, just as you asked for."

Hope clasped her hands together. Then she pointed to the garden beds farthest from the building. "I can see it all now. The tomatoes, peppers, cucumbers, and melons—the fruiting crops— can be out there where they can get as much full sunlight as possible. Then the broccoli, collards, cabbage, and most of the leafy crops can be here—closer to the building—where they can get more shade."

"*Ja.*" Lovina nodded. She kicked off her flip-flops and stepped into the cool grass beside the raised bed. "I'm agreeing with you because you obviously know what you're talking about. I'll stick to the kitchen."

Hope walked to the nearest raised bed. She took a handful of dirt and let it slide through her fingers.

"I'll leave you to your garden, Hope. Just let me know what seeds you'd like to order. There's no time like the present." Lovina moved back toward the side of the building and then paused. "Oh, and Noah had a message for me to give you. Remember Elizabeth Bieler from the fabric store?"

"*Ja.* I've met her a few times, and I asked Joy to return her quilt that she lent me." Hope's mouth circled into an O. "She's okay, isn't she?"

"Oh, *ja.* It's nothing like that. She simply stopped by and asked Noah to tell you to come by the fabric shop sometime. She says she has something for you."

Hope smiled. "That is nice of her." She crossed her arms over her chest. "I wonder what it could be?"

"Quilted garden stakes?" Lovina laughed. "Then again, I'm surprised no one has thought of that yet."

"*Ja*, well, that would be interesting. I'll stop by later today, after I write up my seed order. I've been looking through the catalogs at every chance."

Lovina pointed to a gray folding chair leaning against the back of the warehouse. "I brought that for you. I thought it would make it easier to sit and write everything out."

Hope stroked her chin. "You think of everything, don't you? I can't imagine a better big sister."

"Took me twenty-five years to hear you say that!" Lovina chuckled as she called back over her shoulder. "Enjoy your dirt."

"It's soil," Hope mumbled as she sat down with a notebook. "Dirt is what four-year-old boys dig around in." And she couldn't help but smile, too, as Lovina disappeared around the corner.

Hope eyed the beds, feeling as if she'd just been given the greatest gift of her life. She'd been thinking about what she wanted to plant over the last two weeks. She'd even looked up planting schedules for Florida gardens at the library, but she'd almost been afraid to plan. But now she could get started in earnest. With the large raised boxes she had as much space as a large garden, half of her space back home. She copied the layout on the notebook, and then began to fill the boxes.

Pole beans, okra, eggplant, and green peppers in one box. Lima beans and cantaloupe in another. She was writing "tomatoes and green onions" in a third box when footsteps sounded behind her. It was an older gentleman, one she'd seen around town. She believed he was a full-time resident, but she couldn't be sure. He was a shorter man, and instead of an Amish shirt he wore a short-sleeved shirt in plaid. He wore dark rimmed glasses, and his short cropped hair was more gray than brown. She guessed him to be one of the Mennonite men in town.

The man pushed his glasses farther up his nose. "I hear that you're putting in a garden here."

"*Ja*, it's so *wunderbar*. My sister set it up for me."

He approached and stood over her shoulder, reading her notes. He nodded in approval. "*Ja*, that will work."

"Why, thank you…" She grimaced. *I didn't realize this was a joint effort.*

"Are you going to plant asparagus? Rhubarb?"

"I wasn't thinking rhubarb, but asparagus could be a possibility."

"*Ne*, don't do that. Neither of them grow well in Florida. Don't even waste your time."

She nodded. "*Ja*, okay. I won't."

She waited for him to leave. When he didn't, she pretended he wasn't there. She wrote "carrots and radishes" in another box and tried to think through the rest of the spaces. It didn't work. His nearness caused her chest to tighten. She forced calm, rhythmic breaths and told herself to focus on the stillness of this place. On the quiet.

"It's good to see that the boxes run north and south…"

"*Ja*, then the exposure to sunlight is even for all rows."

"You know a bit about gardening." His glasses slid down his nose, and she resisted the urge to push them back up for him.

Then, over the noise of a truck rumbling down the road in front of the pie shop, she heard more voices approaching. Two women were talking loudly and discussing gardening. Hope heard one urging the other to join her in walking behind the pie shop to take a look at the new garden there.

Please keep going. Please keep going.

She turned back to her new friend, who continued to hover close. "Gardening is my favorite thing to do." Hope caught the man's gaze and forced a smile. "I love the stillness. I love working *alone* with nature…" She rose. Would it be rude to excuse herself and finish her planning at home? Would it be rude to put up a *NO TRESPASSING* sign? If she were back in Ohio no one would dream of going onto another person's property and walking through their garden. What made it all right here?

As expected, two women rounded the corner, approaching. They paused, and smiles filled their faces to see the nine long raised garden beds.

Hope recognized one of the woman as Vera Chupp, their

neighbor. The other woman looked so much like Vera that Hope was certain she was a sister or a cousin.

"So it is true?" Vera approached with quickened steps. "It's so exciting to see such a nice garden. I do believe it'll be the largest in Pinecraft."

"It's so wonderful that you're doing this." The other woman wore a forlorn look. "I think all of us miss our gardens back home."

"Oh, and it'll be especially good for the children too." Vera reached down and slid her fingers over the silky soil. "I feel bad for those who are being raised in Pinecraft. They don't know what it's like to explore a farm or help weed a garden. In fact, I was talking to Ruth Ann just yesterday and she was saying that her niece was bored. Can you imagine that? I've never heard of an Amish child on a farm being bored."

Tightness filled Hope's chest. Had a sign been posted near the front door of the pie shop? *We're growing a garden in back. Come take a look and offer some advice or a few precious memories!* No, but that didn't really matter. News quickly spread around Pinecraft. And it was only beginning. She trembled considering that this might be a new destination spot for those in the village.

"I'm sure most of the children who live here visit family up north sometimes," Hope said. "I imagine the children here *are* as connected to their families in Ohio, Indiana, Pennsylvania. Maybe they do chores on vacation. Weeding for them would be fun for them, *ja?* I mean, up there…on vacation. Uh, not here." Her voice trailed off. The last thing she wanted was to have her garden invaded by children. A shudder traveled down her spine as she imagined them digging their fingers around her new sprouts.

"*Ja*, that's true," Vera said, "but now there's something closer to home, isn't there?"

The women walked through the cement block rows, and as they did they talked again about their own gardens up in Indiana. The sun beat down on Hope. She touched the top of her kapp, and it was warm. It wasn't even noon, but it was already getting uncomfortable—from the heat and from the visitors. Her perfect morning disappeared just like that.

She made a mental note to herself. On the days when she started planting she'd need to get to the garden early. Not only would it be cooler, but maybe then she'd be able to find the peace she longed for.

Hope rose, folded up the metal chair, and placed it against the back wall of the warehouse.

"I can't wait until you start planting," Vera's friend said. "What fun it will be to observe everything. And I also can't wait to tell Jonas that you're already getting started. Do you mind if he comes by tonight to look?"

Jonas? The woman spoke as if Hope should know who she was talking about. Was she talking about Jonas Sutter, Emma's dat?

The woman nodded expectantly, and Hope smiled, certain that Jonas had to be her brother or some other relative. So many people were related around Pinecraft, it was hard to keep track.

"*Ja*, sure. Jonas is free to stop by, but I doubt I'll be here. And while you're at it don't forget to tell him to stop in for some pie."

"Of course. I know my cousin Clyde told Jonas about the orange cream pie. I'm not sure if he's tried it yet." The woman's smile broadened. "I'm Wilma, by the way. Vera is my sister."

Hope nodded, making the connection. Vera and Wilma were sisters. Clyde, Ruth Ann's husband, was their cousin. That would make Jonas...a distant relation, but that didn't really matter among the Amish.

Hope pressed her notebook to her chest, trying to hurry the

conversation along. "I'm sure Jonas will enjoy seeing that a new garden is going in. I never imagined it would be so exciting."

A few minutes later the women left with a smile and the Mennonite man followed after them, promising to be back tomorrow. Yes, she'd have to get up early to beat this crowd.

She longed for a place of peace. She longed for a bit of quiet. And now Hope longed for the garden to be hers, and hers alone.

Victory Gardening, 1942

Most people in small towns and villages either have suitable garden spots of their own or can obtain the use of conveniently located
small plots of reasonably good soil that are not too steep, too wet,
or too shady. In most cases it is not very satisfactory to attempt gardening at any great distance from home. Inconvenience results in
neglect. However, small-town and village dwellers who can find
good areas near at hand can learn to grow vegetables profitably.
Fresh vegetables out of one's own garden give a particular satisfaction and pleasure.*

---

* Victory R. Boswell, *Victory Gardens*, United States Department of Agriculture Miscellaneous
  Publication No. 483, Washington, D.C., issued February 1942, 2.

Chapter Eleven

You are poor only when you want more than you have.

AMISH PROVERB

‿⟡

The sun was barely on the horizon when Hope entered the garden. Three days had passed since the raised beds had been set up, and she'd spent that time discussing her layout with Dat and waiting for her seed order to be delivered. Yesterday, Hope nearly hugged the mail carrier when it arrived. Then last night she'd labeled her seed packets, collected all her gardening tools in her bucket, and now had everything ready to plant.

The streets had been quiet in Pinecraft on her walk to the warehouse. Although the Amish were known for getting up early, most were still enjoying a cup of coffee, and only a few had been out sitting on their front porches as she'd walked by.

Hope moved to the first raised bed and then paused. Movement caught her attention, and she jumped, realizing someone was already there—squatting by the farthest garden bed. Her heartbeat quickened when she spied the silhouette of a man. She could barely make out his form in the dim, early morning light.

What is he doing here so early? Was it safe?

The man stood, and she still couldn't see his face. He placed an Amish hat on his head, and she felt safer, but still she debated whether to run. Pinecraft was a small village set within the larger city of Sarasota, Florida. News of crimes was often reported in the local paper.

Hope felt more at ease seeing his Amish hat, but it still seemed strange to have someone in her space, especially so early.

Hope cleared her throat. The man turned. She sucked in a breath, recognizing Jonas Sutter. His eyes fixed on hers and a smile touched his lips. Seeing him took her breath away. And in the light of the early morning it was as if she truly saw him for the first time.

He wore the typical white shirt and Amish pants. He wore the same hat every other Amish man did, but he was *unlike* any Amish man she'd ever known. His eyes appeared dark and his eyebrows lowered. It wasn't a frown, but rather curiosity, as if he was wondering what *she* was doing here so early.

"Can I help you?" he asked with a humored smirk on his face. He took two steps toward her, and she found herself taking a step back.

Jonas had a handsome face, boyish almost, but also intelligent. Why hadn't she noticed how handsome he was sooner? Maybe because he was alone, without Emma to draw her attention away. Maybe because she'd gotten used to his beard and saw him not only as someone who'd been married before but rather someone who'd faced unimaginable loss and had carried his daughter through it.

Hope tilted her head to the side. "Help me? I—this is my garden."

"Your garden?" He frowned again, and those eyebrows folded even more, making him even more handsome.

She pointed to the building beside her. "*Ja*, this is my sister's place—Me, Myself, and Pie. She asked me…"

"Oh, Lovina's your sister, *ja*." He held humor in his gaze. "I met her in the pie shop, and I heard of her long before I came to Pinecraft. My sister Ruth Ann wrote letters while it was being remodeled, telling me all about it. From all that she wrote, it seemed as if this warehouse was transformed overnight."

"It wasn't overnight, but it did go fast. Two months I believe. Maybe three." Hope crossed her arms over her chest, still wondering what Jonas was doing here. Wondering why he was so interested in her garden beds. And why he was pretending he didn't realize she and Lovina were sisters.

Jonas glanced at his book bag that he'd set on the dewy ground and then met her gaze once again. "I'm heading to school now, but if you'd don't mind I'd love to stop by later and see what you've planted." He pointed to the seed packets in her hands.

Hope hadn't planned on being there this afternoon. She'd planned on planting early and heading home before it got too hot…and before the garden received too many visitors. Still, this was different. He was different. She swallowed down the emotion balling up in her throat. "*Ja*, of course."

Jonas stepped closer, and he pointed again to the seed packets. Lima beans were on top.

"Did you know that you can plant lima beans in the same furrow as weaker-sprouting vegetables and the lima beans help break up heavy soil, making it easier for the other plants to grow?"

"*Ne*, I didn't know that. I suppose one can learn something new every day."

He picked up his book bag and strode to the edge of the building. Then he paused and looked back over his shoulder. "Just don't do too much planting yet, all right? I'd like the children to get involved."

"The children?"

"*Ja*, the schoolchildren. Speaking of which, I better get going. I need to get everything ready. They're still getting used to me as their teacher, and I'm still getting used to them."

Hope nodded, and her gaze followed his retreat. "I'll see you later then," she called after him.

It was only after Jonas left that Hope realized she had no idea what their conversation had been about. Jonas was the new schoolteacher—at least for this spring—but why was he so interested in her garden? And more than that...why was she so glad that he was?

But then her brow furrowed, just like his had. While she liked the idea of inviting Jonas into her garden, and even having Emma around, why had he said *children*? Surely he wasn't talking about *all* the children he taught, was he? Hope pressed her lips into a tight line.

She rested a hand on her hip, elbow askew, also wondering why Jonas had acted so comfortable around the place. Maybe Lovina knew something about this—more about the handsome widower. *I've got to get to the bottom of this.*

Hope pressed her seed packets to her chest. She'd have time to plant them later today, but first she needed to talk to Lovina. Her oldest sister had been eating a piece of toast and fried egg when she'd first woken up, and she was gone by the time Hope made her own breakfast. Hope guessed that Lovina was already in the pie shop, preparing for the day. Even though Me, Myself, and Pie had four full-time bakers, the shop had brought in many more customers than expected—especially during high season. Grace had even approached Lovina about opening an online shop after a local businessman had suggested it. While the idea was a good one, Lovina was having a hard enough time simply keeping up with the pies sold in the store. Sometimes—like today—she came early to make as many pie crusts as she could to get ahead.

Hope walked around to the front. She set the seed packets in her garden bucket and then left the bucket by the open front door. Even before she entered, she recognized both Lovina and Noah's voices. But there was also another voice that she didn't recognize. It was an older woman, and her voice held a slight quiver from age. Hope entered and all three faces turned to her. Lovina stood behind the baking counter, rolling out pie crusts. Noah leaned against the counter with his arms folded over his chest, and Elizabeth Bieler—Joy's boss from the fabric store—sat on a wooden chair next to the counter. On her lap she held a paper bag that had been rolled down on top, making it looked like an oversized lunch.

"Well, there she is." Elizabeth offered a quick wave. "Just the person I wanted to see." Then she turned back to Lovina. "Oh, I enjoyed talking to you, too…don't feel as if I didn't. And I promise I'll bring by that recipe for orange fritters. I think you'll like it. I found the recipe in one of my mother's old cookbooks. With so much wonderful citrus this time of year you'll just have to give it a try."

"*Ja*, I'd love to. Believe it or not, sometimes I need a break from baking pies." Lovina chuckled. "And if you have any good pie recipes, I'd love to try them too. I love to add a new, special pie every few weeks or so."

Elizabeth lifted her chin. "*Ja*, I'll have to look around and see what I can find. I love being able to give special gifts to friends." She patted the bag on her lap and glanced over at Hope. "Which is why I've come."

Lovina's eyes brightened. "Oh, Hope, do you remember the other day when I told you Elizabeth had something for you? She got tired of waiting for you to stop by." Lovina chuckled and brushed the back of her hand across her forehead, leaving a smudge of flour on her temple. "I told her that I thought you were out back, in the garden, but she insisted on waiting until you finished your conversation."

Noah looked at Hope from the corner of his eyes. "Conversation? Your sister doesn't hide her excitement very well, Hope." He clucked his tongue. "Is it someone we should know about?"

Heat rose to Hope's cheeks. "It was Jonas Sutter. He'd just come by. I hadn't expected him." She shrugged. "Maybe he just wanted to check out the new garden?"

"Check it out?" Noah shook his head as he reached over and snatched a strawberry from the bowl in front of Lovina, taking a bite. "I'm not sure what Jonas needs to check out. He's the one who helped me with the layout. He also designed the irrigation system."

"Jonas did that?" Hope's voice broke, and she quickly looked to the side, embarrassed by the emotion that was evident in her voice. "I—I didn't know." She turned to Lovina. "You told me Noah and the teens were building it. But you didn't say anything about Jonas."

Lovina pressed hard against her rolling pin, not looking up. She worked quickly, rolling with fast movements. "Well, I, uh...I told you that other men from the community were helping too. I didn't know I needed to mention names." The dough under Lovina's rolling pin tore. She picked up the dough and formed it roughly into a ball.

Hope narrowed her gaze. Lovina was usually gentle with her crusts. Lovina had told Hope more than once that being in a hurry made sloppy crusts, which could only mean one thing…Lovina was nervous. Lovina had something to hide.

Noah reached over and placed a hand on Lovina's shoulder. "Lovina, that crust isn't going to get up and crawl away, I promise."

She glanced up, surprised. And then she bit her lower lip. "*Ne*, of course not. I'm not sure what's gotten into me." She looked up at Noah and her face softened. A silent conversation passed between their gazes. Hope placed a hand on her hip. Both of them knew something—something they were hiding from her.

Looking away from Noah, Lovina took a keep breath, and then she turned to Hope. "Actually, I *do* have something that I need to talk to you about." Her cheeks lifted in an attempt at a smile. "Maybe tonight, after dinner?"

What could be so serious, so secret? Hope's mind went blank. By both Noah and Lovina's responses, Hope knew it had something to do with Jonas. Why would he volunteer to help with her garden? And why had he been there this morning, looking it over? Nothing made sense.

"*Ja*. I'd be happy to talk to you tonight." Hope looked to Elizabeth, understanding that whatever Lovina wanted to share didn't need to be discussed in front of their elderly friend.

"I know that the two of you need to have a talk about Jonas Sutter—he is worthy of a conversation—but I have something to talk about too." Elizabeth slowly began to unroll the top of the paper bag. She reached her thin, age-spotted hand inside and pulled out a folded square of fabric.

"First, I made an apron for you, Hope. Your sister Joy designed the aprons for Lovina's pie shop, and I thought I'd try to create my own apron—a garden apron." She handed it over.

"You did this for me?" Hope unfolded the heavy canvas material. It was an apron all right, with thick straps and large pockets in front. But the best part was what Elizabeth had embroidered on front.

"Planted with Hope," Hope read. Emotions surged up through her chest. She'd hardly had more than a few short conversations with Elizabeth, but the thoughtfulness of the gift overwhelmed her.

Hope put the strap over her head. It caught on her *kapp* and then she fixed it. The apron slipped on and she tied it in back.

"I love these pockets." She slid her hands into the deep openings. "These are perfect for my seed packets and my tools."

"And for something else—another special gift. Although this one isn't for you to keep. It's for you to borrow for a time."

Hope's brow furrowed. "Borrow?"

Elizabeth pulled out an old book from the bag. It was the size of a small notebook with a hard cover. The edges were worn, and the green faded cover proved its age. Elizabeth set the paper bag to the side, and she ran her hand over the cover.

Lovina paused in rolling out her crust. "What is that? An old hymnal?"

Noah straightened and stepped forward. He leaned down, excitement clear on his face. "That's an antique. I'm sure of it. It looks like an old journal."

"*Ja*, that's exactly what it is." Elizabeth smiled again, broader, and for the first time Hope noticed the hint of dimples on her aged cheeks. "It belongs to one of my friends—well, a friend who started out as a customer at my fabric shop. She's Englisch, and her family has lived in Sarasota for over a hundred years. They have a beautiful family home by the water."

"But why would she want to lend that to me?"

Elizabeth's eyes twinkled. "It's a garden journal. From 1942. My friend's mother was named Pauline, and in the midst of

World War II she started a Victory Garden—have you ever heard of that? Most families had one during the war. There was rationing back then, since so much food went overseas to the troops. Gardens sprouted up in small backyards, on large estates, and even in parks. People knew if they were going to make it through that war they had to do their part to fill their stomachs."

Hope looked from Lovina to Noah and then back to Elizabeth again. She'd heard about Victory Gardens before, but she hadn't paid much attention.

Lovina placed a perfect crust into a tin plate and started to flute the edges. "That's an amazing gift."

Noah leaned even closer. "I'd love to get my hands on that. Collecting antiques is one thing, but reading about a person's experiences is another."

Hope glanced to Noah, then to her sister, and back to Elizabeth. They all seemed to understand what this was about, but it still wasn't making sense to her. None of it.

"So, you want me to read it…to…to get ideas for my garden?"

"Well, that's part of it, but mostly I just thought you'd enjoy reading about what Pauline faced in 1942. There are many similarities between you and Pauline, even though you may not see them at first. You're an expert in the garden and she…" Elizabeth paused. She flipped open the front cover and traced her hands on the woman's name. "She wasn't a very good gardener at first, but that changed. And more importantly, she changed too." Elizabeth shrugged. "Janet—my friend—told me her mother's story once, and then she let me read this. When I heard that it was time for a garden in this place—behind the pie shop—I knew Pauline's story was one you needed to hear."

Hope nodded, still not understanding. Part of her was afraid to borrow such a priceless heirloom, but in another part of her excitement bubbled up. She'd already skimmed through a few books on gardening in Florida, but maybe Pauline's journal would provide even more tips. It would be worth glancing through if nothing else.

Hope stretched out her hand, and Elizabeth handed over the journal. Then she pointed to Hope's pockets. "I even made sure there was a pocket big enough for the journal to fit inside."

"Oh, I'm not going to carry it into the garden. I don't want to mess it up." Hope opened it. Small, neat handwriting scrolled across yellowed pages. "I'll look through it and get it back to you next week."

"Next week?" Elizabeth shook her head. "You'll never be able to get through it by next week. There is no rush." She reached forward and patted Hope's hand. "Take your time. Savor the stories. There are even some recipes that Pauline wrote down—some of her favorites. I've tried a few."

"Recipes?" Lovina snickered. "Elizabeth, Hope has many talents but she doesn't really enjoy the kitchen very much."

"You never know. I might like these recipes." Hope glanced down at Elizabeth. "Maybe I'd like a copy of your orange fritters recipe too." Then she jokingly raised an eyebrow at her older sister. "Just because I don't spend a lot of time in the kitchen doesn't mean that I *can't* cook."

"And just because I don't garden doesn't mean I can't pull a weed," Lovina huffed with a bit of humor.

Hope chuckled, and it felt good. Lovina had her pie shop, and she had her garden. And together—well, they acted more themselves than they had since leaving Ohio.

Hope held up the book to take a closer look, and she also pushed all the questions about Jonas Sutter to the side. She'd worry about that later too. Today, she was excited to read the journal and to discover its secrets, but for the first time since being in Pinecraft she also felt a small sense of belonging. Elizabeth had lived here for years. There were new people coming and going all the time, yet Elizabeth had thought of *her*. She'd reached out to her. Elizabeth had given her hope…not only for the garden, but in how she was seen in the community.

Hope gazed into Elizabeth's eyes. She tucked the journal into her pocket and then leaned close. "Thank you."

Elizabeth nodded, smiled, and reached out her hand. Hope placed her hand in the older woman's grasp. The woman's skin felt paper thin, yet soft.

Elizabeth squeezed gently. "Enjoy the journal, and know that I am available if you ever need someone to talk to. Each of us needs a listening ear sometimes—someone to help us weigh our options, whether that means staying or leaving."

"Leaving?" The word shot from Lovina's lips, and Hope straightened up. She pulled her hand back, surprised.

"I never heard about you leaving," said Lovina. "You're not leaving Pinecraft, are you? Not now, *ja*?"

Hope's mouth dropped open, and she glanced over at her sister. "I haven't really mentioned it to anyone, but I have to admit it's been on my thoughts." She turned back to Elizabeth. "I haven't told anyone except for Eleanor. Have you talked to her? Do you know my cousin?"

Elizabeth shook her head. "I know many Eleanors, and I'm not sure if any of them are closely related to you. Since most of us came from the same group of Anabaptists, I'm sure that most of us are related to each other somehow, but to answer your question I haven't talked to anyone—well, except to God."

The older woman placed a hand over her heart. "He doesn't spill any secrets, but once in a while I have a sense of something to pray for. Last year I started praying for this warehouse." She swept her arms wide. "And when it was nearly done I felt called to start praying for a garden…" She pointed. "A garden out back. Oh, and once, while in church, I felt God telling me to pray for you, Hope. I started paying attention to you then, even though you like to keep to yourself, and that's when I heard that you'd been a wonderful gardener back in Walnut Creek, but you weren't having much luck here. That made me think that you've most likely started thinking about returning home to Ohio. After all, each of us loves to be in the place where we find the most success."

A cool sensation rushed from Hope's chest and into her limbs. It was the same feeling she had once in a dream where she'd forgotten her dress and covering. In the dream she'd run from hiding place to hiding place but couldn't find any way to cover herself. She felt the same way now, but it wasn't a dream. She felt seen by Elizabeth in a way that she usually wasn't, and it made her uncomfortable. It was as if the wall she'd placed around her had been stripped bare. She felt vulnerable and exposed. Hope tucked the journal into the large front pocket and then crossed her arms over her chest, pulling them close.

Lovina still hadn't picked her rolling pin back up. Instead, she eyed her sister as though seeing her for the first time. She reached her hand to Noah, as if needing support, and he grasped it and took a step closer to her.

"Is this true, Hope?" Lovina asked.

"I have been thinking about going back. Maybe by May. I wrote Eleanor to see if she needed a *maud* and a gardener."

"*This* May?" The color drained from Lovina's face, and Hope wished she'd said something sooner. "But—but we just put so much work into the garden out back. So much…" her voice trailed off.

"It was an idea, nothing more." Hope pulled her arms tighter against her chest and shrugged. "I was simply testing the waters to see what Eleanor thought. I have no specific plans." She thought about the entry she'd written in her journal and backpedaled, trying to tell the truth in a way that didn't hurt her sister even more. "Or rather, maybe it *is* a goal—a dream for the year—but that doesn't mean I don't appreciate the gift you've given me with the garden. I appreciate that more than you'll ever know, and I have no plans of leaving soon. It'll be a big decision if I do."

Lovina nodded, and Hope noticed tears welling up in her older sister's eyes. "It seems as if we do have a few things to talk about, Hope. I'll try to see if I can get home early."

"I'd like that." Hope let her eyes flitter closed, and she focused on the pull of the journal in her pocket. Had Pauline faced many questions and doubts? Maybe so. And maybe she needed to understand those even more than receiving gardening tips.

Because harder than getting anything to grow in Pinecraft was trying to understand how to maneuver in this community.

Orange Fritters, 1942

Peel oranges and separate into sections. One orange makes fritters for two or three. Remove seeds, if any, carefully, making the smallest possible incision. Dip sections in batter made of:

¼ tsp. salt
1 cup flour
2 Tbsp sugar
1½ tsp. baking powder
⅓ cup milk
1 egg
1 Tbsp melted butter

Mix salt, flour, sugar and baking powder, add milk gradually, egg well beaten, and melted butter. Fry in deep hot fat. Sprinkle fritters with powdered sugar, to which may be added, if desired, ½ tsp. grated orange rind. Serve hot.*

---

* Marjorie Kinnan Rawlings, *Cross Creek Cookery* (New York: Charles Scribner's Sons, 1942), 197.

Chapter Twelve

Those who fear the future are likely to fumble the present.

AMISH PROVERB

❧

Hope picked up her garden bucket and headed in the direction of home. Her heart ached remembering the pain in Lovina's eyes when she discovered that Hope had thought about leaving. She should have mentioned something sooner. Lovina had just put up a huge expense to create a garden for her. The least she could have done was to tell her sister the truth.

Then again, she didn't think Lovina had been completely truthful either. There was something about Jonas Sutter that Lovina was hiding. Hope just wished she knew what. It would be hard waiting until this evening to know. It would be even harder to get the look of Jonas's gentle eyes gazing at her out of her mind.

An Amish woman walked by in a sea-foam green dress. A small white dog trailed on a leash. The panting dog had a hard time keeping up. Hope smiled and called a greeting, but instead of stopping to chat, the woman continued on.

The streets of Pinecraft were filled with bicycles and those on foot. There were many more people out than when she'd left home this morning. And thankfully by the time she returned home her other sisters and parents had already left for the day. It wasn't that she didn't want time to see them, but she did appreciate the quiet and the time to process her thoughts.

Her guess was that Mem and Dat had gone over to see how things were shaping up for the Haiti mission auction. It was a large event, drawing huge crowds every year and raising hundreds of thousands of dollars for the poor in Haiti. And maybe—with that event coming to the area at the end of the week and drawing attention—she'd have fewer people poking around her garden. One could only hope.

She poured herself a glass of iced tea and sat with the journal. She flipped open the first page and read the woman's name again. *Pauline Spencer. March 10, 1942.* A Scripture passage had been written under her name and the date: *John 12:24.* Hope's Bible was still in her bedroom, and she told herself she'd look up the passage and read it later.

Then she started on the first page.

Tuesday, March 10, 1942

Mother gave me this journal. It's a nice gift, but I'm not much of a writer. She told me to write my deepest thoughts, but maybe I'll use it to record news of the war instead. Last year, on my twenty-seventh birthday, I would never have imagined that we'd be pulled into the war we'd been hearing about in the papers. We had no choice really, after Pearl Harbor. So many lives lost. Such great cost to our naval fleet. I can't understand the horror of knowing one's son, brother, or husband died in such an attack. My heart aches for every one of those who are still trying to imagine their days without someone they love. I do understand that.

Monday, March 30, 1942

I heard from the grocery store clerk that an American ship encountered a German U-boat off the coast of Virginia. Somedays the war seems far away. Not today.

I found this in a book I was reading. It means a lot on days like today.

> In good times and bad, a vegetable garden is a valuable adjunct to the home, financially, physically and spiritually…It makes family income more elastic, it brings health in fresh goods and outdoor exercise, and what is more important, to my way of thinking, it teaches the whole family many wholesome lessons. And now that we have a war to win, a vegetable garden can contribute directly to national safety.

Wednesday, April 1, 1942

Richard would have been 29 years old today. I thought I'd use this new journal to record events from the war, since all this will be part of history someday. But that is too depressing. So for now I'll think about my dear husband and wonder where he'd be now if he hadn't lost his life in that factory accident. Europe? The South Pacific? He wouldn't have sat at home and watched others heading out to fight.

Closer to home, I heard that it's the 97th Bombardment Group who are at the new Sarasota Army Air Field. Janet loves to watch the large B-17s flying over, but she's too young to understand what they mean.

Friday, April 17, 1942

I never thought much about gardens until I decided to grow one. My idea started with a book I found on my mother's kitchen cabinet. I must have read the title of her cookbook a hundred times, Economical War-time Cook Book, but it means something different now that we have a war of our own.

I've started planning the garden, but Mother doesn't know yet. I *had a little money set aside and I've already purchased the seeds. I'm also writing down important information on conservation. This is a much better use of my new journal. And growing a Victory Garden is better than simply moping around this large house all day. Since Richard's death my only purpose has been caring for Janet, but what type of example am I to my daughter by hiding away? I've had enough quiet. I've had enough rest. I need to live life again.*

There are many people doing much more for the war effort, but this is the best thing I can think of to show Janet that we are doing our part. Tomorrow I will plant our garden, and today I will plan and pray. Without food, no man can fight. Without food, a war cannot be won. I have no husband to serve, and with a daughter my fight will look different, but I'm determined to try.

Hope looked through the rest of the journal's pages, hoping for a picture of Pauline or Janet. There was none. Elizabeth had said that Janet was her friend, and she wondered how old the woman would be now. She pictured Janet and tried to imagine her staring up at large planes overhead not truly understanding what they meant. She'd have to ask Elizabeth the next time they were together.

Near the back of the journal, Hope found a piece of paper. It looked as if it had been torn out of a book—maybe the cookbook that Pauline was talking about.

Seven Commands for War-Time Conservation*
Prepared at Cornell University, Ithaca, N.Y.

1. *Set aside enough money to buy 1 quart of milk a day for each child and ⅓ quart of milk a day for each grown person.*

---

* Janet McKenzie Hill, *Economical War-time Cook Book* (New York: George Sully and Co., 1918), 3-4.

The grown person may use some cheese in place of all milk; 1 8/10 ounces of cheese will replace 1/3 pint a day for each grown person.

The grown person may use skim milk. Half of the daily quart for the child may use skim milk, if necessary; but it is not best to feed the child skim milk.

Children suffer more from lack of milk than do grown persons.

2. *Buy 2 to 3 ounces of some fat for each grown person.*

    Children will not need as much as this if they are getting a quart of whole milk a day.

    The best fat is butter, particularly for little children.

3. *If money is scarce, buy only enough sugar to make the meals palatable.*

    One and one-half ounces, or about 3 level Tbspful of sugar, honey, molasses, or syrup a day for each person will do this.

    Sugar is not a necessary food; too much money spent for sugar is likely to deprive the family of more needed foods.

4. *Buy for each day some potatoes and one other vegetable such as cabbage, onions, carrots, turnips, beets, or other available fresh vegetables.*

    The children can eat daily 2 to 3 medium-sized potatoes and 1/2 to 1/2 pound of one of the other vegetables.

    The grown person can eat daily 6 to 8 medium-sized potatoes and 1/2 pound or more of the other vegetables.

5. *Buy only as much wheat and wheat products as the Food Administration rulings allow.*

    The rest of your need for cereal food may be satisfied by

such other cereals as rolled oats, pinhead oatmeal, cornmeal, hominy, barley, rice, and buckwheat.

If possible, buy flours, meals, and breakfast foods made from the entire grain, such as water-ground cornmeal, rolled oats or oatmeal, cracked wheat, graham and whole-wheat flour. They have greater food value than have the refined products.

Less bread and other cereal foods are needed, if some dried beans or peas are eaten and if potatoes are used freely.

One serving of dried beans or peas or one medium-sized potato may replace one serving of cereal or one slice of bread.

6. *If some money still remains, buy a little fruit for each member of your family.*

   Apples, fresh or dried, and dried prunes and raisins are among the cheapest fruits.

7. *If there is more than enough money for this necessary food for all members of the family, spend it to increase the variety and flavor of the meals.*

   The plain but safe diet resulting from following rules 1 to 6 may be made more palatable by spending more money.

   Meat may be added for grown-up members of the family.

   Eggs may be added for all members of the family.

   The amount of money to be spent for milk, cream, butter, cheese, fruits, vegetables, fats, and sweets may be increased.

   This more expensive diet may be more pleasing but not more wholesome than the first one suggested.

Hope read over the rules twice, trying to imagine living during wartime. She chuckled imagining eating six potatoes a day. She also had never considered the numerous sacrifices people made during time of war. The Amish didn't believe in war. They were pacifists, and she'd never known a family member to fight in the Armed Services. Once she'd heard that her own grandfather had served in the Conservation Corps during World War II instead of fighting, but she'd never really considered how everyone in the family had been affected during that time. How ordinary people had to sacrifice.

Growing up on an Amish farm she'd always had food. Her dat had grown wheat and corn on his farm in Ohio. They always had fresh eggs, and Mem had made her own cheese. There had been plenty of milk, and the cellar had been full of jars of home-canned food. Most meals ended with dessert, which seemed like an extravagance after reading about wartime sacrifice.

Even after they'd moved to Pinecraft they'd had plenty of food. They had no garden, but Yoder's Produce Stand had a wide variety of fruits and vegetables. Was it really just seventy years ago when food had to be weighed and measured to make sure that everyone had a little? When meat was only for adults because there wasn't enough to go around?

She flipped through more pages of the journal, noticing descriptions of garden plots, recipes, and lots of personal notes. Hope still didn't understand why Elizabeth had insisted she borrow it, but it was interesting. She read a little bit farther.

Monday, April 20, 1942

Mother was the ultimate penny pincher. "Waste not, want not" was one of her favorite sayings. She liked to repurpose as much as possible, even though Father had a good salary at the bank. She was horrified when she saw that I had dug up her luscious grass today, but she felt slightly better when I told her it was a matter of stewardship. "Why grow grass when we could grow food for ourselves and our community?" I told her.

Wednesday, April 22, 1942

Folks around Sarasota started to wander by around the time I planted the first few rows of seeds. And then it happened: I got my first volunteer. It's an elderly man who moved in with his daughter three houses down. And after that, a mother of three asked if she might have a small area to plant in too. I didn't see a problem with it. Thankfully Mother didn't either. We just dug up more grass and created a plot. Martha told us we'd given her and her children a wonderful gift, but the way I feel tonight—so content and at peace—I feel as if I've been given a great gift too.

There is a new movie out called The Jungle Book. *I'm going to take Janet to see it tonight. She's been working so hard.*

Saturday, April 25, 1942

Today was a good day. Mother came out to help too. She met Ethel and Hazel. They live less than a mile away. The three stood out front and chatted for two hours at least. They're getting together tomorrow to roll bandages for the Red Cross. And just think they've lived just over a half mile from each other their whole lives and never knew each other.

Blackouts have been taken more seriously now. U.S. planes raided Tokyo and most people are sure they're going to respond. I wonder if Janet remembers a time before blackout curtains and rationing.

Sunday, April 26, 1942

I see a lot of posters around town, talking about teamwork and volunteering. When I started the garden it was something that I wanted to do for me...and for Janet. Janet is my biggest helper. She is diligent about pulling every weed. What I didn't realize was that this garden was for more than just me and my daughter. It was for Mother, for our neighbors, and for our community. There have been some who have been gardening for a while, and now they're helping those who are just getting started. It's been a wonderful thing to see.

Hope folded a napkin and used it as a bookmark. Her stomach growled, and she realized it was already lunchtime. She still had no idea where her parents were, and for once she wished the house weren't so quiet. She wished she had someone to talk to about what she was reading in the journal.

Hope walked to their refrigerator. There were leftovers—crisp chicken, mashed potatoes, and carrot pineapple fluff salad, all from last night. It was Thursday, which meant it was Hope's day to cook. Usually she put on a pot of soup. When she used to work, and had a small salary, she used to bring home food from Yoder's restaurant, but once she'd begun saving up money to move she'd stopped doing that.

She pulled out the mashed potatoes, wondering if she should use them to make potato soup once again, and then she remembered a recipe from Pauline's journal. Somewhere in the middle there'd been a potato casserole recipe that looked easy enough. Hope pulled out all the ingredients and set to work. She seasoned and rewhipped the potatoes. Then she layered them into the bottom of the casserole dish. She fried up the bacon and made "nests" in the potatoes. She prepared everything in fifteen minutes, except adding the eggs. She'd do that tonight before she put the casserole in the oven.

Stepping back and pleased that she'd used one of Pauline's recipes, she covered the casserole dish with foil and set it in the bottom of the refrigerator. She made herself a sandwich, thinking about going back to the garden this afternoon. She didn't want to start planting—she'd save that for the morning. But she couldn't help but wonder if Jonas Sutter would stop by. A smile touched her lips when she remembered how he'd looked at her this morning. Hope's smile broadened even more considering that Emma might be there.

Hope quickly made a green salad for dinner and put that in the fridge too. With dinner prepared she enjoyed a piece of cold chicken and grapes. Once all the dishes were washed and the kitchen clean, she slipped on her flip-flops. She was about to head out the door to the garden when she decided it would be best to leave a note.

Dinner is in the fridge. I'll put it in the oven when I get home. She placed the note on the counter and had a strange sense of satisfaction. She'd been discontent for so long that she didn't feel like cooking or spending the time with others, but now…something had changed. It was strange in a way, but she understood a little of what Pauline wrote about. It seemed odd that a few conversations in the garden and in the pie shop and making dinner for her family could make her feel alive again.

- -

Potato Casserole with Eggs in Bacon Nests, 1918

4 cups mashed potatoes
Salt and pepper
Milk or cream, butter
2 eggs, well beaten
12 bacon strips
6 whole eggs

Season potatoes very well with salt, pepper, milk or cream, and butter. Add 2 beaten eggs and beat until light and fluffy. Pile lightly into greased casserole and, with the back of a spoon, make in the surface 6 hollows, each large enough to hold 1 egg. Meanwhile partially cook bacon and line each hollow with 2 strips. Place an egg in each. Bake in moderate oven (350°) until eggs are set and bacon is browned. Season eggs. Grated cheese may be sprinkled over top just before eggs are done. Serves 6.*

---

* Ruth Berolzheimer, *250 Ways of Serving Potatoes* (Consolidated Book Publishers, Inc., 1941), 30.

Chapter Thirteen

The foundation of understanding is
the willingness to listen.

AMISH PROVERB

◦⁓

Hope tried not to hold her breath as she walked to her garden. *Breathe normally.* She told herself it really didn't matter if Jonas and Emma were there or not. But even as she walked, she had a hard time convincing herself. She would be disappointed if they weren't there waiting for her.

Afternoon clouds had rolled in, making it cooler than it had been earlier this morning. Before leaving the house she had slipped on a sweater. She'd also grabbed her bucket with seeds and gardening tools.

The bucket tugged on her arm and swung by her side as she walked. She waved at friends and neighbors as she walked past, but her mind was mostly on Emma. From the way Pauline talked about young Janet in the journal she guessed her to be Emma's age. Something Pauline wrote stuck in Hope's mind. Parents were models for their children. Children learned by what they witnessed. Emma no doubt liked to tag along with Jonas on his farm back home, but maybe Hope could be a positive influence on her while she was in Pinecraft. Hope had already decided that if Emma stopped by with Jonas, she would offer to let the young girl plant some of the seeds.

It only took ten minutes to walk from her house to the garden. Hope rounded the corner and paused in her steps. Her lips opened with excitement.

Jonas and Emma were there.

He was on his knees examining a watering pipe connected to one of the raised concrete beds. Emma was near him, walking along the edge of a concrete block like a gymnast on a balance beam. Her arms spread out to her sides and the slightest breeze ruffled her dark blue dress.

Hope stepped closer to the building, partially hiding in the shadows, and studied them. As she watched, Emma walked to the end of the raised bed, and then she lifted her hands high. "Dat, watch!"

He paused his work, pushed back his hat, and fixed his eyes on her. Jonas's devotion to his little girl was clear.

Emma flapped her arms, as if they were bird wings, and jumped. Despite the effort, her body sank like a rock and she tumbled onto the grass.

"Whoa! I believe you jumped higher that time!"

Unplanned laughter spilled from Hope's lips, and both sets of eyes turned to her.

"Hope!" Emma rose from the ground and raced Hope's direction.

Jonas didn't call Hope's name. He didn't run to her, but his smile—and the happy look in his eyes—offered the same eager welcome.

Her stomach did a little flip as she met Jonas's gaze, and then she turned her attention to the little girl.

"Making yourselves busy, I see," Hope said as Emma approached.

Emma immediately grabbed Hope's hand and tugged. With more strength than Hope expected, Emma dragged her to Jonas. They paused just a few feet away from him.

Jonas pointed to the pipe, but he didn't look up. "Had a little leak, but it's fixed now."

"I appreciate that. I'd expected to be hauling buckets of water from the spigot or setting up sprinklers. The watering system was a nice surprise."

Jonas eyed Hope's bucket. "And I appreciate your waiting to start your planting." He stood, his tall frame towering over her, and placed a hand on Emma's shoulder. Emma hovered by Hope's side with a new unexplained bashfulness.

Hope nodded. She hadn't really waited to plant the first seeds for the reasons he thought—to save the task for when Emma was present—but she didn't need to explain that. She was simply happy now that she had waited.

Hope lifted the bucket. "Ready to get started?"

Emma's eyes widened. "*Ja!*"

Hope pulled off her sweater, revealing her gardening apron.

"Plant-ed wi-th Hope!" Emma read. "Can I get one like that?"

Hope shrugged. "I don't know, but I'll see what we can do. It seems like you would need one if you'd like to be my little helper."

Emma's face brightened in a smile. She looked to her dat, who was smiling too. "*Ja*, I can be your helper!"

Hope glanced down at the long row. "How about we start with carrots?"

Emma reached for the packet of seeds. "Okay."

Hope pulled the bucket back a little. "No, wait. Not yet. We have to make sure the soil is *gut*." She set down the bucket and pulled out two hand rakes. "First, we're going to break up all the lumps. And make sure there are no stones."

Hope kneeled at the side of the raised bed and slowly combed the rake through the dirt. Wherever Noah and Jonas had got the garden soil, they'd found premium dirt. There were few clumps and even fewer stones, but if she was going to model for Emma how to garden she wanted to make sure to do it right.

As Hope worked, Emma watched her, her eyes following Hope's movements, and then did the same.

Side by side they raked through a quarter of the long box. Hope tried to pretend that Jonas wasn't watching. She tried to imagine it was just her and Emma and this was their garden, but the pounding of her heart betrayed her.

When the soil was nice and loose, she tore open a package of seeds and poured some into her hand. "Now we're going to take a pinch—maybe five or six seeds—and poke them into the ground about an inch, which is about as deep as the top part of your thumb." Hope put down the seed packet and modeled it for Emma. She took the seeds between her pointer finger and thumb, pushed them into the loose, moist soil, and released them.

"And make sure you do it in a straight line," Jonas added.

Hope straightened, locking with his gaze. His eyes were smiling today, too, and it was hard not being pulled in to his dark brown eyes. "Oh, you're one of those type of gardeners are you? You don't scatter the seeds, you line them up?"

"And you're not?"

"Of course I am." She grinned. "It's just that every time my dat helps in the garden he likes to work quickly. He's not too concerned about nice, neat rows." She pointed her finger. "But he has taught me a few tricks. Did you know that you can mix in a few quick-growing radish seeds to mark the carrot rows, since the carrots take so much longer to pop up?"

Emma reached into Hope's bucket. She dug around, finding the package of radish seeds. "Can we do that here?"

Hope nodded. "Since we have these raised beds, I didn't think we really needed to do it. It'll be much easier to remember where the rows are here, but I *did* buy some radish seeds because I'm impatient. I don't like to wait two weeks to see sprouts poke up."

They worked side by side, planting the carrots and adding radish seeds sprinkled in.

Jonas watched, and every once in a while he offered help or advice. Hope gladly accepted both. When they were finished with the carrots she considered planting more, but Emma had returned to her balance beam act. Hope wanted this to be fun for the girl, not just work, so she decided to wait. She had plenty of time to plant in the morning, and the many early mornings to follow.

"Hope, what do you love about gardens?" Jonas asked as they watched Emma chase a butterfly.

"I love everything—the soil, new buds, tiny roots, Jerusalem Crickets, roly-polies, the scent of dirt."

He nodded, agreeing. Then he looked at her, lifting his eyebrows. She waited, having a feeling he had something to ask.

"What? What is it?"

"What do you think about the children getting involved in the garden? The children from the Amish school. There are miracles in the soil, don't you think? Art and science too." He winked. "We can measure plant growth and look at root patterns. We can study clouds, weather patterns, and insects. And then when it's time for harvest, the *kinner* can taste their efforts."

The joy of the moment faded as if a dark cloud had moved over her. Feelings of anxiety somersaulted through the pit of her gut. Tension built in the center of her chest and crawled outward—a sharp, creeping heat. Helping one little girl and spending time with Emma was one thing, but she couldn't imagine dozens of students running around, shaking seeds out of packets and climbing over her raised beds. Her stomach ached just thinking about it. The idea of a quiet sanctuary dissipated like the morning dew under the hot Florida sun.

Hoping to hide her worry, Hope pulled a handkerchief from her garden apron and dabbed her forehead.

A brief silence hung over them as she attempted to find her words. "Wouldn't it be hard to walk all this way with the children? It has to be a mile. I'm sure if you asked Noah he could build planters over at the school. There's a grassy area around the side, isn't there?"

Jonas's smile fell. It wasn't the answer he expected.

"That is a possibility, but there isn't great access to a good water source over there. And the only area on the school property that has enough space is on the west side of the building, which is shaded most of the day. I just don't see how that could work."

The tone of Jonas's voice changed too. A stab of regret dug into her heart. Hope scolded herself. *Be more open...don't always think of yourself now.* Wasn't that part of being Amish, living in a community and caring for each other?

Like Vera had mentioned, the Pinecraft children would benefit from growing a garden. They'd be able to learn a lot too. Also, opening up the garden to the schoolchildren meant that she'd have a chance to spend more time with Jonas. Yet even though it logically made sense, her heart cinched up and refused to submit. What purpose would there be for her to stay in Pinecraft if she didn't have a garden of her own? None. None at all.

"Too much shade and no good water source. Those *are* problems." She tucked a strand of hair behind her ear. "Can I think about it?"

The gaiety had disappeared from his eyes, replaced by a troubled frown. "Are you saying you don't want us around?"

Hope bit her lower lip, feeling both selfish and foolish. She'd wanted this garden to be a place of retreat and peace. She was already being invaded by friendly neighbors, and the flow of visitors would most likely increase as word got out.

Bringing children into her space would be even worse. A neighbor might want to watch her work or offer advice, but children could undo her good work. She cringed, thinking of dozens of little hands digging around in her soil, messing with the plants, disturbing new shoots, and interrupting growth cycles as they dug down to check the size of root vegetables or attempted to pull weeds and pulled up the plants instead.

"I'm just saying I want to think about it," Hope finally answered. "And I need to talk to Lovina. After all she's the one who set up all of this. It was her idea to start with."

"*Ja.* Of course." He narrowed his gaze. "So Lovina hasn't talked to you?"

"About what?"

"Oh, just about this garden. About, uh, the ideas for it…"

Hope threw her hands up in the air. "Can you be more specific than that?"

"Why don't you talk to her? I don't want to get in the middle of it." He shrugged. "It's just that when she and I talked, I had a different idea of what this whole thing was about."

Hope glanced up to the sky, wondering when Jonas and Lovina had talked. She was also confused why their conversation hadn't included her. It was as if they had a planned destination when she was just getting used to the idea of going on a journey.

She folded her hands into a tight ball, ignoring the dirt under her fingernails. Then she dared to look at him again. "I will talk to her. We're supposed to talk tonight, in fact. I'll mention what you said—about the children from the school. And I'll be asking some tough questions myself."

"Listen, if it's going to be a problem—"

"I'll talk to her." Hope interrupted his words. She brushed her hands together, wiping off the dirt. Her stomach tightened down again and all the happy feelings of the hours before vanished.

Silence hung in the air, and she turned her back to Jonas. She bent down and sorted through the seed packets, trying to decide what to focus her attention on next. She heard the scraping of a hand rake on the soil, and she glanced up to see that Emma had moved to one of the other garden plots. She pulled the rake through the soil with slow, measured pulls, just as she'd been taught. Her lips were turned down, and Hope had no doubt she'd overheard the conversation.

As Emma worked, her eyes flickered to Hope and then back to her work again. *She just wants my approval. She simply wants to know that things are all right and I'll still be her friend.*

The next time Emma glanced over, Hope offered a smile. "You're doing a *gut* job, Emma—just like you were shown."

The girl nodded, but her sad expression didn't change. Jonas seemed forlorn too. He stood not five feet from her, but they felt worlds apart. He stared up at the tree on the other side of the fence and watched a small cluster of parrots chirping and jumping from branch to branch, but she could tell his thoughts weren't on the birds.

Hope drummed her fingers on the concrete block. Was he thinking about her—thinking about how selfish she was being? It wasn't like she'd asked him to take ownership in this or to help. Maybe Lovina had, but she hadn't. Yet even as she tried to justify her words and actions, she didn't feel better. She'd do anything to go back to the laughter and smiles from earlier. Emma's slumped shoulders broke Hope's heart.

Hope sighed. She should have held her tongue. She should have told Jonas that they could discuss this later, when Emma wasn't around. Just because Hope didn't want dozens of kids in her garden didn't mean she didn't want Emma around. She hoped the young girl knew that.

Jonas moved down the row, checking all the connections of the pipes to the raised beds as if it were the most important task in the world. A weight settled in the pit of her stomach. She wanted to help him, but something held her back.

Watching him, there was an even bigger conflict in her soul than whether or not she wanted the children in the garden. It was Jonas. The schoolteacher was handsome—too handsome. And the way he looked at her with those dark eyes, it was as if he was peering right into her soul. The more she was around him the more she wanted to be around him, and that didn't make sense for someone who liked to be alone, liked her peace. The more she let him in—let anyone in—the more conflict she'd have in her life. Working alone in her garden was so much easier than letting others in.

Should I open my life to him? My heart to him? What would come of it if I spent more time with him? Is that what I want—who I want—for my future?

Just a few weeks ago she knew what she wanted for her year. She'd made a plan. She'd move in May. She'd already sent a letter asking Eleanor for work, but now she didn't know what she wanted—except to know what Lovina and Jonas were up to.

"I'll talk to Lovina tonight," she repeated again. "She's too busy at the pie shop during the day."

"*Ja.* That's fine. Maybe I'll stop by tomorrow to check."

Hope released a breath, wondering why this was such a pressing matter. "*Ja*, fine."

She straightened and tried to think of something else to talk about. "So, how's Hannah?"

"My cousin?" He stroked his chin, letting his hand brush down his beard. "Fine, I suppose. She's on bed rest—still has three months to go with her pregnancy. With Ruth Ann tending her, the doctors believe she should be able to make it to 35 weeks…I think that's how you say it."

"And school's going well?"

"*Ja*. Better than I expected. I teach fourth through eighth graders, mostly girls. They like to read and we're reading some books together. I started reading *Rascal* to the class."

"I remember our teacher reading that one. Do you change your voice as you read?"

"Of course."

"That's kind of you. I can't think of many brothers who would do the same."

"Changing voices?" Finally a smile broke, and Hope was happy to see it.

"*Ne*, teaching school." She chuckled. Her heartbeat slowed to normal, and it felt good not to have the tension tightening her gut.

"The truth is it was as much for Emma as it was for Ruth Ann. It's been a hard few years, and my sister reminded me that she's just a little girl. I thought the sunshine and meeting new friends would be good for her…and then there's the garden."

"The garden?"

"It's all she talked about when she found out we were putting it in. I'll apologize in advance—I'm sorry if she doesn't give you a moment's peace."

"Oh, I won't mind." Hope glanced over to see Emma studying a ladybug on her finger. "I enjoy having her around. She could be my sidekick every day." And as Hope said those words their truth resonated within her. She smiled. "I've never had a shadow like her before, and I think I'm going to like it."

It's just everyone else I have to worry about.

Sowing

Nearly all gardeners waste seed by sowing it too thickly. This also wastes labor as the seedlings later must be thinned by hand to a spacing that will allow proper development. Poor growth and poor-quality vegetables are obtained if the seed is sown too thick and the plants are not thinned out to proper spacing in the row. Don't buy more seed than you need to plant. Don't plant more seed than you need to get started.*

---

* Victory R. Boswell, *Victory Gardens*, United States Department of Agriculture Miscellaneous Publication No. 483, Washington, D.C., Issued February 1942, 9.

Chapter Fourteen

A man who gives his children habits of industry provides
for them better than by giving them a fortune.

AMISH PROVERB

ᕫ

Realizing that she hadn't made dessert for the family dinner, Hope paused on the walk home by a small sign: "Whoopie Pies for Sale." She bought seven of them from the sweet lady inside, taking them home. Faith and Joy were sitting on the front porch when she arrived. She approached with her garden tool bucket in one hand and the box of whoopie pies in the other.

Seeing her, Faith stood and rushed over. She took the box of whoopie pies from Hope and eyed her curiously.

"What? What's wrong?"

Faith reached up and touched Hope's forehead with the back of her hand. "Are you feeling all right?"

"*Ja?*" Hope pulled her head back. "I'm feeling fine. Why?"

"You made dinner—there was a note on the counter. And you brought home whoopie pies?"

Hope smiled at the curiosity in her sister's gaze. "I make dinner most weeks."

"*Ja*, but this is *gut* food. And you actually cooked something."

"I cook."

"Soup. You make soup." Faith turned toward the house. "Joy

and I have come to call Thursdays 'Soup Day.' But not today. What are we going to call Thursdays now?"

Hope followed her. "I came across an interesting recipe, that's all."

Joy watched as they approached. She had an embroidery hoop on her lap and was putting the finishing touches on a palm tree.

"I told you she was sick…" Joy put the hoop down on her lap and touched her cheek dramatically. "Lovesick."

Laughter burst from her sisters, and Hope sighed. She moved toward the house. "I don't know what you're talking about."

"Oh, really now. And who were you just spending the last two hours with?" Joy asked. "Emma Sutter is adorable…and her dat is handsome too."

Hope turned. "They're friends, nothing more." Hope hid her smile as she said those words. From her sisters' wide-eyed expressions she could tell they didn't believe her.

"*Ja*, and Lucy and Virginia are your friends, too, but you haven't been spending time with them lately. These new friends seem so much more interesting, don't you think?"

Hope pressed her free hand to her cheek, hoping it wasn't turning pink. "Do we really need to talk about this now? I need to get dinner in the oven."

"Exactly." Faith pointed into the air. "See, right there. You're saying stuff like that. That's how I—we—know you're lovesick."

"Fine, if that's what you want to think." She set her garden tool bucket right inside the door. "Just know that if I am interested in Jonas Sutter nothing will happen quickly. His heart has been hurt, and then there's his little girl to think about. I wouldn't want her to get the wrong idea. I wouldn't want to do anything to hurt her heart. I care about them like I would any other Amish family."

Joy nodded. "You may say that, Hope, but with those very

words—with your concern for their hearts—it's proving how much you care. Lots. You care lots." Joy shrugged. "We don't mean to tease you, really we don't. Faith and I just rather enjoy our older sister falling in love."

⌒

Voices rose and conversation filled the room around the dinner table. Everyone loved the new recipe, and Hope promised to try something new the following Thursday. There were lots in Pauline's garden journal to choose from.

Joy had finished eating, and she now looked through the journal. "Oh, here's a recipe for pea-pod soup."

"Pea-pod soup?" Mem leaned closer. "I've never heard of such a thing."

"This journal was written during World War Two," Hope explained. "Many people started vegetable gardens because so much of their food was being shipped away to the troops. They had to use everything—nothing went to waste."

Joy stood and began to gather up the dirty dishes. "I just don't understand. I've met Janet before a few times. She's a sweet older lady, but I never heard about her Victory Garden before now. I'm just a little hurt that she let you borrow the journal and not me."

"It makes sense." Grace turned on the warm water for the dishes. "Hope is the gardener. Maybe Elizabeth heard about the garden and told Janet about it."

Hope nodded, and she looked over to where Lovina was sitting. Her oldest sister looked weary. It was from the busy days at the pie shop, yes, but from Lovina's slumped shoulders she guessed it was something else too.

When the dinner dishes were done and put away Hope approached her sister. "Is this a good time to talk?"

Lovina glanced up from *The Budget* newspaper she had on her lap. In the fifteen minutes while Hope had been doing dishes she hadn't turned one page.

"*Ja*, please. Let's go sit in the backyard."

Hope followed her sister to the backyard and sat next to her on the swing. Was it just a few weeks ago that Jonas and Emma had sat on this swing and they'd started to get to know one another? That didn't seem possible. They'd already captured a small part of her heart.

Lovina had barely sat onto the swing when the words poured out of her mouth. "Okay, I just have to tell you…it wasn't my idea to put a garden in the back of the pie shop. I just wanted you to believe it was."

Hope's mouth fell open. Her mind raced, trying to make sense of her sister's words. Who else would be interested in starting a garden? Who else would be able to advise Lovina on such matters. Noah? Mem? Dat? But why? Had someone else—like Elizabeth—guessed that she had thoughts of leaving? Did they think a garden would cause her to stay?

Even after her confession, Lovina stayed on the swing. Her back was slumped, and she stared at the grass under her feet.

"Well, are you going to tell me whose idea it was?"

Lovina sighed. "It was Jonas Sutter's idea. He came to me about three weeks ago. He said he'd been thinking about the students here in Pinecraft. He'd been talking to his sister and brother-in-law and they felt bad that the children here missed so much because they didn't grow up on a farm. Jonas liked the idea of a garden, but he told me he'd be leaving in May. He said he could help as needed, but with his job and caring for Emma he couldn't oversee the whole thing. He asked if I knew anyone who'd be interested. Of course I thought of you."

Hope tried to wrap her mind around her sister's words. "So when Jonas talked to you, did he mention me?"

"*Ne*. He'd just been here a few days when he asked. I don't think he had any idea about how much you loved gardening."

"Okay, but why didn't you tell me from the beginning it was his idea? Why did you make it seem like it was yours?" The pieces of the puzzle clicked together in Hope's mind. It started to make sense. "Wait." Hope held up a hand. "If you'd told me it had been Jonas's idea—"

"You would have refused," Lovina said. "The reason you love gardening is because it gives you time alone. It gives you peace. And…" She let her voice trail off.

"And that's not what Jonas had in mind, was it?"

Lovina shook her head. "*Ne*. He had other plans…getting more people involved."

Hope placed a hand on her hip. She pushed the swing so that it started to rock. "And when were you going to tell me that Jonas wanted to have the schoolchildren involved in the garden?"

Lovina shrugged. "It would have come up sooner or later."

"Well, it has. Jonas asked me about it today. He seemed eager for them to get started 'helping me.'"

"Really, *ach*. What did you tell him?"

"I told him I'd talk to you, since it was *your* garden."

"Did he believe you? Or did he realize you were just trying to stall?"

"Trying to stall, of course. And he knew that."

Lovina lifted her face to the fading sunlight. "I have no problem with children being back there…you're the one with the problem. Or rather…you're the one who has her own ideas of how to use the garden. And I'm not going to stand against that. I've given the garden to you, Hope. It's a gift. You can use it as you'd like."

Hope lifted her hands in frustration. Then she placed both hands on the side of her face. "But you set me up for this. Now, if I say no I'm going to seem like the heartless one." She released a breath and lowered her hands.

"It's just a few children." Lovina sighed, as if wearied from the conversation. Her eyes looked puffy, and Hope wondered if she'd been up late trying to figure out how to tell Hope the truth.

"I'm sure it wouldn't be more than an hour a few times a week," Lovina continued. "And then you can have the garden to yourself the rest of the time. If I had a child and lived in Pinecraft I would appreciate it."

Hope jutted out her chin. "Oh, you would? And I'm sure those parents would also love for their children to learn to make thirty different types of pies. How would you like it if they took over your kitchen in the pie shop?"

"That's different. Every home has a kitchen where a mem can teach her daughters to bake pies, but not every home in Pinecraft has a garden—most don't."

Hope continued her swinging, more violently than the porch swing was designed for.

"Hey, hey." Lovina waved her hands. "Can you let me off this ride?"

Hope stopped the rocking.

Lovina stood. "Listen, I'm sorry. I handled things the wrong way. If you'd like I can go to Jonas and tell him that I put you in a bad spot. We can even put up signs if you'd like, and a gate, stating that it's a private garden. I would do it if I knew it would help. If I knew it would make you…" Lovina's words trailed off.

Hope continued the motion of the swing, softer this time. An emptiness echoed in her chest and she wondered how long it had been there, and if a move would really make it go away. "If it would make me what?" she asked.

Lovina peered down at Hope. The moonlight colored her face a pale shade of gray. Her eyes were as large and round as the moon above. Sadness filled her sister's gaze.

"If it would make you stay," Lovina finally said.

Hope reached up and placed a hand over her heart and the growing pain that pinched and tugged.

"I'm not sure if anything can. Pinecraft is a nice place, but it's just not where I plan on spending the rest of my life. I'm going to leave sometime, Lovina. I just don't know when."

"*Ja.* I understand. I just don't like the thought of that. We've been together our whole lives."

Hope released a long sigh, and then she patted the seat beside her. "Come, sit. I promise not to rock too hard this time." She wanted her sister close. She wanted all her sisters close, but they had to understand she didn't fit in in a place like Pinecraft.

Lovina sat. "And I promise to be more truthful from the beginning."

Hope pushed her feet against the ground, rocking them slower this time.

"When did you tell Jonas you'd give him an answer?" Lovina asked.

"Soon."

"What are you going to say?"

"I haven't decided yet."

From somewhere down the street laughter erupted, and Hope guessed it was a group of teens leaving the volleyball game. She liked the sound, but her heart ached for the sound of crickets and pond frogs.

"I know I said it before, but now I mean it. The garden is yours, Hope. You can do with it as you will."

"*Danke.* It means a lot."

She looked up at the stars, wondering what God had planned

for her. She'd planned on leaving, and God had given her a garden here. She wanted to be alone, and He'd given her Jonas and Emma. He'd given her a new friendship with Elizabeth. And He'd put a journal in her hands. She didn't know what it all meant, but she *did* know that she couldn't leave yet. Even if Eleanor did write back with a job for her, there was too much around here that she needed to figure out first. If only she could do it without hurting those she cared for in the process. And if only she could have a bit of the peace and quiet in her garden—peace that she craved.

- -

Pea-Pod Soup

Pods from 2 quarts peas
1 onion, diced
1 tsp. salt
1 tsp. pepper
1 tsp. sugar
Dash nutmeg
2 cups milk
3 Tbsp butter
3 Tbsp flour

Wash pea pods and cut into pieces, cover with water and boil with the onion for 1 hour. Puree mixture, add seasonings, sugar, nutmeg and hot milk. Heat to boiling and thicken with butter and flour mixture. Serves 4.*

---

* Ruth Berolzheimer, *250 Delicious Soups* (Consolidated Book Publishers, Inc., 1940), 29.

Chapter Fifteen

The right to do something doesn't always
make it the right thing to do.
AMISH PROVERB

◦⌒◦

The aroma of coffee filled the morning air. Hope laid out her garden stakes on the kitchen table. With a permanent marker she wrote out the vegetables' names to match the seed packets: turnips, potatoes, peas, kale, celery, cauliflower, carrots, cabbage, broccoli, beets. She smiled when she read the last one. One of the very first things that Emma had told her about Jonas was that her father didn't like beets. Little did Hope know when she saw that messy girl with an ice cream cone that Emma would become an important part of her life. But just how important? Hope was still trying to decide. She also wondered when she'd see them again and hoped it would be soon. She couldn't help but smile when thinking about them, especially Jonas.

Hope had always just assumed that she'd marry a bachelor. It seemed strange to think of dating a man who already had a beard. A man who'd already been married before. She finished her garden stakes and poured herself a cup of coffee. She'd wanted to get out to the garden early, but when she heard her mem getting ready for the day she considered asking her for advice. She needed someone to talk to. She needed to make sense of her thoughts, her heart.

She poured Mem a cup of coffee and buttered two slices of toast.

Mem exited from the bathroom, and when she entered the kitchen her face brightened. "Oh, breakfast with one of my favorite daughters. What a wonderful surprise. Is that for me?" She pointed to the coffee and toast.

"*Ja*, of course."

Mem sat. "So what do you want to talk about?"

"How do you know that I want to talk?"

"Ever since you were a child you've always gotten up early and waited for me when you wanted to talk. The other girls can spill their hearts among the noise and commotion, but not you."

"Well, *ja*, you do know me." Hope sucked in a deep breath and then released it slowly. "Mem, what do you know about Jonas Sutter?"

"He seems like a nice enough man, but my opinion is that he needs to get himself a wife to help him care for that little girl. I've heard of a few times that she's gotten into trouble around Pinecraft, not counting the time she flipped over that canoe. Now we know why God assigned *two* parents to children—some of them need two sets of eyes on them." Mem sighed. "I'm just sorry that it's come to this. Jonas should have made sure that Emma had a mother before now. It's the right thing to do…I mean after what happened."

Hope put the lid on the marker and stacked her garden stakes into a pile. "But it's not Jonas's fault that his wife died. Maybe he's just waiting for time to heal his heart. Maybe he's trying to find love again."

"*Ja*, but surely there is a nice woman his age who lost her husband. Do you know anyone, Hope? I do remember that you had a friend in Walnut Creek who lost her husband in a buggy and car accident."

Hope sat silent. She knew who Mem was speaking of, but that friend had three very active boys. Joining a family like that would be hard on Emma.

With Hope's silence Mem paused and looked at Hope. "Why are you asking?" Mem asked.

"Oh, I was just wondering."

Mem pushed her glasses up on her nose and leaned forward, peering deep into Hope's eyes. "You're not smart on Jonas Sutter, are you?"

"I wouldn't say that." Hope nibbled at her lower lip. "But I do like many of his qualities. I'd like to find someone like him—a bachelor like him to marry," she added for her mem's benefit…even though she wasn't convinced of that herself.

Mem picked up her toast and took a bite. She nodded and held her gaze. "*Ja*, I see."

Hope packed up all of her things in her gardening bucket, not sure if her mother's answer helped or hurt. Did that mean Mem liked him? Or did she have concerns? Mem nibbled on her toast again but remained silent, which was very unlike her. Maybe she'd learned from trying to persuade Lovina not to get involved with Noah Yoder at first.

"I suppose I'll just have to keep looking," Hope finally said. *And watching Jonas, getting to know him better, too,* she added to herself. Hope rose and placed her garden stakes into her bucket, eager to get to the garden spot. Eager to see what the day held.

Jonas would be a good husband to a widow, she thought as she offered her mem a quick wave goodbye. He'd be a good husband to anyone. She sighed thinking about that. *Ja,* if she could marry anyone, it would be someone just like Jonas Sutter.

∽◯

On the walk to the garden, Hope steered clear of the people and the workers setting up for the Haiti Auction. She'd gone to the auction last year, and while she enjoyed the food and seeing all the items up for auction, she didn't like the crowds. The Haiti Auction was held in three giant tents where they offered quilts, tools, tractors, tiny houses for Haiti, Amish-made furniture, and more. The many food stations offered homemade glazed donuts, pretzel dogs, Brazilian chicken, fried fish, blooming onions, and other wonderful food. Each of these stations was manned by the Amish from out of state, joined by Mennonite volunteer helpers who lived in Pinecraft year-round. Her guess was that by the time the auction started later that day she'd be able to hear the auctioneers over the loudspeakers. Hope was thankful that she had her quiet garden to retreat to until then.

She'd just settled down to start planting lettuce when she heard a voice call to her from the side of the building.

"There you are. I was hoping I'd find you around here."

Hope struggled for something to say as an older man rounded the corner. He pulled off his hat with a smile and ran his fingers through his flyaway gray hair.

"I've been here for a little while," Hope said. "There's nothing quite like fresh dew on a morning garden."

"I heard that you were the young lady behind the garden. I came by and was poking around yesterday. Your sister Lovina said that you like to garden early in the morning. I know that's how people like to do it up in Ohio where you're from, but around Pinecraft there are very few people out and around at 6:00 a.m."

"It's a habit, I guess." She raked her hand through the dirt, making sure to break up the clumps. Then, with the edge of the trowel, she made a long line in the dirt and tried to pretend she didn't have an audience.

It didn't work. He ambled closer, and his gray eyes appeared amused. "You're going to have quite the garden here, once you get everything growing."

She opened the seed packet and sprinkled the seeds in her hand.

"What are you planting?" the man asked.

"Arugula."

"Oh, I just love homegrown lettuce. It's so much better than the store-bought stuff. They have to grow that lettuce so it's tough enough to handle being transported and shelved for weeks."

She forced a smile. "*Ja*, homegrown lettuce is better."

"I've lived here for five years, and I've never seen a garden like this," he said, looking around. "You know that the city council came to us a while back and asked us if we wanted a community garden here in Pinecraft. I liked the idea, but since most of the folks only come during the winter months it's a lot of work for the few who stay here year-round. I'm glad to see that someone's committed to this. I'm glad someone's planning to stick around."

Guilt plagued Hope at his words. People assumed that because she was planting this garden that she was staying. Of course that only made sense. Who planted and did all the work without waiting for the harvest? Not that many people she supposed.

"A garden is a big commitment," she finally said. And as she planted the lettuce seeds in the ground she wondered if she was sinking her roots in this place one seed at a time, whether she intended to or not.

⌒

Hope saw Jonas and Emma briefly at the church service, and by Monday afternoon she kept wondering if they would come by after school. She still hadn't given Jonas an answer about the schoolchildren. Maybe she was just hesitating. If she told him she didn't want the children to help out would she lose him and Emma, too?

Over the weekend, while everyone else was attending the Haiti Auction, Hope planted beets, radishes, and potatoes. And as the morning slipped away and afternoon came, she found herself with senses peaked, watching for footsteps or voices, but no one came. Had Jonas given up on her?

When she was certain that school was out, Hope went into the pie shop to check the time. It was four o'clock. If Jonas and Emma didn't come in the next thirty minutes they never would.

Then, as she was making her way back to the garden, Hope saw her. Emma was walking down the street holding Ruth Ann's hand.

Hope paused in front of Me, Myself, and Pie. Disappointment tugged at her lips. Where was Jonas? She pushed them up into a smile.

"Hope!" Emma called. Ruth Ann released the young girl's hand and she raced up the road toward Hope. Hope bent down and opened her arms. Ten seconds later Emma jumped into her embrace. Warmth spread through her.

"I told *Aenti* Ruth Ann that I need to come—needed to be your helper."

Hope gave Emma one more squeeze, and then she straightened up. "*Ja*, I was hoping you would come by."

Ruth Ann approached. She looked down at Emma and then eyed Hope. "Is it okay if she stays a while? She has been talking about the garden ever since she got home from school. Jonas stayed over to help one of his students with his math."

Hope tried to hide her disappointment that Jonas wasn't with Emma. "*Ja*, I've missed Emma. I've been waiting for her so I can plant the beets."

Emma wrinkled her nose. "Beets?"

Ruth Ann gave the girl no mind. "Well, if she's not too much of a bother."

"*Ne*, I love having her." Hope took Emma's hand. "Are you ready to do some planting?"

For the next hour, Emma and Hope planted turnips, peas, beets, and cauliflower. When they finished, Hope dropped down onto the blanket on the grass next to Emma. They sat on the blanket and stared up at the clouds, trying to find pictures in the white forms.

Then, just when Hope was about to suggest that they go get ice cream, Jonas walked around the corner, carrying a book bag.

Hope quickly sat up and tucked her skirt around her legs.

His smile was large. "The garden looks good. Did you work on it all afternoon?"

"Over the weekend most. I worked on it by myself, but this afternoon I had help." She brushed away dirt from Emma's cheek. "Emma is the best helper."

"Have you had any other helpers? Or advisors?"

Hope smiled up at them. "Oh, I had plenty of advisors this weekend. Lots of friends from the village have stopped by."

Jonas chuckled. "Was the advice welcomed?"

"I'd never send anyone away."

Jonas smiled and nodded as if he understood.

Emma rose to her knees. "Hope let me put seeds in the holes!"

"I imagine you did a wonderful job." Jonas reached over and gently tweaked Emma's ear. There was a comfortable ease between father and daughter that Hope didn't often see. It was a relationship forged with time. Amish men loved their children, but they were often many of them. It was hard to give too much attention to just one.

Amish men were also busy in everyday tasks or they were at work all day, and they especially didn't spend a lot of time with their daughters. Yet the relationship between Jonas and Emma was different. She smiled, imagining the young girl tagging along with her father as he worked on the farm.

They sat and chatted for a while longer, and then Jonas took his daughter's hand. "Well, we need to get going. Ruth Ann is planning dinner."

"Oh, all right." Hope looked at him, wondering if he was going to ask about the schoolchildren being allowed to help in the garden, but he didn't say a word.

"Hope, I wanted to check with you—do you mind if we stop by tomorrow afternoon? I have something I want to do for you."

"For me?"

"*Ja.*"

"I will be here." She didn't know what else to say. *I always want to see you, Jonas.* "You really don't need to do—"

Jonas held up a hand, halting her words. "*Gut.* I'm looking forward to it."

"Me too."

Emma gave Hope another squeeze.

And as they walked away Hope was certain they were taking a piece of her heart with them.

Working with Mother Nature

Almost any kind of care will produce vegetables of a sort; in fact
there are some kinds that are difficult to kill after they once have
a start. But you do not want just vegetables; one of the objectives
of vegetable-gardening is the enjoyment of a better quality than is
found in products purchased from the stores. To produce vegetables
of good quality and texture you must work sympathetically with
Old Mother Nature, with a knowledge of her processes, so that the
plants under your care will grow.*

---

* Ross H. Gast, *Vegetables in the California Garden: A Home Gardener's Guide, with Notes on the Planting and Care of Fruits and Berries and an Introduction to the Small-home* (Stanford, CA: Stanford University Press, 1933), 1.

Chapter Sixteen

It's better to give others a piece of your
heart than a piece of your mind.

AMISH PROVERB

❧

The sound of a hammer rang out from the back of the garden area when Hope arrived the next afternoon. She waved at the customers sitting near the front window of Me, Myself, and Pie, and then she quickened her steps. What was going on? Was Noah building or remodeling something?

She rounded the corner of the building, and it wasn't Noah there, but Jonas. Hope paused her steps and her heartbeat quickened seeing him there. He was framing something. This must have been what Jonas meant when he said that he had something for her. She clasped her hands in front of her. It was almost too much to believe. Jonas had already worked all day teaching school, and now this. She'd never known someone so giving and kind.

"What is this?" She eyed it curiously. "Maybe a playhouse for Emma?"

He turned to her and grinned, but he didn't answer.

"Well." She crossed her arms over her chest. "Are you going to keep me in suspense?" She gently reached out with her thumb and wiped at the sawdust that had accumulated on the plank at the top of the pile. "It looks *gut*, whatever it is."

Jonas pulled a red handkerchief from his back pocket and wiped his brow. "*Danke*. I'm making a tool shed."

"A tool shed?"

He glanced down at the bucket that she'd set at her feet. "Aren't you getting tired of lugging that bucket around? And I thought we could get some donations of tools for the children too."

She cringed again, thinking of those children digging in her soil. "I—I haven't really decided about that yet."

"I know. But if you do decide, I'll be here to help you oversee them. They're not going to hurt your plants."

"Can you promise that?"

Jonas winked. "Well, not all of them."

"You make me wonderful mad sometimes, Jonas Sutter."

"Is that why you're smiling at me?"

"*Ja*, I suppose it is."

She watched as Jonas built the tool shed. It was larger than she needed for the items from the tool bucket. But as much as she wanted to tell Jonas that it would be all right for the children to come and help, she couldn't.

"Where's Emma?" she asked.

"She and Ruth Ann are visiting neighbors today. As much as I like Emma's help I thought it best she not hang around when I'm hammering." Then he looked back at the hammer and nails as if trying to decide if he had more to say. "Besides, I thought it would be nice to just spend some time with you, Hope."

Her eyebrows shot up and her stomach flipped once and then twice. "Really?"

"*Ja*." He nodded. "I'd like to hear more about your life in Ohio and what it was like growing up with four sisters."

And so Hope told him. She told him about their farm in Walnut Creek, about the vegetable stand by the road and about her dat's illness that he couldn't shake. "When the doctor told us Dat wouldn't last another winter up north, we had no choice but to move."

"And he's doing better now—your dat."

"*Ja*, thankfully. I appreciate your asking."

Jonas shared too about being one of the youngest in a large family. "I'd get into more trouble than any kid, I think. I've gotten stuck in dry wells and had to get stitched from falling out of trees a few times. I suppose I know where Emma got her adventurous nature."

Picturing Jonas as a little boy getting into all types of trouble made her laugh. And as they talked he built the tool shed with ease. She supposed he learned all types of skills taking care of his own farm.

As it neared dinnertime, Hope waved as Jonas headed out. She hated to see him go. She also hated to give him the answer she wanted to give. As much as she appreciated his help—and the tool shed—she still did not like the idea of allowing children into her garden.

At home, it was Grace's turn to make dinner, and she was grinning from ear to ear as Hope walked through the front door of the Miller house.

Grace turned, wiping her hands on a dish towel. "Guess what, Hope? We're having soup tonight, and it's not Thursday, it's Tuesday."

Hope sniffed the air. "Soup?"

"*Ja*, I got the recipe from your journal. Onion soup gratinée. Doesn't that sound fancy?"

Hope glanced over to the kitchen table where she'd left the

journal. Thankfully it was still there. "You were careful with the journal, weren't you? I'd hate anything to happen to it."

"I actually wrote the recipe on a piece of paper first. I didn't want to have the journal in the kitchen getting splatters on it. I hope that's all right."

Hope nodded. "*Ja*. It smells amazing. I can't wait to try it."

Joy was setting the table. "Oh, guess who I saw today, Hope? Janet came in today for more fabric for a quilt project. She wanted to meet you. She also wanted to see what you thought of the journal so far."

Excitement bubbled in Hope's stomach. In her mind Janet had become a hero, of sorts, working alongside her mother during the war. "She wants to meet me?"

"*Ja*. Do you think tomorrow at lunch would work?" Joy asked. "She said she'd be happy to meet us at Yoder's. If it doesn't work we just need to let Elizabeth know."

Hope nodded. "I'd love to." She clasped her hands together, trying to picture Janet in her mind's eye. She was Englisch, not Amish, but Hope pictured someone with a fun, spunky attitude, just like it seemed her mother had.

The onion soup tasted wonderful, and Faith asked if she could look through the journal for ideas for her cooking night.

"*Ja*, of course, but can I let you look through the journal tomorrow night? I'd like to do a little reading tonight. After all, I'll be meeting Janet tomorrow."

After the kitchen was cleaned up from dinner, Hope went to the living room and sat down with the journal once again.

Friday, May 1, 1942
Before two months ago the only time I'd ever seen the neighbor boy from next door was when he occasionally snaked under the fence to

retrieve his baseball, hoping my mother didn't see him in her prized flower garden. Today he came over to check out the garden with me. Now I know that his name is Tommy. He has a great sense of humor, and he even loves sitting down and reading books to Janet. Tommy is nine years old, and he can read much better than Janet, who just turned six. She loves listening to stories too. Then, last month, Tommy came over with his mother and I offered a plot in the garden.

Today the new green sprouts were evidence of their hard work. Tommy was very excited to see the first new sprouts come up. We had our first harvest too. We had a wonderful salad for dinner, and Janet said she'd never tasted one so good. Even my mother noted that the vegetables from the garden tasted better than those she usually bought in the store. She seemed surprised by that. To tell you the truth, I was surprised by it too. It's amazing to think how much has changed in just a few short months, and all because of a garden.

The day before I planted my garden I'd walked around town and checked out jobs, thinking I should join the workforce. Daddy has been so generous since Richard died, promising to care for Janet and me. Still, I had to find something to do. The jobs available were a pin girl at the bowling alley and a job in the 10-cent store. There were jobs at their air force base, but after Richard's accident I was pretty sure that my heart couldn't take being around all the soldiers. Now the garden is my work. These neighbors are my co-laborers. No, more than that…they are friends.

Friday, May 15, 1942

Yesterday we had someone new at our garden. His name was Henry, and he trains pilots over at the airfield. He heard about the garden from one of our neighbors who serves at other USO dances. Henry had a garden back in Kansas, and he's been missing it.

With the two new airfields, men from around the country can be *found all over town, enjoying the good weather and wide-open spaces. Sometimes I see a group of them having a night out in town. At times like that it's hard to remember there's a war still on. Then I'm knocked in the head again with food rationing, gas shortages, and travel limits. Thankfully, we have the garden.*

When my parents have friends over they always love to come over and see it. Maybe it's making a positive influence. I think it is. I recently heard that my father's friend, Powell Crosley, offered his mansion to be used as an officer's club for the Sarasota Army base. This war is bringing about a lot of loss and a lot of pain, but it's bringing together our community in ways I never expected. Makes me think we're sowing more than vegetable seeds. Sometimes I think we're sowing a legacy.

Tonight I might go to the USO dance with a friend. Henry said he'd be there. Part of me feels like I'm too old to be there. I'm a mother of a little girl after all, but Henry is someone worth getting to know, and Janet likes him too.

Hope closed the journal. The aroma of the onion soup still filled the room. She breathed it in, trying to imagine Pauline cooking the same soup. She tried to imagine Janet again. In her mind, she pictured a young girl, but tomorrow she'd meet Janet grown up. Janet shared all the memories that Hope was reading about.

And tomorrow history would come to life in a person.

Onion Soup Gratinée

3 onions
3 Tbsp butter or other fat
3 pints beef stock
¾ tsp. salt, dash pepper
⅛ clove garlic
¼ loaf French bread
3 Tbsp grated cheese

Slice onions thin and simmer in butter until soft and slightly browned. Add beef stock, boil 10 minutes, add salt, pepper, and garlic. Cut bread into thin slices, dry in the oven a few minutes, pour soup into a casserole, place bread on top, sprinkle with grated cheese, and set in a very hot oven (450° to 500°) just long enough to brown the cheese. Serves 6.*

---

* Ruth Berolzheimer, 250 Delicious Soups (Consolidated Book Publishers, Inc., 1940), 12.

Chapter Seventeen

Courage is faith singing in the rain.

AMISH PROVERB

◦○◦

Rain poured outside of Yoder's Restaurant, and Hope watched a group of Amish women walking down the street with umbrellas—two women under each. She sat at the table and watched the door, looking for Joy and Janet. Her heart leapt when she saw Joy holding an umbrella high over the woman's head, leading her inside.

Janet was tall and thin. She walked with a cane, but it looked as if she was only using it for decoration. Joy paused and pointed Hope's direction, and Janet hurried toward her. Hope stood as the older woman approached, and Janet offered a quick squeeze.

"Oh, there you are. Elizabeth has told me so much about you. She said that you were lovely, but I never imagined you'd have such beautiful hair. It's such a nice shade of red."

"Thank you." Hope gazed into the woman's blue eyes, and she tried to imagine all that the woman had seen over the years. She swallowed and told herself not to say anything foolish. "It's so wonderful to meet you. I've been enjoying your mother's journal. She sounds like she was an amazing woman."

"She was." Janet gazed over Hope's head with a wistful look. "She loved to garden, and she passed that love on to me." Then, with a shrug of her shoulders, Janet sat in the chair across from Hope and patted the seat beside her, motioning for Joy to sit. "Whenever one wanted to talk to my mother he or she just had to go to the garden—that was where she could be found. I've often thought before what a shame it would have been if she'd never discovered the joy of planting and growing. The war brought many painful things, but it also changed us in ways that we couldn't have imagined. Change does that. Often we grow the best in the places we don't want to be."

Hope nodded and she wondered if Elizabeth had been talking to Janet. Did Elizabeth know that Hope was planning on leaving Pinecraft? Did Janet know?

The waitress came, and they ordered. Asian chicken salad for Janet, smoked ham for Joy, and a stuffed tomato with tuna salad for Hope.

"If my mother was here she would have ordered the BLT with sliced turkey—the bacon extra crisp," Janet said with a laugh. "Growing up I'd be so embarrassed we'd go to these nice, fancy restaurants and she'd always ask for a BLT." Janet's smile softened. "That was my mother. She was raised in high society and could waltz with the best of them, but she was most comfortable around ordinary folks. She'd make a best friend out of anyone she met— that's something the war years taught her too. We all needed each other back then, all of us from rich to poor. The war was an amazing leveling field."

Janet asked about Hope's garden, and Hope enjoyed telling her about all she'd done so far.

"I'm eager to see the first sprouts. I've never planted in January before. There's always still snow on the ground this time of year back home in Ohio," Hope said.

Janet focused on Hope's gaze, and it was as if the woman was trying to read something deeper there. And instead of asking about Ohio Janet turned the topic of conversation. "And it sounds like you have a little helper in Emma."

"Oh, *ja*. I just love that little girl, but she is mischievous."

"She sounds like me when I was her age." She chuckled. "Thankfully my mother didn't write as much about me in the journal as she could have—like the time I hid worms in my grandmother's shoes." Janet wrinkled her nose and fanned her face as the memories obviously reeled through her mind. "If all my exploits were recorded in the Victory Journal I might not have allowed you to read it."

"I'm so glad you did. I think about your mother's garden when I'm working in my own." Hope took a sip from her raspberry iced tea. "But as much as I love reading it, I love hearing about it more." Hope leaned close.

"Oh, you don't want to hear all about the good ol' days, do you?"

"*Ja*. I do. Very much."

Janet nodded and smiled, and from the light in her eyes Hope could see that she was back there again...back in the garden with her mother.

Their lunch arrived, and Hope and Joy said a silent prayer. When they were finished Janet prayed out loud for them all. The food smelled wonderful, but Hope was more interested in Janet than the food.

Janet picked up her fork, but instead of eating she let out a soft sigh. "One of my earliest memories was watching my mother walk down the manicured law of my grandparents' estate with a shovel in her hand. My grandfather was a banker, and they had numerous yard men to care for their estate. I'm not sure why

Mother picked the spot to stop and start digging. But all of a sudden—with nothing but a sea of grass all around her—she stopped, jabbed the tip of that shovel into the ground, and pushed it down with her foot." Janet chuckled again. "If she'd been smarter she would have started the garden closer to the house, and then we wouldn't have had to drag those water buckets so far. But thankfully she put the garden closer to the front gate where everyone in the neighborhood could see it. It became more *theirs* than ours that way, and looking back, the relationships we built over the years were worth every bucket of water hauled."

Janet paused, but Hope could see there was more of the story running through the older woman's mind, so instead of asking more questions she just waited. Joy must have realized it, too, because she didn't say a word either. Instead she poked her fork into her green beans, stacking them up before putting them in her mouth.

"When Mother pulled the shovel out there was a clod of dirt and grass. Mother flung it over her shoulder and it landed not far from me," Janet said.

"What did you do?" Joy asked. "I'm sure that was a big surprise."

"Yes, it was. I picked it up, and turned it over in my hands. The roots held the clump together. The dirt was warm. I squeezed and some of the dirt broke apart. I was horrified because dirt got on my dress. I tried to wipe it away, but it just made it worse." She pouted, and Hope could see five-year-old Janet in her gaze. "I thought I'd go to bed without dinner for certain when I went inside with that dirty dress."

The waitress came and refilled their drinks, and Janet finally started on her salad. Hope and Joy shared a little about their growing-up years and their garden back in Walnut Creek, but Hope had many more questions for Janet too. From the interest in Joy's eyes Hope knew that her sister was enjoying this as much as she was.

"Were you afraid your mother was going to be upset by the dirt that you got on your dress?" Joy asked, taking them back to the story of a moment before.

"Not my mother, my grandmother. Like I said before, she was from high society. She believed little girls should be seen and not heard. We always dressed for dinner...and after we moved back in with my grandparents my mother conformed back to that. If it wasn't for Mother's determination that lawn would have stayed pristine all through the war, and all those children would have gone to bed hungry."

Hope cocked an eyebrow. "Children?"

Janet smiled. "Why, I'm getting ahead of myself, aren't I?" Then she sighed. "Actually, I could tell you about it, but I'd love for you to read about it first...in the journal."

"There is so much to read. I'm just thankful that you're giving me the chance. I never knew so much about Victory Gardens, or World War Two. Amish are pacifists, you know."

"Oh, I didn't lend you the journal so that you could learn more about the war, but about the garden. The community garden."

"Oh Hope, are you going to create a community garden? That would be so wonderful." Joy put down her fork and clapped her hands together. "I'm sure there are so many people around Pinecraft who'd like to be a part."

Heat crept up Hope's neck. Did Janet know about Jonas wanting the children to help with her garden too? Was that what this was about...a way to try to convince her? Her back stiffened and she pressed against the chair.

"I've thought about that. It seems like it would be a lot of work to me." Hope took a bite of her tuna salad and then looked from

Joy to Janet. "Maybe next year we—someone—can grow it into a community garden." She leaned back on the seat. "This year I just need…more quiet. More peace."

Janet used a knife and a fork to eat her salad. She made neat, small bites, and Hope could tell she'd been trained with fine manners.

"You remind me of my mother. So independent." Janet took a bite of her salad. A wistful look filled her eyes. "The war was hard, but my mother discovered a part of herself that she never knew before. It caused her to be a stronger person. It caused her to depend on God more too." There was a twinkle in Janet's eyes. "Just remember, Hope, that although giving ourselves to others is hard, and takes work, in the end it's better than being independent. As we learn to depend on others we learn to depend on God too."

"You think I'm independent? Really? I've never really heard people call me that before." Hope forced a smile. How much did this woman know about Amish communities? The Amish lived a life of conformity. They worked together and depended on each other. She'd grown up that way, but maybe Janet didn't understand.

As if reading her mind, Janet nodded. "Even those who live in a conformist society find their own ways of living independently. If it hadn't been for the war I'm not sure my mother would have been brave enough to step out and change. She married my father, the man my grandmother wished her to marry. He owned a huge factory and usually stayed up in the office, but one day when he went down to check on a complaint on the floor there was an accidental explosion. He was killed—him and two of his workers. Even as a married woman, my mother went to all the right luncheons and social events, but when my father was killed, and the United States entered the war, she realized that each person needed to do her part to serve others, including her. She realized there were more important things in life than being seen by the right people or attending the right events."

"And that garden…that's where she served?" Joy asked.

"Yes, it was a great contribution." Janet smiled, and then she turned back to Hope. "But don't take my word for it. Read it for yourself. You'll enjoy the rest of the story."

"Thank you. I will."

Joy looked at the clock on the wall. "Oh!" She sat up straighter in her chair. "I need to get to work. I told Elizabeth that I'd come in today." She motioned to their waitress. "Can you get me a box? I'll take the rest of this to go."

Hope put down her fork too. She was full. Full of tuna salad, full of wonder over the stories she'd just heard, and in a strange way full of questions about her own garden—her own motives. She was also full of awe over the fact that Janet chose to share them with her. She turned to Joy. "Speaking of Elizabeth, I need to talk to her. Emma just loved my garden apron. I wanted to see if Elizabeth could make another one—a smaller one."

Janet nodded. "Yes, I would have loved a garden apron when I was that age. Maybe I wouldn't have gotten in trouble for so many dirty dresses."

"Emma and Hope have become quite close," Joy explained. "Emma's dat is a widower. He's the new schoolteacher for this semester. Jonas and Hope have become *gut* friends…"

Janet pushed her salad to her side. Then she reached across the table and took Hope's hand. "I hope that means what I think that means."

Hope forced a smile. "We're just friends for now. We haven't known each other very long. But I do enjoy spending time with Jonas and Emma."

"Oh, that does my heart good, Hope. You know my step-father dared to love a widow. My mother had given up on love until he came along. He was a wonderful father. I'm very thankful that I had him in my life."

Hope's eyebrows lifted. "Wait, your step-father?" She squeezed Janet's hand. "Was it Henry?"

"Oh, Henry. You've read about him, have you?" Janet winked. "I'd hate to tell you more and give it away. You'll just have to read it—"

"In the Victory Journal, I know." Hope stood. She reached out a hand to help Janet to stand too. The woman seemed a little more unsteady on her feet than when she first arrived.

"I do have one more question before we part," Hope said. "Can you tell me—out of all the recipes in the Victory Journal, which are your favorite?"

Janet smiled thoughtfully. "Oh, I have two. Aunt Effie's Custard Johnny Cake and Steamed Pudding. I make both often myself. My mother found them in one of her grandmother's cookbooks. You'll have to try them both."

"I will." Hope nodded and accepted Janet's hug. "In fact, I might go home and try them now. In addition to reading more of the journal, I have to find out who your step-father turned out to be. I can't wait to find out."

Aunt Effie's Custard Johnny Cake

1 cup cornmeal
½ cup flour
1 tsp. baking soda
1 tsp. salt
2 Tbsp sugar
1 cup buttermilk
2 eggs
1 cup whole milk

Mix and sift together the cornmeal, flour, soda, salt and sugar. Beat
in the buttermilk, then stir in the well-beaten eggs. Add the whole
milk last, blending quickly. Pour into a greased rectangular pan
and bake in a hot oven about 35 minutes. Serve immediately, cutting in squares at the table. The custard will rise to the top in baking.
Serves four to six.*

---

* Marjorie Kinnan Rawlings, *Cross Creek Cookery* (New York: Charles Scribner's Sons, 1942), 26.

Chapter Eighteen

Were we meant to talk more than listen, we
would have one ear and two tongues.

AMISH PROVERB

⌇

In the early morning Hope was already at work in the garden, but for some reason the quiet didn't seem right this morning. She hadn't read more of the journal last night—she couldn't—even though she wanted to find out if Henry was the one Pauline married. Instead, it was as if fear kept her from opening those pages.

What if everyone—Janet, Elizabeth—expected Pauline's story to become her own? Just because Pauline found friendship and joy in creating a community garden didn't mean that she would too.

Instead, last night she tried to go to bed early. But instead of sleeping, all she could think about were Janet's stories, Janet's words.

The garden changed my mother. The friendships we made were worth every bucket of water we hauled. My mother was a different person because of the war. She learned to depend on others and depend on God.

The first sprouts of radishes poked through in her raised beds, and the smallest carrot tops were following. According to what she read in a book on Florida gardening, she'd be able to start planting melons soon. But would she be around for the harvest? Hope still wasn't sure.

A whistling came from around the corner, and Hope looked up. Her sister Grace approached with a hop to her step. As the youngest daughter, Grace was a spot of sunshine for all of them. She was almost always in a happy mood. Grace enjoyed being around people, and sometimes Hope wished that she had Grace's ease with others—her approachability.

"There you are. I knew you would be back here."

"Of course." Hope looked around at the long rows of raised beds, teeming with new life. "Ever since we moved to Pinecraft this was exactly what I wanted—just where I wanted to be."

"Oh, I love that, Hope. I love how both you and Lovina dared to follow your dreams." Grace spread her arms, as if taking it all in. She lifted her face to the sun and soaked it in before turning back to Hope. "And I love how all this turned out. In fact, I think this is a story worth sharing."

Hope frowned. "You're not thinking about writing about it in *The Budget*, are you?"

"Well, you know I'm the youngest scribe in Pinecraft, and I'm one of the youngest in the nation. I have to come up with *gut* stories, and there are none better than those close to home. You know how much everyone loved the story about Me, Myself, and Pie, *ja*?"

Hope twisted her lips. "I know, I know…but if you wrote a story…"

"Actually, it's not just a story I want. I want to introduce you around. We're having a *Budget* scribe meeting here in Pinecraft.

They have it the first Saturday of every month. I've been there a few times, but I'd like to bring you as my guest."

"A guest?" Hope didn't like the sound of where this was going.

"Yes, and then I thought the other scribes would like to come by after the meeting to see the garden. This is the newest feature to Pinecraft. *Ja*, I want to write about it, but maybe they do too."

"No." The word shot from Hope's mouth. "It's not a big deal, really." A thousand needles crept up her arms. The sun suddenly felt way too warm. Grace's presence overbearing. If Grace wrote about the garden—and if the other scribes wrote about it too— then the word would get out. And once the word got out more people would come. It would be a regular place to visit here in Pinecraft, and Hope didn't like that idea one bit.

"No, please…I don't think I'd like to come to the meeting. In fact, I beg you not to write about it. This garden, it's no big deal," she repeated again.

"No big deal…then why that reaction? Are you all right?" Grace leaned down and placed a hand on Hope's shoulder.

"There are already so many people stopping by as it is. I'm not like you, Grace. I need quiet. I need space."

"But haven't you considered making this a community garden? It seems like so much work for one person."

Hope refused to answer that. She was sick of the words *community garden*, just sick of them. She just shook her head. "Enjoy your meeting, Grace. I'm sure you can find something else to write about."

Grace left with a mere wave, and then Hope's lunch with Janet came to mind. Why did everyone have to bring up the same thing? Why did everyone think she needed to bring people in? She was not Pauline. She was not Grace. God had created her differently. He had His own story for her. Why did everyone else try to write hers?

Hope attacked the weeds with renewed diligence and prayed that her cousin Eleanor's response would come quickly. It was clear that even if Hope didn't have very many visitors here in Pinecraft she'd have no peace. The only way was to go to Ohio where everyone gave a woman working in her garden no attention whatsoever.

~

Hope's resolve to not read any more of the journal only lasted one evening. By the next morning she couldn't ignore it. She was fearful of the story, but she longed for it too. She wanted to know how that garden had made such a huge difference to a community. She wondered why people kept talking about it, especially when it was planted over seventy years ago.

Monday, May 18, 1942

Mother bought me a gas mask. Father is having an air raid shelter built in the backyard. Cook's newest kitchen gadget is a ration book, and I'm the proud owner of an identity card—as if everyone in Sarasota didn't know me already.

Everyone knows Mother. She's done her part in helping Madira Bickel organize the Sarasota County unit of the British War Relief and worked with James Haley for the Sarasota Red Cross, and I was just her daughter—a miniature version of Mother, so they assumed. Until I started my garden and I became my own person. Some thought I was foolish. Others crazy. Some believe I was simply acting out against my mother's traditional ways, but at least they thought of me. At least I wasn't a shadow, a clone.

Hope's mouth opened slightly and she pressed the journal to her chest. It smelled like dust and old leather, but she also felt a special connection with those words.

She had never told those things to anybody, but she'd felt the same way. In Walnut Creek she was known for her garden, and here…she was just another woman in an apron and kapp.

And that was what bothered her too. Wasn't it being prideful to want to be noticed? It was. But still…still she wanted to feel like herself again. She wanted to feel as if she had meaning and purpose. She wanted to be known for her garden…if only she didn't have to have so much company while she worked in it.

Hope put down the journal and decided to make a new treat. The recipe for Upside-Down Vegetable Cake was too interesting not to try, and then—when it was in the refrigerator and ready to put in the oven for dinner tonight—she'd head over to Elizabeth's. She wanted to purchase an apron for Emma, but even as she walked to the kitchen she worried. Would Elizabeth talk about a community garden too? Hope didn't know how she'd handle it if she would. And she was certain that if others knew of Jonas's request to get the children involved, too, she'd never hear the end of it.

~⊘

Jonas sat inside the classroom eating his lunch and watching the children playing in the grassy area behind the school. They didn't have fancy playground equipment like the public schools, but a while back some men had put up swings. There was also an area used for jump rope or tag. It didn't take much for Amish kids to find a way to entertain themselves.

"I have a garden!" Emma's voice rose above the noise.

"Back where you came from…" Sadie, who was a couple of years older than Emma, wasn't impressed.

"*Ne*, I have a garden here. It's mine and Hope's. We planted a hundred million plants and it's going to take a lot of work."

Jonas smiled to himself and took another bite from his

111

1111

1111

sandwich, sure that Emma had no idea that he was sitting inside, right by the window, and could hear every word.

"I want to help in the garden," a younger boy named Elmer piped up.

"Oh, you can help. Dat says that we can all go there for school."

"For school?" A chorus of voices rang out.

Jonas jumped to his feet and strode away leaving his lunch on the desk. He walked outside. Almost the whole group of kids had gathered around Emma. Eyes were fixed on her as she shared about the seeds that were beginning to sprout and the shed her dat had built.

Jack, a tall boy from Pennsylvania, turned to Jonas as he neared. "Is it true? Is there a garden behind the pie shop?"

Jonas released a slow breath. He had to be truthful, but he knew the last thing Hope wanted was more uninvited visitors. He understood that in a way. After Sarah's death the people hadn't stopped coming by for months. As much as he liked being around people, there were just some days he wanted to be alone.

"*Ja*, there's a garden, but it's a private garden. Emma and I are thankful that Hope has invited us to help."

"*Ja*, but Aenti Ruth Ann said…"

Jonas placed a hand on his daughter's shoulder. She looked up and he fixed his eyes on hers. "I know what your aenti has said, but having others work in the garden is Hope's decision."

Emma nodded. "I know, but I don't know why she would want to do all that work by herself."

"It's not up to us, Emma." Jonas spoke in a deeper tone.

Emma sighed and returned her gaze to the jump rope in her hands. "Yes, Dat."

Then Jonas scanned the crowd of children, making eye contact with as many of them as he could. "There *is* a garden behind the pie shop, and we might get to go see it, but for right now please don't bother it. There are some people who like their quiet, their space, understand?"

The children nodded, and a few seconds later they went back to their play. It was only Emma who stood to the side with her head lowered and her arms crossed over her chest as if her feelings had just been crushed.

Emma's lower lip began to quiver. "I thought Hope was nice."

"She is nice."

"If she was nice she'd let us help."

"She lets *you* help, doesn't she?"

Emma lifted her eyebrows and turned to him. "Am I the only kid she likes?"

Jonas opened his mouth to respond and then closed it again. How could he answer that? "I—I really don't know. I'm sure there are a lot of kids that Hope likes. Now run and play. We only have a few minutes of recess left." He reached over and patted her shoulder.

Emma scampered off to join the other girls who were jumping rope, but her questions wouldn't leave Jonas's mind. How much did he really know about Hope? Did she like children? Would she want to have more someday? Was she a good choice for a wife?

Jonas sauntered back to the classroom, wondering if his attraction to Hope was getting in the way of logic. His heart was drawn to her—that was certain—but would Hope ever be willing to open up her heart? She was having a hard enough time just opening her garden. If she couldn't allow people into her private spaces, what type of wife would she be within the Amish community? Would she always feel distant and aloof? As Jonas returned and sat at his desk he knew he had a lot to think about. And for the first time since meeting Hope he worried about where his feelings for her would take him.

Upside-Down Vegetable Cake

2 cups sifted flour
2 tsp. baking powder
½ tsp. salt
¼ cup shortening
1 egg, beaten
1 cup milk
4 cups mixed cooked vegetables (peas, carrots, celery, lima beans)
½ cup vegetable stock
2 Tbsp butter

Mix and sift dry ingredients together and cut in shortening. Combine egg and milk; add to dry ingredients, stirring until mixed. Arrange hot seasoned vegetables in bottom of a greased shallow baking pan, add vegetable stock, dot with butter, cover with first mixture, and bake in hot oven (425°) 20 to 25 minutes. Turn out on hot serving plate with vegetables on top and serve with tomato or mushroom sauce. Serves 6.*

---

* Ruth Berolzheimer, *250 Ways to Serve Fresh Vegetables* (Culinary Arts Institute, 1940), 45.

Chapter Nineteen

God puts us on our backs at times so we may look up.

AMISH PROVERB

∼

The fabric store was quiet as Hope entered. Joy had the day off, and Elizabeth was the only one behind the counter. She was looking through some swatches of blue, as if trying to find the perfect shade.

"There she is!" Elizabeth said as if she'd been waiting for her all day.

"Hello, Elizabeth." Hope approached the counter with a smile. "It looks like you're busy with a project."

The fabric store smelled of cinnamon from the candle Elizabeth had burning near the cash register. The large window in front welcomed in the Florida sun, which splashed across the neat bolts arranged by color along the aisles. Elizabeth sat behind the counter on a high stool with a back. On the wall behind her a beautiful antique quilt was displayed, in purples, pinks and dark grays. It reminded Hope of the quilt that used to be on her grandmother's bed, and she was thankful for the memory and thankful for the peace she felt in this shop.

"Busy? I don't believe in being busy at my age. Life is too

short not to enjoy each day. I have been messing with these colors though—just trying to find the right fabric to start piecing together a wedding quilt."

"A wedding quilt." Hope's eyes widened. "Do I know the happy couple?"

"Well, last I heard you share a room with Lovina." She winked. "I know the wedding isn't published yet, but every time I see that couple I know that it won't be long now before we hear the *gut* news. I've seen many couples, and those two seem to complement each other so well." She reached across the counter and patted Hope's hand. "But enough about that. Tell me why you've come."

Hope took the older woman's hand and gave it a gentle squeeze. Elizabeth's skin on the back of her hand was soft and thin like the breezy white cotton she sold.

"Oh, I'd like to order another gardening apron. Little Emma Sutter saw mine, and she just loved it. I think she'd be excited if I had one made for her."

A smile filled Elizabeth's face, and the lines around the corners of her eyes stretched outward as her cheeks pushed up. "Oh, that would be a fun project to make. I just love when new friendships are made. That little girl looks up to you, you know. Every time I see her she has something to say about Hope or the garden. Is it going well with them? I hear Jonas is doing a fine job as our teacher."

Is what going well? she wanted to ask. *It's just a friendship.* But from the sparkle in Elizabeth's eyes she knew she'd never fool the woman.

"*Ja*, it is." Hope's stomach tightened and she nearly held her breath as she thought of a way to cause the conversation to shift. "I enjoy…them. We enjoy being in the garden together."

"And is the garden everything you'd hoped for?" Elizabeth asked.

"*Ja*, except…well, I'm getting a lot of visitors. Just this morning two Englisch ladies were at the pie shop and they got so excited when they heard there was an Amish garden out back. I was just leaving when they came back there and asked if they could take photos. I told them I didn't mind if they took photos of the garden, but I didn't want any of me." She sighed. "Though I guarantee they did when they didn't think I was looking. I thought there were a lot of tourists in Walnut Creek, but I'm seeing them more and more around Pinecraft. Who thought being Amish would be so popular?"

Elizabeth nodded. "I think people are drawn to our simple ways. There is so much busyness and hurry in our world. The Englischers like to know that some people are making different choices."

Hope snickered. "It's not so simple sometimes, being Amish. At least it hasn't felt that way lately. Sometimes I wonder if we're really that different at all."

Elizabeth cocked an eyebrow. "What do you feel is most important about being Amish?"

Hope paused, having to think about it. This wasn't the question that she expected from Elizabeth, not today. "Being Amish is living plain. Not putting ourselves over others. It's living in humility and making one's family the center of your life. It's loving God, too, which I should have said first."

"That's very good. And all those are important things. But there's something you forgot. Something important."

"What's that?"

"Before I answer that I have to tell you a little story." Elizabeth pushed aside the scraps of fabric, folded her hands, and leaned against the top of the counter. "Hope, there was a time when I questioned if I should remain Amish. After forty years of marriage my husband died, and that whole time God never did bless us with children. It was just a few years after we moved to Pinecraft, so this didn't feel really much like home yet, and the home I had in Indiana was gone—sold to a young couple starting their lives.

"I didn't want to feel like an outsider, but I did. When I sat at sewing frolics everyone talked about their children and grandchildren. When I attended weddings I always found myself seated with other widows, but even they had family to talk about. At the same time, my shop started doing well, and I had a growing customer base, not only from the Amish, but the Englisch too. Women like Janet."

Hope nodded, listening. She imagined if she spent more time with Janet she'd consider her a good friend too.

"She became a *gut* friend, and I knew she loved God. I believed that because of Jesus—what He'd done for both of us and our acceptance of salvation through Him—both Janet and I would go to heaven at the end of our lives. I've never been foolish enough to believe that only Amish did things the right way in God's eyes. Or believe that only Amish had any hope of heaven. So then I wondered, *Why remain?* If living plain didn't save my soul, then why do it?"

Elizabeth smiled. "I was being rebellious one quiet, Saturday evening, and I took off my *kapp*, just to see how it felt. And as I did I thought about the things Janet and I talked about most. The times in her life that she shared the most stories from—the war years. They should have been considered the hardest years of her life, but there was good mixed with the hardship and pain. And the person Janet admired most was the woman who'd faced very hard trials. Her mother, Pauline, was a widow. She had a child to raise on her own, and there was a war. She had to ration and raise her own food, but looking back it's a time that Janet never forgot."

"Because of the garden?" Hope asked. Warmth filled Hope's chest, and she had a feeling that it was. She remembered again why gardening had become so important to her in the first place. It was a place of life, of growth, and connection with God. And she supposed all those things could be found in a garden even during a time of war.

Elizabeth didn't answer right away. Instead, she looked into Hope's eyes and offered the slightest smile, as if reading Hope's thoughts.

"No, it wasn't the garden that left such a strong impression," Elizabeth said. She brushed a strand of white hair back from her forehead. It was light and wispy. Hope wondered if it felt like cotton. It sure looked as if it would.

"Not a garden," Elizabeth said again. "A garden only grows for a season and fills our stomachs for a season too. The part that Janet will never forget is the people. Strangers who came together to make the garden grow and became friends." Elizabeth's smile grew. "Those friendships lasted longer than one season. They lasted long after the war. Who the neighbors became *together* was the most important part. What they did together bonded them for a lifetime."

Hope nodded, forcing a smile. She crossed her arms over her apron and wondered how long Elizabeth had been planning this talk. Did Lovina put her up to it?

Yet just because something was right for someone else didn't mean it was right for her. Still, she stood there and listened to Elizabeth. If it wasn't the message, it was the conviction in the woman's words that she'd pay attention to.

"Janet was telling me about her mother's garden during the time I considered leaving. It was so much easier just to be alone than to be around others and pretend I was happy for them every time they announced a new wedding, a new grandchild, or a new marriage," Elizabeth continued. "And then, that's when I felt my good God asking me to recite the Lord's Prayer."

Tears filled Elizabeth's eyes and her lower lip quivered. Tenderness and vulnerability filled her face. Hope shifted on her feet. She wanted to look away, and as she glanced to the blue printed fabric on the bolt on the counter, Elizabeth's hand touched hers, pulling her back in.

Hope cautiously looked back to Elizabeth, focusing on her eyes, tears and all.

"Hope, will you say the first line of the Lord's Prayer with me—just the first line?"

Together their voices rang out in the quiet of the fabric shop. "Our Father who art in heaven."

Hope's brow furrowed, and she wasn't sure what Elizabeth was getting at.

"Now, my sweet girl, will you just say the first word?"

The word replayed in her mind, and then, as if someone had opened a spigot, it dripped down into her heart. Heat filled her chest, and she tried to open her lips, but they felt dry and almost stuck together. Hope licked them with the tip of her tongue and she swallowed hard. "Our?"

"*Our*, yes, that is the word the Lord had for me. That was the reason He needed me to remain Amish. Many people today believe in God, but they think of it as a solo pursuit. They think of it as just between them and God. But Jesus reminds us of 'our' in this model of how we pray. It's not just *my* God who art in heaven. It's *our* God, and it's a message that wearing this *kapp* displays, even when I'm not thinking about it. The *kapp* takes away my individuality, but for a good reason. It's a symbol to our world—to the customers who come into my shop—that living in unity and serving one another is important.

"Janet and I have talked about this and we agree that people are at their best for God when they are serving—not alone—but with others," Elizabeth continued, emotion heavy on her lips. "God chose the nation of Israel. Jesus died for a sea of sinners. Most gardens don't just feed one, but many, and sometimes the hardest part of being Amish, opening ourselves to others—allowing them to press in and mess up our order and our plans—becomes the best thing. Not only for them. Not only for us. But for a whole world that needs to be reminded not to think of God as mine but ours. We, Hope, are a symbol of what happens when we all unite—together—in God's bigger plan for this world."

Hope nodded, taking in Elizabeth's words. They spoke truth, but she also knew what it would require. If she followed this directive she'd have no quiet. She'd have no peace.

"All of that makes sense. You've given me something to think about, Elizabeth."

"And pray about, I hope."

"*Ja*, of course."

"I'm not going to tell you to do anything—make any decisions for you—but I learned long ago that in order to get a *gut* picture of what God's doing in a place, you have to look back and see what He's already done. How He's already worked.

"God's been at work in this community long before you came, Hope. Long before I came too. And long before that Victory Garden was planted back in 1942. Maybe we can see more clearly when we turn back the pages of time…that's all."

"And is that why you asked if I could borrow—could read the Victory Journal?"

Elizabeth winked. "It just might be."

Hope sighed. "It wasn't about the garden tips and the recipes after all, was it?"

"Those don't hurt. I'm sure you found some good things to try, some good advice. But, *ja*, now you know the real reason."

Hope took the Victory Journal out of the pocket of her garden apron, and she flipped through the pages, seeing the book in a whole new light. She paused at the Grapefruit Pie recipe that she'd shown Lovina just last night. And her breath caught.

"And Lovina…the pie shop…this is part of it too. It's a gathering place. Pulling people together."

A slow smile crept up Elizabeth's face. She nodded and released a sigh. "*Ja*, isn't the Lord *gut*? God urged me to pray for that place, and I've been doing it for a while. But until a few months ago I was just focused on the building itself." She pushed her glasses farther up on her nose. "But I have a feeling that my prayers spilled over to the back—to the garden area too."

Hope nodded, and deep down she knew what she needed to do. To hear Elizabeth explain the importance of community proved her garden was just part of what God was doing. What He'd be doing for a while. She would have to pray that God would change her, soften her heart, and make her not so concerned if her carrot tops popped up in nice, straight rows.

Oh Lord, I want to be willing. Please make me so.

- -

Grapefruit Pie, 1940

⅓ cup cornstarch

1¼ cups sugar

¼ tsp. salt

1¾ cups boiling water

3 eggs, divided

1 Tbsp butter

½ cup fresh grapefruit juice

1 tsp. grated grapefruit rind

1 baked pastry shell

grapefruit segments

6 Tbsp sugar

½ tsp. vanilla

Mix cornstarch, sugar, and salt. Add water slowly, stirring until well blended. Cook over boiling water for 15 minutes, stirring until thick and smooth. Pour into egg yolks slowly, return to heat and cook 2 minutes longer. Remove from heat and add butter, grapefruit juice, and rind. Cool. Pour into pastry shell and arrange grapefruit segments around edge of pie.

For meringue, beat egg whites until frothy. Add sugar gradually and continue beating until stiff. Add vanilla. Pile on pie and bake in slow oven (325°) 15 to 18 minutes.*

---

* Ruth Berolzheimer, *250 Superb Pies and Pastries* (Culinary Arts Institute, 1940), 27.

Chapter Twenty

Anyone who practices what he preaches
doesn't have to preach much.

AMISH PROVERB

❦

Hope tossed the journal onto her bed, thankful that Lovina had gone to a volleyball game with Noah. Thankful that she had their bedroom all to herself. She sighed and sank down on the bed next to it. As much as she'd like to go to the garden and enjoy the cool of the evening, she had a lot of thinking to do. Pauline's story had stirred up so much inside her—so much that Elizabeth had confirmed today.

Sure it was easy for Pauline to welcome people to help in her garden. There had been a war going on. They needed the food back then. They needed to work together.

"This is different," Hope mumbled to herself. "Is it too much to ask for a place to retreat? Is it too much to have a space just for me?"

Guilt weighed on her shoulders as soon as the words were out, and her eyes fluttered closed. She wanted her own space. She wanted her own work. She wanted to look out at the garden and have evidence to what she'd accomplished…and that spoke of one thing: pride.

Tears filled Hope's eyes and she lay back against her pillow, allowing her body to sink deeper. Her chest tightened as she remembered her earliest memory—walking behind Mem to church at a neighbor's house. They'd been walking from the buggy to the house where church was being held. Instead of paying attention to Mem she'd gotten distracted by two puppies in the barn, and when she looked up all she could see was a sea of Amish dresses and men's pants. Hope remembered how her heart had pounded. She remembered how she'd cried out for Mem. She remembered her tears. Her gut tightened at the memories.

Then, finally amidst the noise, someone heard her voice. It was an older Amish man with a long beard. He'd taken her to his wife—a lady with a round face and large blue eyes. "Oh, it's just one of the Miller girls," the woman had said.

It had been the first time she'd heard that term—"Just one of the Miller girls"—but it hadn't been the last. She and her sisters were more different than similar—in looks and talents—but that didn't stop those in their community from lumping them together. Hope liked to be by herself, and that was hard to do in a home with four sisters and a mother who loved getting together with other women and serving in her community.

Instead, she'd found solace in the quiet of the garden. And even though she hadn't expected it, her gardening skills in Walnut Creek had also given Hope her name back. When slow buggies drove by, the drivers had plenty of time to appreciate her hard work. She was no longer just one of the Miller girls, she was Hope Miller, and everyone in Walnut Creek had come to know Hope's garden.

Even as a young teenager she was often stopped at the grocery store by other Amish women asking for gardening tips. And when Grace had convinced the sisters to open a garden stand on the roadway near their home, business had gone well. People had driven out of their way for her produce. Yet when Hope moved to Pinecraft she not only felt as if she lost her garden, but lost herself too—lost her worth. Was it prideful to want to reclaim that here?

Who am I without a garden? Who am I? The questions filled her mind, and with them came a rush of pain, like a knife to her heart. Hope didn't want to walk through this world feeling like that young, lost girl. She didn't want to relive the same emptiness she'd experienced during the last year in Pinecraft. In both cases she'd felt alone, unknown, and unnamed.

I want to be Hope. I want to have hope.

She leaned back against the wall, picking up her pillow and pressing it against her chest. She didn't want to share her garden, but what choice did she have? She could continue to put up walls and push everyone away, but what good did that do? It was just making her miserable. And maybe she'd lose any chance with Jonas in the process too.

She could continue to push people away. She could move back to Ohio, and she could leave the garden behind to everyone who wanted to run it. Or she could…submit. She could open herself up to others. She could forget about having her own garden and just enjoy being with others during the time she had.

She could still go back to Ohio when the time was right, but until then she'd see the garden as *theirs,* not just *hers.* Just like Pauline.

The idea of welcoming others, their opinions, and their ideas into the garden was a hard one. Still, it was the right thing to do. It was what God would want. *Our* Father.

Hope closed her eyes and imagined people gathering around the garden beds. She imagined children poking their fingers into the soil, and she imagined Jonas there with them. At least that last thought made her smile.

She enjoyed being with Jonas. She enjoyed seeing him with Emma, but also ached at the pain and loss in his gaze at times. She liked the idea of building a closer friendship with him—maybe something more—but another fear plagued her. Would she ever be able to replace the loving wife that he'd lost? She didn't think so.

God, I'm tired of thinking about all this, worrying about all this. She clenched her fists and then released them. *I'm tired of figuring out the perfect plan for the garden, or if I should move back to Ohio, or… or open my heart to Jonas. I'm tired of feeling as if I'll never be enough. Lord…*

It wasn't much of a prayer, and Hope wasn't expecting an answer, but a sweet, gentle voice filled her mind all the same. A voice that didn't come from her mind, but one that did speak to her heart.

I know your name.

Emotion filled her throat and tingles danced on the back of her neck, down her spine, and to her limbs. For most of her life God seemed distant and far away, but in this moment—when she felt weak and confused—He suddenly felt close. Very close. As if He was sitting right next to her on this bed.

God had created her. He knew her fears and worries. God knew how much joy she'd found in her garden back in Ohio. He'd given that garden to her.

God was with her, and she wasn't forgotten. God knew her name. She just wasn't one of the Miller girls. She was Hope.

God… Tears filled her eyes, and she covered her face with her hands. *Are You doing this to grow me and change me? Is this garden a way to make me more like You… more like Your Son?*

It was easy living life within one's premade boundaries, but was that what God called her to? Was that what He called anyone to?

Just in the weeks she'd started this new garden she'd had to learn to be more patient. She'd listened to others, and she learned to give—of her time, of herself, of her space in small ways. She'd carried on conversations with strangers. She'd planted seeds with Emma, sharing her favorite activity. Yet she also hadn't given her whole heart to these tasks. How would things change if she did?

Hope thought of Jonas again too. Hadn't he said he'd given up his farm for a season to help his sister? He'd left the place he loved to help his daughter too. And that was what attracted her to him. He was willing to put his desires aside to help others.

She also thought about Pauline's garden journal. In 1942 the young mother had started out wanting to prove herself—to prove that she could help with the war effort too—but God had given her so much more. He'd given her friends. He'd given her a community, and He'd given her a heritage to pass on.

Forgive me for being so selfish, God. Forgive me for trying to keep this gift to myself. I know opening up the garden also means opening up my heart. I know it will be messy. I know it will be noisy. But I also know there are lessons there I will learn no other way.

Hope paused and took a deep breath. "And…" she whispered, "I will accept all this as a gift instead of a burden. I will embrace others instead of pushing them away. And I pray, Lord, that You will do Your work in all of us."

A gentle peace came then, like the soft, warm spring breeze that had blown through the maple trees and over her garden back in Walnut Creek. That garden was still there, being tended by someone else. And for the first time, she was at peace with that.

Hope reached over and picked up the journal. She turned to the back page where she'd tucked Janet's phone number. She also remembered the last words Janet had spoken when they parted. "If you'd ever like to see Mother's garden, just let me know."

It had been three weeks since Elizabeth had given her the journal and she'd first started reading about Pauline's story. Yet she never considered visiting the garden until now. And deep down she knew why. Pauline had taken what she had and she'd freely offered it to others, and to see her garden would convict Hope to do the same.

But God had already done the convicting, and maybe she did need to go see the garden—see what God had continued to do in the years since Pauline had dug up that first clump of grass. Because maybe God had bigger plans for Hope too. Plans she couldn't even wrap her mind around.

Hope rose from her bed, wondering if Dat was still out back, and wondering if she could use his cell phone to call Janet. Would it be possible for her to visit the garden sometime soon?

An urgency stirred in her heart that surprised her. Once she submitted to God's voice, there was nothing holding her back.

⌒

May 20, 1942

Henry Coulter won my heart by weeding my garden on the one Saturday I dared to sleep in. He'd come by with a single rose to thank me for the wonderful evening at the dance, and when our housekeeper told him that I was still in bed he decided to tackle the weeds. It was Janet who saw him first and woke me up to tell me. By the time I dressed and tied a scarf around my hair Henry and Janet had finished the job. And for the next few hours we lay on the grass and watched the planes flying overhead. Henry described the B-17 Flying Fortresses. He described how the 97th Bombardment Group, which

*had been training since March, were now in England. And now it
was the 92nd Bombardment Group who flew overhead. Henry is a
mechanic and guesses he'll stay around Florida a while taking care of
the airplanes. For a while we sat in silence—even Janet—because we
all know how quickly things can change.*

*When Janet went to lunch Henry asked about my husband's death.
He assumed that Richard had been a soldier or pilot. It was strange
how easy it was to tell Henry about Richard. It wasn't until the end
of our time together that I realized I'd done most of the talking. Just
as I started asking him questions, a neighbor came by to pick beans.
We all picked them for a while, but somehow Henry ended up doing
most of the work. He was fast too. Said it was due to all the contests
he had with his brothers growing up. Henry also recommended that
I plant sweet potatoes. He guessed they would thrive. I told him I'd try
it. I also invited him to stay for dinner. I miss cooking for Richard and
since our cook had the day off, Mother said I could take command of
the kitchen for the night. I made poppy seed chicken and baked corn.
Both turned out delicious, if I say so myself.*

*I had a smile on my face after Henry left—or so my mother told
me. Even Janet fell asleep tonight without worries of bad people coming to attack us. I know it might be too early to write this—since I've
only seen Henry a dozen times—but the world seems like a safer place
tonight knowing he's out there, doing his part.*

✏

Hope yawned as she walked into Elizabeth's fabric shop. She'd
been up late into the night reading the Victory Journal. Thankfully Lovina had drifted right off to sleep and the light from the
lamp hadn't bothered her sister. Lovina had been working long
hours at the pie shop lately and she often went straight to sleep.

Hope missed the long chats she used to have with her sister at night, but in a strange way a lot of her questions—about relationships and following God's call—were being answered within the pages of the journal.

Hope loved reading the recipes, the gardening tips, and the way neighbors were turning into friends, but even more she appreciated reading about Pauline's growing relationship with Henry. Like rose petals unfolding, it was sweet to read about how their relationship bloomed. At times, Hope felt embarrassed as she read about USO dances, walks on the beach, first kisses, and the time they spent together in the garden. Hope didn't know if Pauline ever planned on having her journal being read by others, especially by a stranger, yet Hope was thankful to read about the woman's tentative steps and even her questions concerning the relationship.

Hope had always believed that when one found the person he or she should be with for life, everything would just make sense and fall into place, but maybe that wasn't true. Maybe the path to love was more crooked than straight at times.

Even as Pauline felt herself growing closer to Henry, she took time to also write out her worries and fears. Should she think about marriage again? Was it foolish to allow herself to fall in love, knowing that Henry would most likely be shipped overseas to fight the Nazis? And what about Janet—what if things didn't work out with her and Henry? Pauline didn't want her little girl's heart to break too.

In the fabric store, Elizabeth was busy helping a customer look at some of the handmade quilts, and so Hope took it upon herself to start straightening the bolts. As she did her own questions—similar to Pauline's—played in her mind:

Was there a reason Jonas hadn't remarried? Was he worried

about Emma? Was his heart still so broken from his loss that he couldn't think about opening it up again?

And what about her? Was she ready to be a wife, a mother? She knew that once she had a husband and children she wouldn't be able to use her garden as an escape. She couldn't run from people who depended on her. Her life would have to be more than just planting the right vegetables and keeping the rows weed-free.

The customer purchased a beautiful wedding-ring quilt, and Hope helped her carry the bulky package to her car. When Hope returned Elizabeth was just hanging up the phone.

Elizabeth motioned Hope to join her at the counter. "I have sad news, I'm afraid."

Hope approached and paused before the older woman. "Is everything okay? You're not ill, are you? Is everything all right with Janet?"

"*Ja*, with Janet everything is good, but her daughter in Tampa had an episode and needs surgery. Janet's going to help with her grandchild. Her friend is driving her up, and she'll be gone for the rest of the week. I'm afraid she's not able to show us her garden today."

Disappointment caused the brightness of the room to fade slightly. Hope's shoulders slumped. "I understand. I hope her daughter starts feeling well soon."

"I hope so too. Janet says she'll call me when she returns to set up a time for us to visit."

"And what about this week? Will she need someone to tend to her garden? That sure is a long time to leave it alone."

Elizabeth's eyes sparkled. She pressed her thin lips together but a hint of a grin poked through. Thin lines spread from her lips up to her cheeks, and finally she spoke. "Janet has no need to worry about her garden while she's gone. It'll be well tended. Janet—like her mother—has made many friends in her neighborhood."

"That's *gut* to know."

"I suppose the blessing is that you can spend time in your own garden today," Elizabeth added.

Hope winced slightly at those words. She did need to do some weeding, but she usually enjoyed being there earlier in the day—to miss the crowds. And then she remembered her thoughts from yesterday. God had given her a garden not to keep to herself, but to open it up. Her job was to be faithful in the small things, even if it meant opening her garden up instead of hiding it away.

"*Ja*, I think I will enjoy time in my garden today. I think I'll even stop by the school when it is done. There is something I need to talk to Jonas—I mean Brother Sutter—about." Hope lowered her head and brushed her hands on her skirt as if brushing away invisible lint.

"It sounds like it'll be a *gut* day then." Elizabeth's voice rose an octave as if she was holding in laughter. "Just the day that the Lord has made. But why wait until after school? The kids won't be arriving for another twenty minutes yet. I'm sure Brother Sutter would be pleased to have you visit."

Baked Corn

1 pint corn, drained
2 eggs, beaten
2 Tbsp granulated sugar
2 Tbsp all-purpose flour
¼ cup butter, melted
1½ cups milk
1 tsp. salt
ground black pepper to taste

Preheat oven to 400°. Combine all ingredients in a 9x9-inch baking dish. Bake until top turns brown. Lower oven temperature to 300° and continue baking for one hour.

Poppy Seed Chicken

6 cups cooked and deboned chicken, cut into chunks
2 cans cream of mushroom soup
8 ounces cream cheese, softened
12 ounces sour cream
2 heaping Tbsp poppy seeds
2 sleeves crackers, crushed
½ cup butter

Preheat oven to 350°. Spoon chicken into bottom of 9x13-inch baking dish; set aside. In a large bowl, mix soup, cream cheese, and sour cream. Pour over chicken. Mix together cracker crumbs, butter, and poppy seeds. Sprinkle on top of casserole. Bake for 45 minutes. Makes 6 to 8 servings.

Chapter Twenty-One

The best way to succeed in life is to act
on the advice you give others.

AMISH PROVERB

⌒

Hope walked to the Golden Coast Amish School with quickened steps. She paused as she neared the door to Jonas's classroom. Excitement and nervousness knotted together in the pit of her stomach. Taking a deep breath Hope knocked, but no one answered. Tentatively, she turned the knob. It was unlocked. She peeked inside. The lights were on.

Hope walked into the small schoolroom, guessing that Jonas had just stepped out for a minute.

The room was neat and orderly. Twenty wood and metal desks were lined in rows. The metal part of the desks was painted pink, and Hope was sure the Amish school had bought them from a public school sale sometime in the past. She turned a slow circle, taking it all in. This was where Jonas worked, yet this wasn't his life. His life was different. He was a farmer, and soon he'd be returning to his real place on earth.

She closed her eyes and pictured Jonas plowing behind a team of horses, turning the earth into rich brown furrows. She pictured

Emma barefoot in the garden, her small footprints showing up beside Hope's larger ones. She imagined the soil soft underfoot and warmth from the sun on her shoulders.

She pictured Kentucky, and this time she pictured herself there with them. Hope opened her eyes, gasping at the possibility. Then she crossed her arms over her chest. She didn't know if Kentucky was going to be possible. She didn't know if Jonas did indeed care for her and wanted things to move that direction, but she didn't need to know that now. Today she had something else on her heart. She looked to Jonas's desk and then to the smaller ones. She'd sit in one of the student's desks and wait.

The school was both similar and different from the schools she had attended in Walnut Creek and the one where Lovina had taught for two years. Drawings and paintings from the children decorated the walls. On the white board someone had written a prayer. It wasn't the typical, perfect script that her teacher used to write in, but rather it was written in printed blocky letters—a man's handwriting. Hope's heart warmed thinking of the rugged farmer taking the time to write the prayer in such neat letters. As she read it, she recognized it as one of the songs of the Ordnung—songs from their ancestors that had been passed down for generations.

> Copy the Lord Jesus like a mirror,
> And also live without evil craftiness,
> Slander you shall avoid.
> Keep yourself pure, undefiled, chaste, and clean,
> Turn everything into the best.
> Also abstain from all appearance of evil.
> Let the kindness of the Lord
> Be known to everyone.
> What you desire from me,
> You shall also do to another.

Out of the whole song one line was underlined: "Copy the Lord Jesus like a mirror." There was an arrow away from that line and Jonas had jotted more notes, as if they were written in the midst of a class discussion: *forgiving, compassionate, pure, kind, loving, gentle,* and *truthful.* Ways they must live to follow Jesus.

Hope smiled seeing that. She thought back to her teachers growing up. They were all female and all young. As a class, they had said morning prayers and had memorized Scripture passages, but from looking around at that song on the whiteboard—and on other Scripture passages that the children had written out and posted around the room—Brother Sutter put more attention to the children's spiritual growth than most. It seemed the widower taught much more than reading, writing, and math. Ruth Ann had made a good choice in asking her brother to teach. Perhaps because of what Jonas had gone through with his wife's sickness and death he'd grown deep in his relationship with the Lord.

As Hope considered that, a new emotion filled her. An empty longing overtook Hope at the thought of Jonas returning to Kentucky. Many people came and went in Pinecraft, and while she missed some of her friends, an ache had already begun at the thought of his leaving...and he was still here.

Footsteps sounded behind her, and Hope turned as Jonas stepped through the door. He wore a soft grin on his face and a Bible was tucked under his arm. His smile widened upon seeing her.

"Hope, what a pleasant surprise this morning!" The grin on his face told her that he meant those words.

She stood from the desk. "Jonas, I want to talk to you. I..." She let her voice trail off, and doubts rose up in her mind. Hope took a deep breath. "Jonas, I want to know..."

He lifted his eyebrows and waited. "*Ja*, Hope? What do you want to know?"

Hope's eyes darted around the room, as if she were searching for an answer in the children's artwork.

"Do you like teaching?"

Laughter burst from his lips. "Hope, is that really what you were going to ask? Because in the last thirty seconds all the color just drained from your face. It seems a pretty serious response for a question like that."

"*Ja*." She nodded. "I've been curious."

Jonas shrugged. "I do like it, and it would be better if it weren't for all that book learnin' stuff."

His words surprised her and laughter burst from her lips.

"If only it weren't for that." The laughter caused some of the tension to release from her chest.

"The way I see it, it's my job to bring some Amish culture into our school day too," said Jonas. "We've been whittling, and the other day I spent an hour talking about crop rotation. It doesn't seem right for these children to be raised so far from Amish farms. They know how to push *walk* buttons and cross busy streets, but they don't know how to milk cows. They buy their vegetables at Yoder's Produce Stand…"

Jonas let his voice trail off then, and she knew what he was getting at. But then he closed his lips, pressing them tight. She had to give it to him, Jonas wasn't going to pester her. He wasn't going to ask again.

"That *is* a shame that all the vegetables the children eat are from a market. I've been thinking about it—I told you I would—but I'd like to come and have the children work in my garden. I'd like—"

A whoop erupted from Jonas's lips, and then he'd wrapped his arms around her and swung her once around. Then, as if realizing what he was doing, Jonas quickly set her down. Hope struggled to catch her breath and try to remain on her feet—not just because he'd just spun her, but because of his closeness.

Jonas released his grasp and he took a step back. "I—I'm so sorry."

Hope reached out her hand and clung to his arm, holding herself steady. "Well, Brother Sutter," she said, using the name his students called him. "I have to admit I never expected *that* reaction."

He looked away, but redness crept up his neck.

"The students can come and start tomorrow," said Hope. "I think by then I can ask around and get some garden tools donated. I'll ask my sister Grace to help. It's the perfect type of task for her."

"Really? That would be wonderful!"

She took a step back, chuckling. "You're not going to throw me into the air now, are you?"

"*Ne*, Hope." Jonas shook his head. "But I will thank you." He reached forward and took her hand. "And I will admit that I'm going to enjoy spending this time with you. I—"

The sound of the classroom door opening caught their attention. Jonas quickly released Hope's hand and turned. Hope followed his gaze. Emma stood at the door.

Emma wore a big smile. Without hesitation she raced toward Hope, wrapping her arms around Hope's legs.

"Hope, are you going to be my new mem?" Emma asked.

This time it was Hope who felt the heat rising up the back of her neck. "I...I think..." She carefully avoided looking at Jonas. "Maybe we should just focus on spending time together in the garden, *ja*?"

Hope only had to ask once for Grace's help. Two hours later her industrious sister had returned with two buckets filled with garden tools. Hope looked into the bucket and found hand trowels, hand weeders, soil scoops, and more.

"Oh Grace, these are wonderful! I didn't realize there were so many hidden treasures around Pinecraft."

"Everyone was eager to donate." Grace went to the kitchen sink, washed her hands, and then wiped a wet towel over her face and neck. "It is warm out there though, and it seemed everywhere I went people either wanted to hear more about the garden or wanted to offer me their gardening advice. Since I don't know much about either I just said a little and moved on. I wouldn't be surprised if you have a lot of folks coming by to watch."

Hope nodded and sighed. "It wouldn't be Pinecraft without that, would it?"

"Oh!" Grace reached into her apron pocket. "There's something else. I have a letter from Eleanor." She pulled out a white envelope and handed it to Hope. "I hope she's doing well. I haven't heard much from her since she had her newest baby—although I suppose that is to be expected."

Hope's hand trembled slightly as she reached for the envelope. She thought back to the goals she'd written at the beginning of the year: move away from Pinecraft and grow a garden. The latter had happened in an unexpected way. And only a month passed and suddenly the former didn't seem as important. In fact, she hoped that Eleanor was writing to tell her that she *didn't* need help—at least not until Hope could sort out her feelings for Jonas.

She took the envelope and tucked it in her apron pocket. "Uh, thank you."

Dat eyed her curiously. "Well, aren't you going to read it, yet?"

Hope nodded. "I will. I'm going to pour some lemonade and

sit in the back. There's an ocean breeze blowing and I thought I'd enjoy it."

"Makes sense," Dat said, but his eyes still held worry. Grace watched her too as she escaped to the yard. It wasn't until she was outside that Hope realized she'd forgotten her lemonade.

"Oh well," she mumbled. She'd rather stay parched than fall under their questioning gazes again.

Instead of walking to the swing where she'd be in full view of the kitchen, Hope walked around the side of the house to the little garden table and chair that the last owners of the house had left behind. They were dirty, but at least they were in the shade. She brushed the seat off with her hand and then sat.

Dear Hope,

Greetings in the name of our Lord Jesus who blesses us with family and friends who help us wait out every winter and rejoice with us in spring's return.

It was so gut to receive your note. I am sorry that it took so long to respond. When I first received your letter I was going to write you back immediately and tell you to come. Roy and I had just been talking about my need for extra help, but when I showed him the letter he said that we had to wait. He'd just received news at work that there would be layoffs coming. If you remember, Roy works at one of the trailer factories in town and because of the economy their company has been facing hardship. I was disappointed by the news, but I understand the need to wait. I understand we must be frugal during these times. I wouldn't want to do that to you Hope—have you move all the way up here only to have Roy lose his job—and have us be unable to offer you a wage.

Roy did say that by spring we should know more. I will write you again in April or May and tell you if things have changed at his work.

I would like to see you and all your sisters again. I miss quiet days like the ones we spent at the creek as children—Lovina making mud pies, you pulling up small plants and studying their roots, and Faith drawing sketches of the creek. When I was cleaning out my hope chest a few weeks ago I found a dandelion crown that Joy had woven together. I had dried it, and it has held up amazingly well. Also tell Grace hello too. I do enjoy the letters that she writes for The Budget. *If Grace's plan is make everyone wish for a visit to Pinecraft—to escape winter's grasp—she's doing a wonderful job.*

As for us, the snow keeps coming and the world around us is dusted with white. I haven't been out much since Baby Katie's birth. She has a more delicate health than my others. I even had to miss church last week. Spring cannot come soon enough.

Know, cousin, that you will be hearing from me again in April. Give everyone our love.

Your dear cousin,
Eleanor

Hope released the breath she'd been holding. She'd prayed for an answer—for God to make things clear—and in a way He had. He'd asked her to wait.

"Hope, it's not time to leave," she felt the stirring inside her say. "Not yet."

For this season of her life she was needed in Pinecraft. Children from the school needed her. Emma did too. And maybe Jonas? Was it too much to hope for?

So instead of packing, Hope rose with new determination. She had to make a plan for her garden, and she had to think of a way to have the children help. Even though opening up her garden would be hard, Hope had peace knowing it was what God was asking her to do.

Chapter Twenty-Two

True worth is doing each day some little good, not
dreaming of great things to do by and by.

AMISH PROVERB

〜

Hope turned off the sprinkler that had been watering two of the long planters. She gathered the hose, coiling it by the faucet. She had to get the last details organized. The kids would be there before she knew it. She held the sprinkler head in her hand, and a lightness filled her chest remembering Jonas's excitement when she'd told him that she'd like to work with him—that she had some ideas for working with the children in the garden. His eyes had been so bright. His toothy smile so large. He'd seemed like a different person, and she got a glimpse of the young man he must have been before dealing with the long illness and death of his wife.

The faucet dripped in a steady rhythm, and Hope pictured Jonas jumping off rope swings and climbing to the tops of hay wagons as a young boy. She pictured life in his eyes, not just loss, and it was more attractive than she could have imagined.

A dog's bark somewhere in the next neighborhood broke her trance, and Hope's foot felt cold. She glanced down to notice that cool water from the sprinkler head had been dripping water on her foot. Her mind had been so lost with thoughts of Jonas she hadn't noticed. She dropped the sprinkler and placed a hand over her heart. Was this what it was like to be attracted to someone? It had come on so fast, so unexpected. Or had it?

Hope heard the chatter of voices even before she saw the children. Then a loose train of bouncing bodies rounded the corner. Hands pointed to the long boxes filled with soil. A bee buzzed by and a few of the children shrieked. The younger *kinner*—not just Jonas's older class—had come today too.

A little girl ran over to her pot of marigolds and plucked off two heads. She turned to Hope with wide eyes and beamed, as if she'd just done something wonderful.

"Oh no, Andrea. We look at the flowers. We don't pick them," Jonas said.

Andrea's smile faded, and then her lower lip puckered. Tears welled up in her eyes and her whole body slumped.

Hope hurried over to her. "Oh, it's all right, Andrea. You didn't know, but Brother Sutter is right. We just want to *look* at the flowers and all of the plants."

One boy ran up to her and placed a hand on her arms. "Can I help you pull weeds?"

"*Ja.*" Hope nodded, and she held up her hand. "But not yet. Today we're going to look at the different plants. We're going to learn which are vegetables and which are weeds. Then we're going to play a game to see who remembers."

Emma's hand shot into the air. "I want to play a game!"

Hope laughed. "Of course, everyone will play."

"Even Brother Sutter?" an older boy asked.

Hope turned to find Jonas's face. His eyes were already on her. His smile was large.

"Brother Sutter is actually going to help me teach you about the plants. He's a great gardener too." She pointed. "Jonas, why don't you take those rows and I'll take these closest to me, and then we'll meet in the middle and trade."

"That sounds like a good idea, Hope. I'd be happy to help."

Hope moved to the first row of plants, and the children gathered around her. She wanted to reach out and touch each one. They were focused and quiet. They were also excited—she could see it from their smiles. Joy lifted and flooded her heart, and she wondered why she'd pushed this away for so long. Could it be that God had been wanting to bless her with the very thing she'd been pushing away?

~⌒⌒

Jonas had walked all the children back to the school just in time for the day to end. Emma went home with Ruth Ann, who promised that they would head back to the house and make ranger cookies. After watching them walk away, Jonas headed back to Hope's garden. And with every step the questions he had earlier about Hope faded. She was wonderful with children, tender and thoughtful. And as she helped them with the raised beds, she also talked about the gardens in the north too. She'd talked with longing in her voice, and seeing that—hearing that—made up his mind. He wanted to pursue Hope for more than a friend. He wanted more.

Jonas walked around to the back of the pie shop and smiled when he saw that Hope was still there.

Jonas strode up to her. "I think the garden is a success."

"Already?" Hope smiled. "But we haven't even had a harvest yet. And I'm still not sure I trust most of your students to be able to know the difference between a vegetable and a weed."

He chuckled. "I'm talking about my daughter. You should have heard Emma at dinner last night. Ruth Ann served carrots but Emma called them 'yummy orange roots.' She has already learned so much. I know the other kids will catch on too."

"They should make me a banner." Hope winked at him, and emotion flipped in Jonas's stomach. "I'll forever be known as the woman who taught an eight-year-old that the carrot is the root of the plant."

Jonas laughed, and his heart felt light and happy. "All the children had a *gut* time in the garden today. Thank you so much for agreeing to this. I know Emma will be even more excited about our own garden when we get back to Kentucky."

The brightness in Hope's eyes faded at his words, and she looked away.

"But we're not leaving for a while yet," he quickly added.

Hope gave him a tender smile, yet there was hesitation in her gaze. "Oh, I'm glad to help, but anyone in Pinecraft could do the same. I'm sure that anyone you stop on the street could tell you about their favorite plants to grow and their best tips. What I've done is nothing special."

Jonas took a step forward. He wanted to reach for her hand but then changed his mind. He balled his hands into a fist instead, wishing he could share his true heart without scaring her away. "There are many gardeners, Hope, but only one who I know who comes alive when she digs into the soil. Before I met you I thought a garden was about the end result—about having a stocked pantry before the first snow fell. Until I knew you, I didn't know such joy could be found in the process. I didn't know that I'd get so excited to see the first sprouts of new growth. I haven't treated my own garden very well back home, but that's going to change."

She smiled at him, broader this time. Her gaze softened and

became wistful. Was she thinking about his garden—trying to picture it? More than anything he wanted to show her. He wanted to take her to Kentucky and show her who he truly was there. Yes, he enjoyed teaching, but that job was only for a season. Who he was in Kentucky was who he was for a lifetime.

"When I look at you, Hope, I appreciate the cycle of life that we all take for granted. I know you probably don't realize this, but there are a least a hundred expressions that cross your face in one afternoon. The way you look at the plants, at the children, at Emma, and…" He was going to say *and me*, but Jonas stopped short.

Her cheeks turned pink under his gaze. "What do you mean?"

He chuckled. "Don't be embarrassed. It's a good thing."

"I do love this." She swept her arm around the garden. "And I love having a garden even more after not having it for a year. The move to Pinecraft was harder than I thought." She shrugged. "And this isn't all that I want—I hope that doesn't sound greedy—but I'd love a garden up north. A real garden that I can walk around in barefoot and line up row after row." Her voice filled with so much longing that the last words came out in a whisper.

Jonas couldn't help but again think of her in his garden. And when he did he pictured Emma by Hope's side. He'd come to Pinecraft to see Emma smile again, but her smile was never brighter than when she was with Hope.

"You know what I see when I look in your eyes?"

She shook her head and lowered her gaze to the bright green grass under her feet.

"I see gentleness and dedication. Intelligence and an eye for the simple things that most of us forget to pause and wonder at. I see a little girl, like Emma, who wasn't content sitting in a sewing circle and just listening to the latest chatter. I see a daughter and sister who loves her family and walked away from where she felt comfortable and safe to be with them. I see a woman who is going to make a fine wife someday for the mere fact that she rejoices in new life and new seasons. And I see someone who is going to teach her children that it's okay to be different and to trust who God made you to be."

The words came too easily, and part of Jonas told himself to stop. His mind raced ahead, and he knew where he wanted this conversation to go. And from the look in Hope's eyes she didn't want him to stop either. She soaked up his words like parched ground soaked up water, and he knew if he continued there would be no going back, but at this moment Jonas couldn't have kept the words in if he tried.

"This might be happening too fast, Hope, but I've learned not to waste a day. Life is too precious. You never know what a day will hold.

"After losing Sarah I never dreamed I'd want to open my heart to another again, but to tell you the truth, after meeting you that's not my biggest worry. My biggest worry isn't risking the chance of a broken heart. Instead it's trying to imagine a future without you in it. I never imagined a more fitting person to welcome into Emma's life."

Hope's eyebrows lifted as if she was taking everything in. And then her smile faded. "Into Emma's life?" she questioned.

"*Ja*, you can imagine how hard it has been for me. It's not myself that I think of first, but her. I've been praying for the perfect mother for my daughter—"

Hope's brows furrowed and Jonas paused. What was wrong? Had he jumped to conclusions? Even though Hope cared about Emma, maybe she wasn't ready to be a mother yet.

"Jonas, I wanted to hear those words. It's *gut* to know that it's not just my heart that is being drawn this direction. But when it comes to a relationship I want to be more than just someone's—"

"Hope!" Lovina's voice interrupted their conversation, and her sister strode around the corner. "There is a car waiting outside for you. Janet sent it. From what the driver said she's not doing well. She fell while helping her daughter. She broke her hip and she'll be going into surgery in the morning."

"Oh, no! I'm so sorry to hear that. Is there a reason the driver is here?"

"You can talk to him, but from what he said, Janet sent for you because she wants to show you her mother's garden before she goes into surgery. She wants to tell you more of the story—something that is not in the Victory Journal."

"*Ja*, of course." Hope turned to Jonas, but he noted tears in her eyes. Tears for her friend.

Compassion swelled in his chest, mixing with both care and confusion. Even though he'd confessed his heart, something was bothering Hope. Something only time and patience would reveal. "Do you want me to go with you, Hope?"

Hope nodded. She reached out her hand and he took it. "I'm not sure what to expect, but I want you to meet her. Janet—my friend—and her mother's journal did so much to change my heart about the children. Maybe hearing her yourself will help you understand."

Ranger Cookies

1 cup shortening

1 cup brown sugar

1 cup sugar

2 beaten eggs

1 tsp. vanilla

2 cups flour

½ tsp. baking powder

1 tsp. baking soda

½ tsp. salt

2 cups oatmeal

2 cups crisp rice cereal

1 cup coconut flakes

1 cup nuts

Preheat oven to 350 degrees. Cream together the shortening, brown sugar, and sugar. Add the beaten eggs and vanilla. In a separate bowl, combine the flour, baking powder, baking soda, and salt, and add that to the sugar and eggs mixture. Stir in oatmeal, rice cereal, coconut flakes, and nuts. Drop heaping spoonfuls onto greased cookie sheet. Bake 7 to 9 minutes. Makes 4 dozen large cookies.*

---

* Sherry Gore, *Simply Delicious Amish Cooking* (Grand Rapids, MI: Zondervan, 2013), 157.

Chapter Twenty-Three

A happy memory never wears out.

AMISH PROVERB

⁓

Hope looked out the window, nearly touching it with her nose as she looked to see where the driver was taking them. They drove toward the ocean, and the busy streets with gas stations and small strip malls transformed into a neighborhood of older homes. They were set back from the road by large lawns. Tree-lined paths also dotted the property. She'd never been in such a nice neighborhood, and she certainly couldn't imagine living in one. Then, after driving a few more minutes, they came into a public area with a large garden, a picnic area, and a playground.

The driver turned in to the park, and Hope's brow furrowed. "I thought we were going to Janet's house," she said under her breath. Just beyond the park was a large white house with a sweeping porch. The circle driveway was made of paving stones, and tall pine trees graced both sides of the entrance.

"Could this be Janet's house, next to the park?" Hope asked Jonas.

"Yes, miss, this is her home," the driver said, overhearing. "And that park used to be part of Ms. Spencer-Rushing's property until it was gifted to the city as a community park."

"Her property, a community park?" Hope turned back around in her seat at the realization of what the one small victory garden had become.

The car parked, and the driver opened the door for Hope. Jonas got out the other side and she joined him. Down the path Hope saw a wheelchair and she immediately recognized the older woman inside.

Janet waved them forward. "Come, you two. Please, I have so much to show you."

Hope hurried forward and accepted Janet's extended hand.

"Are you feeling well?" Hope asked, even though she could see Janet wasn't. Her face was pale and dark circles hung under her eyes. She still wore a beautiful, colorful outfit, but her hair was done hastily, brushed back from her face and held back by a few bobby pins.

"It's my hip," Janet complained. "I was trying to carry a lunch tray to my daughter and I fell going upstairs." Janet sighed. "Who in their right mind falls going *up*?"

"I'm so sorry to hear that." Hope noticed Janet's eyes moving to Jonas, and she turned to introduce him. "And this, Janet, is Jonas. He's a friend and—"

A brightness filled Janet's eyes. "And the handsome, unmarried schoolteacher." She winked. "There isn't much that happens in Pinecraft that I don't hear about. Elizabeth does a wonderful job filling me in."

"I'm glad to meet you, ma'am," Jonas said. "Hope told me a bit about you on the drive here. You have a beautiful home."

She clasped her hands together and smiled. "Jonas, would you push me? I'd like to go to the garden, which is truly more beautiful than my home."

He began to push her down the sidewalk toward the garden, and Hope followed. The path wove around, lined by small flower beds. "All of this used to be grass, can you imagine? So boring." She waved her hand toward a small plot of strawberry plants. "As a child I used to run and play with my friends down the long green slope, but it wasn't much use for anything other than that. Our lawn used to look like any other lawn in the neighborhood, but I like it so much better now. Don't you?"

When they approached the garden area Hope noticed people squatting or standing among the rows and working. There were people of all ages, from young toddlers to older men. They were from all ethnicities too.

"Our first garden was just a fraction of this size, but over the years it has grown. I enjoy meeting all the folk who come to garden here, although these days it's hard to remember everyone's name."

As they watched, a truck pulled up and parked. Two men moved to the back, opened the tailgate, and started to shovel out mulch.

Next to her Jonas shifted his weight from foot to foot. Hope looked at him. "Would it be all right if I went to help?"

"Of course I don't mind." Janet waved him forward. "It'll give Hope and I more time to chat."

Jonas hurried forward, rolling up his sleeves as he walked. Within no time he had his own shovel and was helping spread the mulch that the other two men were unloading.

"He looks like a special young man there," Janet said.

"He is special, although he's not going to be in Pinecraft too much longer. Jonas is only here to teach school for the semester. He'll be heading back to Kentucky in April, but I have to say that I wouldn't have the garden without him."

"And what about you, Hope?" Janet looked up at her, blocking the sun with her hand.

Hope moved Janet to a shady spot and then sat down on a park bench facing her.

"I'm glad the garden is up and going, but I can't imagine myself in Pinecraft—not long term. I miss the seasons up north. I miss the farms and sprawled-out Amish communities. I miss gardening and the cows and..." Hope smiled. "Well, you understand."

Janet nodded. "Hope, sometimes God calls us to a specific place, but other times He simply asks us to cast the vision. My mother is no longer with us, but her garden is. God has brought amazing people with knowledge and skill to help with this garden. Maybe the seeds you've planted with your garden will be harvested by someone else, and that's fine too."

"I have a feeling that's the way it's going to be. It's bittersweet, *ja?*" Hope plucked a small leaf from a strawberry plant and turned it over in her hand. "Even as I plant the seeds and line up the rows I have a feeling someone else will be eating the produce." She shrugged and ran her hands over her skirt. "My cousin Eleanor is interested in having me come and help with her children, her garden. I should know in a few months."

"Even if you do leave, look what you started—just like this garden here." Janet placed a hand to her cheek. "Oh my, my mother would have loved to see how this turned out." She sighed.

"And just think, if it wasn't for the war none of this would have happened. Who knows what would have happened to your mother..." Hope wanted to ask about Henry, but she was almost afraid to. Either things didn't work out with them and she'd be disappointed, or things had worked out and she'd ruin the rest of the journal. She never was one who read the last chapter of a book first.

"The way I see it there's a war now that's just as great a threat. It's a threat to our communities. People don't think about their neighbors anymore. They don't even know their neighbors. I used to know every person up and down my street, but as the old folks have died or moved away new people moved it. They pull into their garages and quickly shut the doors. Or they put up fences and gates. They're trying to protect themselves, so they say, but they're missing out." Janet rubbed her hip, but continued on.

"Children today watch more television than they play outside. Families eat in separate rooms of the house. That's why I'm drawn to Pinecraft—drawn to the families there. Neighbors still know each other. They sit on front porches or meet at the park to chat. And that's why I got so excited when Elizabeth told me about your garden. It took me back." Janet paused and looked at Hope. "You remind me so much of her. You'd have liked my mother, and she would have liked you."

Hope nodded. "I have a feeling I would." Hope looked around again.

"We donated our garden to the city, but hearing about your garden reminded me of my mother's first efforts, and I wanted to be a part of that. I know she'd like knowing that you read her story. Now I want to hear more of yours, especially if it has some romance. Romance books have always been my favorite."

Hope rose and pushed Janet over to the rows of melons, hoping to get a better view of how they were growing.

"I'd love to share my story, but there isn't much romance in it. Jonas and I do have a growing friendship."

The disappointment was clear on Janet's face. "I understand, but please tell me what you've learned—even if it's not about love."

"Well, because of your mother's journal I decided to open up the garden to the community. Yesterday children from the Amish school came to help me. Jonas—as you know—is one of the teachers there."

Hearing his name, Jonas approached. His hands and pants were covered in mulch, but a huge smile filled his face.

"Having the garden open to the community is better than I expected," Hope continued. "I thought I loved gardening before, but I'm discovering new things to enjoy now. Like yesterday, I realized that gardening can be enjoyed by all ages. We had a gardener who'd been gardening for sixty years, at least, and today we had children who were doing it for the first time. And for both the process is the same—digging the soil, planting the seed, watering."

"Sort of like prayer," Jonas cut in.

"Excuse me?" Hope asked.

"I was thinking about that when I heard Emma praying the other night," Jonas explained. "Ruth Ann sometimes prays aloud while she's cooking, and Emma picked it up. She was talking to God as if He was sitting right there next to her, and it reminded me of my grandmother. Even when she tried to pray silently, her lips always moved and I'd watch them, trying to figure out what she was saying. Anyone, any age can come to God."

"I suppose we're the ones who try to make things more complicated."

Janet leaned back in the chair and lifted her face to the breeze. "You two are so wise for being so young." She chuckled. "It took me many years to figure all this out."

Hope wanted to tell Janet about Jonas's loss. There was no doubt that as he drew closer to God for comfort and strength, he was changed too.

"I've learned that if it's not a matter of life and death, it's not worth fighting about…and it's not worth putting a barrier between you and the one you love," said Janet. "Which brings me to the story of the children."

"The children?" Hope asked.

"Remember when we had lunch I told you that the garden would have an effect on the children? When school started in

1942 my mother got an idea. She got those in my class involved in helping with the harvest. And the best part was that all of them took home a lot of produce that fall. With so much rationing it was a huge blessing for those families. Even now when I talk to old schoolmates they always mention the garden."

"Well, I suppose our idea wasn't too unique then?"

"Just goes to show that a good idea is timeless." Janet smiled again, but weariness was clear on her face.

"Thank you, Janet, for inviting us. Seeing all this has confirmed what God has been telling me," said Hope.

Jonas wheeled Janet back to the house, and a nurse was waiting next to the ramp by the front door.

"There you are," the nurse called. "I was just coming to get you for a nap."

They said a quick goodbye and then the driver pulled up to take them home.

"That's a special lady," Hope said as they pulled away. "I'm so thankful that Elizabeth introduced us."

"*Ja*, she is special." Jonas reached over and placed his hand on Hope's. "And speaking of special ladies, I think you're one, too, Hope. Would you like to come over to my sister's house tomorrow night? I already talked to Ruth Ann. She will watch Emma so you and I can spend some time together. I'd love to get to know you better."

"*Ja*, Jonas. *Danke*."

The sunshine filling her up inside seemed brighter than that outside the car window. She'd never planned on having a garden in Pinecraft. She'd never planned on meeting someone like Janet. She never planned on being pursued by someone like Jonas, and for the first time in a long time Hope was thankful that her plans hadn't worked out.

❦

June 12, 1942

Eight army fliers were killed when a bomber crashed into Sarasota Bay. I heard there were others injured, but I'm not sure how many. The news has rattled all of us. That's all everyone can talk about. The workers at the garden today were somber. All of us are thinking of those men's families. All of us are thinking of our own.

Hearing about those deaths has helped me to make a decision. I'm going to tell Henry I love him. He's told me twice, and I haven't been sure of it myself. But today, as I thought about the men who lost their lives, all I could think about was having Henry close—not just today but every day of my life. I think this is a sign of love. And I'm going to tell Henry tonight. Lord, please don't let me lose him too. I'm not sure my heart can handle it.

- -

Every Small Thing

Rare indeed is the day when a modern housewife could not find
in her refrigerator all sorts of odds and ends in the way of food.
And it is these leftovers that challenge the imagination of the alert
homemaker. She has learned the importance of their utilization for
food value as well as economy. She knows, for instance, that the
liquids from cooked or canned vegetables are full of vitamins and
minerals, and so they go into cocktails and soups instead of down
the sink. She has become aware of the value of saving everything
from peapods to grapefruit and melon rinds and of preparing and
presenting them at the table with eye and appetite appeal.

Never a piece of vegetable so small but that it can go into the salad
or be made into a garnish or added to the soup. No bit of fruit, but
it can be made to brighten an aspic, garnish a chop plate, top a
meringue or decorate a cake.*

---

* Ruth Berolzheimer, *250 Ways to Serve Fresh Vegetables* (Culinary Arts Institute, 1940), 2.

Chapter Twenty-Four

The best things in life are not things.

AMISH PROVERB

⤳◦⤳

Hope put on her blue dress and walked to Ruth Ann's house with a lightness to her steps. Jonas must have been watching for her because he opened the door even before she knocked.

"Ruth Ann and Emma insist that you and I have dinner with everyone at the big table, but I have something special set up in the backyard for after. I hope you don't mind."

"Of course I don't mind." She stepped inside and breathed in deeply. "I'm looking forward to spending time with your family."

Within minutes Ruth Ann had filled the table with all the fixings for a haystack supper. She watched as Jonas piled up the rice, cauliflower, ground beef, and so much more. He wasn't shy about eating. Hope tucked away that knowledge for future use. Ruth Ann seemed especially pleased with Hope's presence. Every one of Hope's comments was met with a nod of approval and a smile. There was no room to doubt what Jonas's sister thought of their growing relationship.

Ruth Ann's daughter Hannah joined them halfway through. She still had two months to go before the birth of her twins, and she looked larger than almost any pregnant woman Hope had seen. She looked uncomfortable and picked at everything on her plate. Though she tried to be cheerful, Hope had compassion for the woman who was just her age. And just to think, the pregnancy was just the beginning. Soon she'd have two infants to care for, with a husband who often left town for construction jobs.

Maybe Ruth Ann will be so busy still helping her daughter there will be need for Jonas to return to Pinecraft in the fall. But the thought was futile. Where would *she* be in the fall? That had yet to be determined.

"Oh Hope, I wish that I could come and see your garden. Being on bedrest sure isn't fun. I'm tired of lying on my back all day."

Hope thought about Janet and their stroll in the garden. "What about a wheelchair? My dat has one he doesn't use much. I'm sure you could borrow it."

"Really?" Hannah's face brightened. "I would love that."

Jonas paused from his meal. "It's a good idea, Hope. When I walk you home later, maybe I could pick it up."

When I walk you home. The sentence was music to her ears.

Hope smiled. "It sounds like a wonderful plan." Her stomach tumbled at his eyes on her from across the table, and she was thankful she hadn't served herself too much. She'd be lucky if she'd be able to finish the food on her plate with all the attention he gave her.

Less than a month ago she'd been counting down the days until she could leave Pinecraft and move north, but now? Now she wished time would slow. She wanted to spend as much time with Jonas as she could before he returned to Kentucky.

And Emma too. She glanced over at the young girl, realizing how quiet she was being. Her eyes were wide, and her cheeks flushed pink. She looked from Hope to her dat, and the girl's desire was clear. *She wants this as much as I do…*

Dusk fell, and Ruth Ann ushered Hope and Jonas outside, refusing to let Hope help with the dishes. Jonas lit a hurricane candle. Then he motioned for her to wait a moment, and he went into the house through the back door. The candle flickered, just like the stars overhead. Jonas returned a few minutes later with a plate of chocolate chip cookies. A smile touched his lips.

Hope cocked her head. "I thought Emma was going to bring the cookies out?"

"Ruth Ann said Emma didn't want to interrupt us. But…" He lifted a piece of folded-up paper and handed it to her. "I think this is for you."

Hope took the paper from his hand, unfolded it, and moved it closer to the light. "Dear Hope. Do you like oak meal cookies? Yes. No. Circle one. P.S. Come by tomorrow if the answer is yes."

She chuckled. "So it seems I'm invited back."

"So it seems."

"I'll have to tell Emma that I love both oak meal and oatmeal cookies, especially if they have raisins." She looked to the door. "Emma's pretty thoughtful. Not wanting to interrupt us like that."

"She *is* thoughtful. She had to grow up too fast."

"I'm sure that's true. I can understand…" Hope started and then paused. "No, I take that back. Dat's only been sick—really sick—the last four years or so. When I was a child I…I had no idea how much his illness—his weak lungs—was taking a toll on him. He hid it well."

"I think you can understand in part, Hope. I believe most of us see our parents as strong and indestructible. It's hard for anyone to see a parent in poor health."

"What was she like—Sarah?" The question was out before Hope had a chance to censor herself.

Jonas sucked in a breath and looked away.

Hope reached over and touched the cuff of his shirt. "I'm sorry. I shouldn't have…"

"No, I'm glad you did. It's strange that, well, most people are afraid to say her name. People who knew her their whole life will carry on a conversation with me and not mention her once. It doesn't seem right."

"Maybe they don't know what to say."

"Maybe not, but I'd rather they say something—anything—than pretend that she didn't exist." He took in a deep breath and then turned to her. "Sarah grew up on a farm just down the road from ours. The first time I saw her she was just starting school and she passed us as we walked. She was driving a pony cart and acted as if she owned the road."

Jonas chuckled and Hope joined him. "I can imagine Emma doing that."

Jonas's eyes widened and he looked at her. "You know what? I can too. I was worried about that, you know, Emma not getting the chance to know her mem's personality as she grew, but I think God took care of that. Emma is like Sarah in so many ways."

"That's beautiful, that God gave her that."

"So it doesn't bother you, my—our memories of Sarah."

Hope paused before she answered, not because she didn't know her response, but because she was trying to put it into the right words.

"Not at all. In fact I'd be more worried if you didn't mention her. The look in your eyes when you talk about Sarah shows me that you're a man who can love deeply." She pressed her lips together and added to herself, *Someone who could love me deeply too.*

They talked more about their memories during their growing-up years, and Emma was already in bed when Jonas went inside for a flashlight to walk Hope home.

When he'd finally left with the wheelchair, Hope got ready for bed, but she had a hard time falling asleep. Her thoughts of the past continued, taking her back to their home in Walnut Creek. When they moved to Pinecraft they'd sold most of their things, including the large hutch in the dining room. It had been filled with china, most of which Mem had picked up at auctions. The hutch had glass doors, and the inside of the doors had been lined with obituary cards. Since the Amish didn't take photos, it was one way they remembered those they'd lost.

Sarah Sutter. What had she been like as a wife? But as quickly as that thought entered her mind another was added to it: *Hope Sutter.* She liked the ring of that, but heat rose to her cheeks, and she was glad that Lovina was asleep not to hear her gasp. If she and Jonas fell in love, would that love ever match up to his first wife? Hope wished it would. Wished it more than anything. Wished it enough to put aside all her plans to see what God's plans for them together were.

Haystack Supper

1½ cups evaporated milk

2 cups finely shredded cheddar or American cheese

Salt and pepper to taste

⅛ tsp. paprika

Cracker crumbs

Cooked brown or white rice

Shredded lettuce

Onions, chopped

Tomatoes, chopped

Cauliflower, chopped

Green bell peppers, chopped

Corn chips

Taco-seasoned browned ground beef

Salsa

First, make cheese sauce. Heat evaporated milk in saucepan until very hot, but not boiling. Add cheese and stir until it begins melting. Remove from heat and continue stirring until sauce is smooth and creamy. Add spices to taste.

Layer remaining ingredients on plates or in a large bowl in order given. Top with cheese sauce.

Chapter Twenty-Five

You only live once, but if you work it right once is enough.

AMISH PROVERB

⁓

Hope had slept in, mostly because she was dreaming of a beautiful farm—maybe in Kentucky. She wasn't sure, but it slowed her pace, and she didn't arrive at the garden until nearly 7:30. Her breath caught when she rounded the corner and saw a surprise guest. Emma stood in the garden, pressing a small box to her chest. Her shoulders slumped forward and her head was lowered. She looked like a statue she stood so still.

Hope stepped forward. "Emma?"

Emma's head lifted, and she turned. She extended her hands out as if offering the box to Hope. "I—I brought this to show you. I—I wanted to share a secret." Her words came out with a sob and Hope took the box from her hands. It was the size of a cigar box but it looked handmade of pine.

"Did you want me to open it?"

Emma nodded. "*Ja*...but something fell out. I don't know where it is."

Hope lifted the top of the box. There was no hinge and the top slipped off easily. Inside was a collection of things—a bird's tiny egg shell, a keychain from Shipshewana, a recipe for humming-bird cake, a small autograph book that she guessed was filled with signatures and poems from Emma's friends. There were also a few letters. She glanced at the return address. Both letters were from a girl named Emma—most likely pen pals. And in the corner of the box was a pretty marble and a piece of yarn tied at the ends so Emma could play cat's cradle.

"These are wonderful keepsakes. I had a box of treasures just like this when I was a little girl."

Emma's hand covered her face, and her shoulders shook.

Hope bent down on one knee beside her. "What's missing, what did you lose?"

"Mem's card…It had her name on it. I got it when she…she…"

Emma didn't continue, but Hope understood. A lump formed in her throat as she looked into the little girl's dark brown eyes. "Was it your mem's funeral card?"

Emma nodded. "*Ja.*"

"That was so special that you wanted to share it with me. I would love to see it."

"But it's gone. I lost it. I dropped my box…"

Hope stood. "Will you show me where? I can go with you. We can look together."

Emma wiped her eyes and nodded. Hope put the lid on the box and tucked it under her arm. She then extended her hand and smiled as Emma put her small hand in Hope's larger one. They walked together back toward Ruth Ann's house. About halfway there Emma rushed forward. She pointed to a small hedge next to the road. Hope quickened her steps. They paused in front of the hedge.

"A bike was coming," Emma said. "I went to move out of the way and my box spilled."

On the ground a flash of something glimmered in the sunlight. Hope bent down. There was a marble on the ground, similar to the one in Emma's box. Hope looked around, but she didn't see anything else. She opened the lid and added the marble to the box, and just as she was about to tell Emma that she didn't see it, a card caught her attention. It had somehow gotten stuck in the hedge. Hope reached out and picked it out of the branches. It was off-white and the size of a small envelope. She turned it over.

In Loving Memory of Sarah A. Sutter
July 17, 1986 – January 10, 2013

Visitation Tuesday, January 13, 2013
to be held at the late home, 156 Lawson Lane, Guthrie, KY 42234

Funeral Wednesday, January 14, 2013
Northwest District Amish Church, Crofton, KY

Officiating Bishop Jonathan Kanagy

Burial to follow at Northwest Amish Church Cemetery,
Guthrie KY 42234

"For the hope which is laid up for you in heaven,
whereof ye heard before in the word of the truth of the Gospel."
Colossians 1:5

Tears filled Hope's eyes as she read the card. There was a poem there, but Hope didn't take time to read it. Seeing the card, Emma's face brightened. She smiled and her nose wrinkled. She took the card from Hope. Hope opened the box, and Emma put it inside.

Hope blinked back her tears. "I'm so happy that you brought this to share with me, Emma. From now on we'd better keep it at your house. I don't want you to lose any of this. These things are special."

"I just wanted to show you." Emma's lower lip trembled. "Dat told *Aenti* Ruth Ann that you were special."

"He did?"

Emma nodded.

"Well, I think your dat is special too. Does he know where you are?"

"He knows I was going to the garden. He said he'll meet me there and we'd walk to school together."

"Well, in that case we should get back to the garden. I also have a feeling that more people will start showing up soon. We get a lot of visitors."

Emma walked beside Hope, holding her hand. "Do you like visitors, Hope?"

"You know, it used to bother me, but it doesn't much anymore. God has helped me with that."

"Did you pray about it?" Emma's eyes widened.

"*Ja*, I did. And I can tell God is at work in my heart, Emma." Hope glanced down at the girl, wondering if she understood.

"I'm praying about something too." Emma reached up, taking Hope's hand. She squeezed it tight.

From the look on Emma's face it was clear what she was praying for. Emma wanted a new mem. And she'd brought the funeral card to show Hope that she still had a place in her heart saved for her biological mother too.

Hope lowered herself onto one knee and allowed the young girl to wrap her arms around her shoulders. Hope took Emma into her embrace and squeezed. "I'll pray with you, sweet girl. I will pray that God gives you the desires of your heart, if that is in line with His perfect plan." She closed her eyes, breathing in the scent of her, and it was only the sound of footsteps that caused her to open them. There, at the corner of the building, Jonas stood watching them. Hope offered him a smile, and he smiled back. He looked like a pleased father, thankful that she was caring for his little girl. Yet deep inside Hope's question remained. Did he only want a mem for Emma? Or did he want her for himself as his bride? Would their relationship be moving at the same pace if it was just the two of them? Hope wasn't certain, but she liked to think so. She wanted to be loved by this man as a wife, not just someone's mother. As much as she loved Emma, she needed to know that Jonas was offering his hand not because of what she could provide for Emma, but what Hope could give to him—her heart, her life, her future. Until the last breath she breathed, just like Sarah had.

Hummingbird Cake

3 cups all-purpose flour
1 tsp. baking soda
1 tsp. salt
2 cups granulated sugar
1 tsp. cinnamon
3 eggs, beaten
1 cup vegetable oil
1½ tsp. vanilla extract
1 8-ounce can crushed pineapple (with juice)
1 cup chopped pecans
2 cups chopped bananas
Cream cheese
Butter
Powdered sugar
Vanilla extract

Combine flour, baking soda, salt, sugar, and cinnamon in a large bowl. Add eggs and oil, stirring until moistened. Do not overmix. Stir in vanilla, pineapple, ½ cup pecans, and bananas. Pour batter into 3 greased and floured round cake pans. Bake for 25-30 minutes. Cool for 10 minutes before removing from pans. When completely cooled, combine cream cheese, butter, powdered sugar, and vanilla to make icing. Spread over top and sides. Sprinkle top with remainder of pecans.

Chapter Twenty-Six

There is no beauty without purpose.

AMISH PROVERB

～⊃

It was hard to believe that nearly two months had passed since Hope had first written her goals for the year, and now February was nearly through. She'd spent at least part of each day with Jonas and Emma. They had become as close to her as family. It seemed as if she'd known the two her whole life, and Hope didn't want it any other way.

The house was quiet, except for a slight shuffling in the kitchen, when Hope rose. It was late—nearly six o'clock. Back in Ohio the days had started early, spring, summer, fall, or winter. Dat had been up before four o'clock, feeding livestock and milking the cows. She and her sisters always helped with chores too. Sometimes they helped with the milking or gathering the eggs. Lovina usually stayed inside and helped in the kitchen, and when winter slipped into spring Hope found herself in the garden. In Pinecraft it seemed almost every day was a good one to be in the garden.

It was going to be a big day with the Gospel Express auction, and Mem was already up and making breakfast. Oatmeal was on the stove, and she was scrambling eggs. Hope considered stopping by the auction later. It depended on who would show up at the garden. The children weren't coming today, but there were always new tourists in town. A smile touched her lips as she considered that. She still enjoyed her quiet and peace, but she'd made many new friends from Amish communities all over the United States.

Mem glanced over her shoulder as Hope entered. "Do you know what sounds good? Something we haven't had in a while: fried cornmeal mush and tomato gravy. Oh, or some Florida vegetable medley, especially with your home-grown tomatoes."

Hope chuckled. "Oh, it'll be a while yet. I haven't even put in tomatoes, and I can't plant them for a while."

Mem lifted her spoon into the air. "So you *are* going to be planting tomatoes?"

There was tension in her voice. Hopefully it was just that she was busy and in a hurry to get out the door.

Hope eyed her mom. "*Ja.* I hope so."

But when Mem turned and caught her eye, Hope knew that the tension wasn't about the auction. There was something more.

Mem cocked an eyebrow. "You're telling me that you're definitely going to be planting tomatoes here in Pinecraft?"

"Well…I'm not sure where else I would plant them."

"I imagine you don't. I've heard from two of my sisters that you've written to Eleanor, asking if they need a *maud.*"

Hope's stomach tumbled, and she again wondered why she hadn't said anything sooner to her parents. It wasn't a secret, was it? She was surprised Lovina hadn't said anything to Mem. "*Ja,* that is so. I wrote to Eleanor."

Mem pointed to the kitchen table. "Do you have a minute to talk, Hope?" She turned off the burner on the cooked eggs and put the pan on a trivet.

"Of course. I was just going to the garden."

Mem poured two cups of coffee, added cream, and carried them to the table. They settled across from each other, and Mem released a low sigh.

"Hope, it is no surprise that you want to move back. Dat and I considered this very thing when we decided to sell the farm and move. We were thankful when all five of our daughters decided to follow us down here. We knew that all of you were old enough that you could have made a different decision. We also knew that in comparison to Ohio, there wouldn't be much to keep you here."

Hope released the breath she'd been holding. "So you're not upset that I want to leave?"

"*Ach*, no. I've lived my life, daughter, and I don't want to live your life too. I know that I sometimes stick in my nose where it doesn't belong. I also know that maybe I'm too concerned about finding the right husband for my daughters, and stirring up all sorts of worries, but I understand that you have your own dreams, just like Lovina had hers."

"*Danke*, Mem. For a while I thought I'd be able to stay here. I thought the garden at Lovina's pie shop would be able to satisfy me. I thought it would be enough."

"And it's not?"

"Well, for now it is. But I can't say it's what I'd want forever." Hope shrugged. "I love the garden space, and I'm even starting to enjoy the community—getting to know everyone. But I can't stop thinking about spring on a farm. A real spring. If not this year, definitely next. I'm sorry I didn't tell you sooner."

"I understand, Hope. But are you honestly thinking of returning to Walnut Creek, or would you go someplace else?"

Hope lowered her gaze to the pattern of the wooden table, using her fingers to trace the lines. "I'm not sure what you mean."

"Well, according to Lovina and Noah there have been many volunteers, but none as dedicated as Jonas Sutter."

Heat rose to Hope's cheeks, and she folded her hands on her lap. "Of course. After all, the schoolchildren have been helping out. He's made the garden part of their lessons."

"Of course he has."

"Jonas is a friend, Mem, nothing more." *At least not yet,* she wanted to add.

"Dat seems to think Jonas would like it to be more than that."

"So Dat is talking about this, too?"

"Everyone is."

Hope placed her elbows on the table and her hands on her forehead. "Which is another reason to move away from Pinecraft. This place is just too small. I can't even walk to Yoder's Restaurant without everyone knowing about it."

"So you're *not* interested in Jonas?"

"I—I do enjoy being with Jonas very much." She sighed. "I can see he has feelings for me too. It's just going slow. We're enjoying our friendship. Besides, there is much to consider for things to move forward, considering he is a widower."

Mem was silent for a moment, as if she was considering her words. "There are many young women who marry widowers. I just don't know if it's right for one of my daughters."

Hope sat up straighter, shocked by her mother's words. "Mem, I didn't know you thought that way. To be truthful I have wondered at times of Jonas's true intentions. Is he interested in me for himself—as someone to love—or does he just need a mother for his daughter?"

Mem nodded and took a sip of her coffee. "Surely there are other men—single men who've never been married—around here. Maybe getting to know a few of them better would help with your decision. Have you spent time with any of those bachelors from Indiana who are here visiting?"

"*Ne*, Mem…and I'm not worried about finding a husband. God will show me in the right time."

"It's true."

Her mother's confirmation hurt, but Hope had to face reality. She cared for Jonas, and he cared for her, but was it enough to build a marriage on? They enjoyed spending time together, but was it love? She'd never really been in love before and didn't know how it was meant to feel. Maybe she'd been right when she first thought about moving. Maybe she did need to go back to Walnut Creek for a time, just to be sure.

Hope stood. She took a bowl from the cupboard and scooped up a helping of oatmeal. "So, since you've been talking to your sisters, do you know if any of them need my help as a maud?"

"I can write and ask. There are lots of your younger cousins in Ohio too. Maybe you should write a few more letters. Although they might feel that they'd need to pay you more because you're…"

"Because I'm older?"

"Yes."

Hope set the bowl down and threw up her hands. "What if I don't need money? What if I just need a garden?"

Mem lifted an eyebrow. "And where would you sleep?"

Tears filled her eyes, and she wondered why she'd even bothered. Would she sound desperate if she wrote to all her cousins to ask them for work? *Lord, why can't this be easy? Why can't I have a clear dream, a clear goal just like Lovina? Being with Jonas seems right…but how can I be certain?*

Hope placed her bowl on the counter. She sprinkled brown sugar on top. "I'm just being foolish, Mem. Don't pay me any mind."

"I know it's hard to figure out a place for us in Pinecraft, but deep down I have a feeling that you'll discover your place when the time is right. And for now you're doing a wonderful thing. Just look at that garden you're growing, and just look at how the community is connecting. This is something that Pinecraft didn't have before…and it wouldn't have if you weren't here."

Hope nodded, and a soft smile touched her lips. Mem was right. She didn't know where she'd be six months from now, but God had a purpose for her today. And for now that had to be enough.

- -

Florida Vegetable Medley

6-8 small squash, sliced
6 ripened tomatoes, sliced and seeded
3 sweet onions, thinly sliced
¼ tsp. salt
¼ - ½ tsp. lemon pepper
½ cup water
1 cup grated sharp cheddar cheese

In a large skillet, layer squash, tomatoes, and onions. Continue layering until all vegetables are used. Add salt, pepper, and water. Steam on medium-high for about 25 minutes. Sprinkle with cheese before serving.

Chapter Twenty-Seven

Preach faith until you have it, and then
preach it because you have it.

AMISH PROVERB

❦

Emma gazed up at Hope with large brown eyes. "Hope, what did you do when you were a little girl?"

Many visitors had come and gone throughout the day, but Hope had been looking forward to this special visitor most. She'd counted down the hours until school was over. Ruth Ann had brought Emma by, and Hope urged the older woman to let her stay. They'd pulled a few weeds, and then Hope decided they needed a change of scenery and they headed to the park.

"Well, I liked to garden. And my sisters and I would try to catch the barn kittens. Sometimes we would name the baby calves or climb into the haystacks."

Emma's face fell. "Is there anything that we can do here...like when you were a kid?"

Hope thought for a minute. She looked around the park. The grass was neatly mowed. There were no barns with barn cats. "I can think of something. I'll try, I promise. For now, why don't we walk to the water and see if anyone is fishing?"

Emma glanced up, and she nibbled on her lower lip.

Hope squatted down. "You're not nervous to go down there by Phillippi Creek, are you? I promise not to let you climb into a canoe."

Emma chuckled. Then she grabbed Hope's hand and led the way.

When they got to the boat ramp they discovered three teenage boys fishing.

"Do you want to try fishin'?" the tallest of the boys asked, handing the pole to Emma.

Emma reached out her hand, but then she paused. She looked at the water and a blank look crossed her face.

"Do you want to?" Hope asked. "Maybe you should try."

"*Ja*," the boy took another step closer. "Your mem already said that it is all right."

Your mem. The words swirled around Hope's mind. Emma didn't correct him. Instead she squeezed Hope's hand just slightly and then released it, reaching for the fishing pole.

The older boy patiently showed her how to cast the line. Emma's mouth opened as she slowly reeled it in. She did it a few more times but didn't catch anything. Emma handed back the pole and then turned to Hope. "Aenti Ruth Ann said I have to be home for dinner." There was a puzzled look on Emma's face, as if she didn't know what to think about the boy's words.

Does she like the idea of getting another mother? Or does it bring her pain? Hope wished she knew.

"*Ja*, of course."

It was a quiet walk home, and Jonas was nowhere to be seen when Hope said goodbye. Emma offered her a small wave, and Hope walked away more confused than ever. Her mem had told her one thing—to start spending time with other Amish bachelors. But whenever Hope was with Jonas or Emma she wanted to ignore that advice. Hope missed them as soon as they were apart.

Lord, please show me the answer.

She turned the corner to Gardenia Street and stopped short. There, on the corner, was a yard full of dandelions, and immediately Hope knew what she wanted to do with Emma. Without hesitating, she hurried up the front steps of the house. Her neighbor Eli must have been watching out the window because he opened the front door before she had a chance to knock.

"Eli, has anyone claimed your dandelion greens yet?"

He stroked his long beard, obviously pleased by her request. "*Ne*, not yet. Are you hungry for some dandelion salad?"

"I am, but even more importantly I thought it would be something that Emma and I could do together. She wanted to do something like what I did when I was a little girl on the farm, and I remember picking the greens."

"I'll save them for you."

"*Wunderbar*! I'll be—we'll be—right back."

Hope half-walked, half-ran back to Ruth Ann's place. She knocked on the door, and Ruth Ann answered.

Hope grinned. "I'm sorry to bother you, but I was wondering if I could have Emma for another thirty minutes or so."

Ruth Ann smiled. "Your cheeks are flushed and you're breathing hard." She smiled. "Whatever it is, I dare not say no."

Emma must have been listening. She hurried outside. "What is it, Hope?"

"We're going to pick dandelions, just like I did when I was a kid."

"Dandelions?"

Hope took Emma's hand. "You'll see."

It took only fifteen minutes for Hope and Emma to clean the yard of dandelions. They first collected the greens in a plastic bag that Eli offered them, and then used the rest of the flowers to make crowns to set on top of their kapps.

They had a full audience at Hope's house when they made a dandelion salad—thankfully Mem already had cooked bacon in the fridge. With eager steps they took it back to Ruth Ann's with a hop in their steps. Emma knocked, and Hope held the bowl out in front of her, waiting for the door to open. But it wasn't Ruth Ann who opened the door. It was Jonas.

"Hope, Emma!" He grinned. "What have you been doing? You have weeds on your kapp."

Hope touched her kapp and considered taking off the wilting crown, but then changed her mind. "We come bearing a gift for the dinner table."

"Dandelion salad?" Jonas held out his hands. "Thank you."

Hope peered over his shoulder and noticed they had already gathered around the table. Had she interrupted their prayer? She took a step back and then bent down to look at Emma. "Let me know what you think, *ja*?"

Emma reached for Hope's hand. "Won't you join us, Hope?"

Hope sighed. "Didn't you see Joy making all that fried chicken? She'd be so disappointed if she didn't have me to help her eat it."

Emma nodded and followed her dat into the house.

Jonas was silent, but when Hope looked up at him she was sure she noticed the hint of tears in his eyes.

"Thank you," he mouthed. It wasn't more than a whisper.

"My pleasure," she responded. And as she turned to walk away Hope realized she meant it. Her arms felt empty when she walked toward home a second time. How would she ever say goodbye to that little girl when the time was right? Or to her father?

Hope attempted to keep her smile as she returned home, but from the looks in her parents' eyes she wasn't doing a good job.

"Hope, I know something that might cheer you up," Dat said after they sat down for dinner and bowed their heads in silent prayer. "A letter from Eleanor has arrived."

Eleanor. Hope looked over to the pile of mail on the kitchen counter. Sure enough there was a letter on top with her cousin's distinct handwriting.

She tried not to think of the letter during dinner, but as soon as she was through she hurried to the letter, taking it out to the backyard. Hope settled into the swing and then opened the envelope.

Dearest Cousin Hope,

Praise be to our Lord Jesus for the ways He continues to provide. Roy discovered at work that he will not be laid off. Instead he was given a promotion, taking over for one of the older men who is going to retire. I've heard you have a wonderful community garden now, but if you're still interested in coming please let me know. I would love help with the kinner, and as you know I have a large garden plot too. Write when you can, and dream of a Northern spring!

Love, Eleanor

Hope read the letter twice, and then she folded it up and put it away. She didn't know what to think of it. She didn't know what to do. She wanted to go, and she wanted to stay. And that was when she knew she must pray.

Lord, I need You to make this clear. Give me an answer. Show me the way.

If it hadn't been for Jonas and Emma there would be no complications. Then again...they were the best type of complications to have.

Dandelion Salad

2 quarts dandelion greens, young
4 thick slices bacon
¼ cup butter or other fat
½ cup cream (scant)
2 eggs
1 tsp. salt
Black pepper
Paprika
1 Tbsp sugar
¼ cup vinegar

Wash dandelions carefully, dry gently in a towel, arrange in a salad bowl, and set in a cool place. Cut bacon in small pieces, fry until crisp, and sprinkle over dandelions. Melt fat with cream in skillet over low heat. Beat eggs, add salt, pepper, paprika, sugar, and vinegar and mix with slightly warm cream mixture. Pour into skillet, increase heat, and stir until dressing becomes thick like custard. Pour piping hot over dandelions. Stir well. Serves 8.*

---

* Ruth Berolzheimer, *500 Snacks* (Culinary Arts Institute, 1940), 31.

Chapter Twenty-Eight

Bend the branch while it is still young.

AMISH PROVERB

⸙

In Ohio, the first planting happened after the snow had melted and the ground was able to be worked. The first things Hope typically put in were spinach, onions, radishes, beets, and carrots. After the danger of frost was gone she put in the green beans, zucchini, peppers, corn, and melons. She smiled thinking about what her grandfather had told her years ago—that is was safe to plant after the first full moon in May.

Back north, sometimes warm April days would lull gardeners into feelings of safety, only to have a late frost come and wipe everything out. Hope had listened to her grandfather's advice. She'd stuck by that rule, and she'd never had frost take her plants. This was the first year that she didn't follow that rule.

In Pinecraft things were different. Frost was rare, and that was why she'd gone to the library and looked up some local gardening books. She'd diligently written down their suggestions of what to plant when, and because she wasn't the expert she wasn't going to argue.

Now, here she was in March harvesting from her first crops. Some of the carrots were ready, and so were the radishes. The schoolchildren arrived and she oversaw the excited group as they picked the ones that were ready, washed them under the faucet, and then ate them right there.

"That's one way to get the children to get their vegetables," Jonas said, sidling up to her.

"*Ja*, and Emma has had three radishes already. I hope they don't make her stomach ache."

Hope didn't have much time for small talk. As soon as they were done with their treats she gathered everyone around to explain their last task of the day.

"We're going to finish the last of our planting." Hope laid out the stakes. "Nellie, it's your job to use this marker to write the type of seeds that are planted on these sticks and make sure they are put next to the right row."

"Back in Tennessee my mem used to put the seed packets on the end of the sticks and put them in the ground like that," one young boy named David said.

"*Ja*, I've seen some gardeners do that, and it's *gut* too. I usually like to use a marker on my stakes because sometimes the seed packets get blown off. Or…" She waved to the corner of the building where a mother stood with her two-year-old son watching. "Or…sometimes the little ones like to come and pull off all the seed packets, and then you're stuck with trying to remember what you planted where."

Emma raised her hand, waving it in the air. "Can I keep the packets?"

"You want to keep them?"

Emma nodded enthusiastically. "*Ja*, I want them for my garden at home."

"Oh, you have a garden at home now, do you? You'll have to tell me about that later, but right now why don't each of you go find a hand rake or a trowel and we'll get started."

The other children rushed toward the buckets, their excited voices filling the air.

"Will you come see my garden, Hope? I planted carrots," Emma said.

"Sure." She nodded and smiled, not knowing if Emma was talking about a real garden or a pretend one. "You'll have to tell me about it later, but right now why don't you go get a garden tool? We need to get started. My guess is that this isn't the only thing your dat has planned for your school day."

Emma nodded and ran to join the others at the buckets.

Jonas came up to her again and leaned in. His presence was overwhelming, and Hope nearly wanted to step away. How could one man cause every nerve in her body to stand on end like that?

"Emma's garden is a few small planters that I found at the Village Cupboard, and we picked up some carrot seeds at the store." He chuckled. "With all the water, love, and attention she gives them I'm not sure if they'll even sprout, but she's having fun. And she tells me, 'I'm just like Hope, Dat.'"

"That's so sweet. I'd love to see her garden sometime."

"*Ja*, I'll ask Ruth Ann if there's a day when you can come to dinner…again."

"Oh no, I didn't want to impose."

Jonas turned to her and smiled with a smile that lit up her heart. "Hope, you won't be imposing. I promise. I can't think of a better person for Emma to model herself after."

"Danke, Jonas. I don't know what to say."

"Say you'll come for dinner?"

"Shouldn't you ask Ruth Ann first?"

"If she hasn't already started dinner I'll offer to pick up dinner from Yoder's."

"Wise man."

"*Ja*." He nodded, peering down at her. "Choosing to have you around as much as possible is very wise indeed."

⌒

Ruth Ann had made enough food to feed a dozen guests. Hope's favorite part of the meal was Ruth Ann's salad with home-made honey-orange dressing.

Jonas chuckled when she went back for thirds on the salad. "I should have guessed that someone who loves gardening would love salad."

"Don't worry, Hope," Ruth Ann said, scooping more salad onto the plate. "I'll be sure to send you home with the recipe for the dressing."

Once the dishes were done Hope went to join Jonas and Emma outside. She closed the screen door silently behind her. Jonas stood straight, peering down and watching Emma dig in her pot with a small trowel. In her mind's eye Hope pictured herself approaching him from behind, slipping her arms around his waist, and laying her cheek between his shoulder blades. She imaged his shirt to be warm from the afternoon sun. She imagined feeling his heartbeat as she pressed close to him, but as soon as those thoughts came in she pushed them away. She should not be having these types of feelings for him—not until she had a clear answer.

She thought back to something her mem had told her: *Love that grows slowly over time, putting down its roots, is a love that will last.* Everyone who she knew who'd had a rush of emotions also found them rushing away just as quickly. Jonas was handsome and that was appealing. He also was a good father and a good teacher, but surely to have real emotions—lasting emotions—would take longer than the few months they'd spent together.

After Emma finished her gardening they played a game of checkers on the table. First Emma played Jonas and then she played Hope. Emma giggled when she won both times.

When the second game finished Ruth Ann came out. "Emma, did you want some homemade ice cream?"

Hope noticed that neither she nor Jonas were invited in. And when Ruth Ann shot Jonas a curious look she guessed why.

He has something to talk to me about.

They sat on two lawn chairs side by side, listening to parrots chatter in a nearby tree. They talked about school and the decrease of visitors, and then Jonas quieted. Hope sucked in a breath, waiting for his words.

"Hope, I want to talk to you about Sarah's death."

It wasn't what she expected, and the sadness that crossed his face nearly broke Hope's heart. "You don't have to. I know it must be hard."

"I loved her. She loved me." He drew in a great sigh and expelled his breath. The shudder moved through his whole body.

"Every marriage should be like that, Jonas." She reached out to take his hand, and then she changed her mind, pulling it back onto her lap.

With words full of sadness he told her about Sarah's stroke, about finding her, and about the hard years to follow that included caring for Sarah, caring for Emma, and trying to keep the farm going.

"But at the end I was so tired. It was so hard to see her suffer. And a few days before her death I prayed that God would take her."

"That's a sign of love, too, don't you think?"

Tears filled his eyes and he nodded. "I just wanted you to know about that. To know about how hard it was. I want you to know that if there are days when I don't seem myself, or days when I'm especially quiet, well, I'm probably thinking about those times. About…"

His voice trailed off, but Hope guessed what he wanted to say. "About her."

He nodded.

"And I'm sure the same can be said about Emma," she said.

"I suppose so."

Jonas reached out and took her hand then, squeezing it as if he was afraid to let go. "It's strange, you know, carrying all of this inside. Most of the time it's like this hat I wear." Jonas placed his free hand on his straw hat. "I'm so used to wearing one that I forget it's there. But then there are times I'm aware of the shade it casts."

"You have a way with words, Jonas Sutter, and I'd be worried if you didn't have those thoughts and feelings."

"But I just want you to know that what I had with Sarah, Hope, takes nothing from what I feel about you. I never thought it would be possible to have such hope for the future."

She smiled then, but she also worried. Were things moving too fast? Did she truly know him? Did he know her? Hope had never had her heart broken, and more than anything she hoped she never would. But that didn't matter to her as much as worries of hurting both Jonas and Emma. He'd already gone through so much loss, and what if this didn't work out? She didn't want to hurt him, and she didn't want to hurt that little girl.

He pulled her hand toward him and kissed the back of it. Hot heat rushed from her hand, down her arm, and to her chest—straight to her heart.

Take things slow, Hope. Don't let his heart become entwined too quick.

But even as she thought that Hope wondered if it was too late. She also wondered what all this meant. But for the moment she was content simply sitting in this backyard with Jonas and feeling the tenderness of his touch.

⁓

September 17, 1942

We planned the wedding in three days. I've known that I loved Henry for months now, and I knew he loved me. I'm not sure why we waited to marry…fear, I suppose. Fear that we were making a mistake. Fear that things were moving too soon.

Uncle Sam was finally the one who stepped in to say, "Enough is enough," and Henry received news he was heading to Europe. I knew before he left that we had to marry. He felt the same.

September 30, 1942

The transport plane that was carrying Henry to his new base crashed. There are survivors. I haven't heard if Henry is one of them.

October 7, 1942

Henry is coming home, but not like I expected.

October 15, 1942

He lost his arm, but my husband will be in my arms soon. I sent him a letter telling him that he can still pull weeds with one arm. I imagined his smile. I hope that letter arrives before he leaves. I want him to know that I love him now just as much as I did before the accident. There is little that can change a love like we have…

Honey Orange Salad Dressing

1¾ cup plain yogurt
¼ cup honey
2 Tbsp frozen orange juice concentrate
2 Tbsp freshly squeezed lemon juice
¾ tsp. grated orange zest
¼ tsp. freshly grated ginger root

Combine all ingredients and serve over fresh green lettuce leaves or fruit chunks.

Chapter Twenty-Nine

May our lives be like arithmetic: friends added, enemies
subtracted, sorrows divided, joys multiplied.

AMISH PROVERB

&

When Joy half-jogged, half-ran around the corner of the pie
shop, Hope knew that something was wrong. She first
thought of Dat, but another name slipped from Joy's lips.

"It's Janet. She had her hip surgery but she took a turn for the
worse. They have her in a rehab center."

A weight sank in the pit of Hope's stomach. Her breath caught
and she extended a hand to Joy. "Is—will she be all right?"

Joy shrugged. "Elizabeth doesn't know. She just asked me to
come and tell you. She knew you'd want to know. She knew you'd
pray."

"*Ja*, of course."

Hope thought of the Victory Journal that she'd left sitting
on her bedside table. Even though she was only borrowing it, it
meant so much that Janet trusted her with it.

"Do you think we'd be able to go see Janet—once she's stable,
of course?"

Joy brushed a strand of dark hair from her face and shrugged.

"I'm not certain, but I'd be happy to ask." Joy looked at the trowel in Hope's hand. "Actually I'm heading there right now if you'd like to join me."

"*Ja.*" Hope brushed a dirty hand on her apron. "I'd be happy to. Just give me a minute to wash up."

Twenty minutes later both of them were sitting near Elizabeth as she hand-stitched a small quilted wall hanging. "I know we won't be able to see Janet until she is stable. She's at a nice place, though. I've visited there before. My husband and I went to visit one of his friends."

Hope's head jerked backward. "Your husband? I am so confused. Didn't you tell me about moving to Pinecraft and feeling so alone?"

"*Ja,* we did talk about that a while ago, didn't we? For a while I even considered leaving the Amish, but I am glad I stayed. I met and married a wonderful man. Amos Bieler. His name was the same as my married name, but we couldn't find any close relations. We only had four years together before his death, but they were a wonderful four years."

"I've always wanted to ask you about Amos." Joy smiled. "I've seen the photograph of him on your desk."

Elizabeth chuckled and pushed her glasses farther up her nose. "The newspaper took that photo when we were meeting the bus. Amos was upset that they published it, but I bought five copies and cut out the photos." She sighed. "I'm secretly thankful."

"And if you hadn't stayed Amish…" Hope's voice trailed off.

"If I hadn't stayed Amish then I would have never married Amos. I thought I was a godly woman until I married a man with two children. I was older, and Abel and Katie were both nearly grown by the time I married their father, but oh the trials. I couldn't just think of myself all the time," Elizabeth said. "And there was so much I needed to learn…"

Hope started to organize the thread spools next to her by color. "What do you mean?"

"Before I got married, sewing was my life. I promise you that after I moved in with Amos my sewing machine sat in the living room with an unfinished project folded up on top of it for three months. I couldn't just be concerned about myself, but those who needed to eat and needed clean clothes. There was that large garden—bigger than anything I'd ever tackled before, and though I loved Amos I'd cry as I watched him leave for work, knowing he'd expect a good hot meal at lunch.

"Looking back now I know I'd placed high expectations on myself. No man expects a perfect wife. I also know that putting myself in the middle of that family, and the new community, was the best thing for me. It was a growing time. It made me realize that I didn't have my act together as much as I thought I did. Before my marriage, God was a nice companion. I knew that He was there. I thanked Him throughout the day. I also prayed for others. Oh, I had troubles in my life to be certain, but for the most part nothing that I couldn't handle. But with a husband and children I needed God. I clung to Him. I turned to Him for wisdom. I cried to Jesus for strength. And, Hope, I'm guessing that you have some worries about your growing relationship too. But dear one, don't be afraid to open your heart."

Hope chuckled. "It sounds as if marriage is hard. Are you really trying to talk me into opening my heart, Elizabeth? Because right now everything within my mind shouts 'run, run.'"

"Oh sweet child, weren't you listening? All my self-concern didn't disappear, but a new name became most important, and that was *Jesus*. I wouldn't trade the close relationship with Him for anything else. Every heartache, every conflict was worth it because it drew me into His arms."

Elizabeth reached over and patted Hope's hand. "Besides, God's going to grow us up somehow. That's what all good parents do. If He's not going to use marriage to change you and mold you into the likeness of His Son, He'll use something else." Elizabeth winked. "And if I were you, I'd sign up for God's classroom of life with a handsome partner like Jonas Sutter."

Heat rose to Hope's cheeks, and she fanned her face with her hand. "Elizabeth," she offered in a shocked whisper.

"I've seen the way he looks at you—"

"Yes, I know. Jonas believes I'll be a *gut* mother for Emma."

Elizabeth clucked her tongue. "Oh dear, is that what you're telling yourself? That's just the half of it. *Ne*, make that a quarter of it." Elizabeth closed her eyes, and she dropped her head. When she noticed the slightest trembling of Elizabeth's shoulders Hope realized she was crying.

Hope squeezed the woman's hand.

"I was married to Amos for four years, and if given the chance I'd go back and do it all again—despite the hard work and the times of heartache. After being single well into my forties there's nothing like knowing you matter most in the world to someone." Elizabeth lifted her face and the rim of tears on her lower lids glimmered. Seeing it, tears filled Hope's eyes too.

"Don't let your fears stop you from giving your heart away, Hope."

"I know I care for Jonas, and I suppose it's growing into love. I'm just afraid that his feelings are moving ahead of mine. How will I know, Elizabeth? How will I know when the time is right for us to make that commitment?"

"Oh, that's easy. When you get to the place when you don't want to be apart from him, and your heart breaks thinking over having to, listen to that. If you're willing to step away from the things you love most to be with the man you love…well, that's a good sign too."

"Are you talking about the community garden?"

"The garden is important all right, but more important are your plans and the dreams you've built around your future. When all the ideas and plans you've been scheming seem like a waste of time without Jonas, then it's a sign you've given him your heart."

Hope took in those words. She let them sink deep. Her heart tightened and ached. Before Jonas she hadn't known this feeling— the pain of both longing and…and what?

Tenderness. Was that it? Was her heart really hurting because she'd come to care for those two people? She didn't even know that was possible.

"Oh!" Elizabeth's eyes brightened. "I know you probably need to get going. No one has all day to sit and chat with an old woman, but before you leave I have something for you. Something you asked for."

Elizabeth rose from her chair and went to the back storeroom. She returned with a paper bag rolled down at the top. She reached inside, pulling out a small apron.

"Oh!" Hope's hands flew to her face. Is that for Emma?"

"*Ja*, it is."

Hope took it from her, and her fingers trembled slightly. She held it up. It was exactly like hers, only smaller. Tears filled Hope's eyes and shimmered on the rim. Emotion grew in her throat when she imagined Emma's expression when Hope gave it to her.

"It is perfect, Elizabeth, just perfect." She pressed the apron to her chest. "Just let me know how much I owe you."

Elizabeth waved a hand in the air. "You don't owe me any-thing, dear girl. You've given so much to our community—with your time, your garden, and your smile. It's the least I could do."

The warmth grew in her chest at her older friend's kindness.

"Can I see it?" Joy held it up. "Maybe we should stock some of these at Me, Myself, and Pie too. The kitchen aprons are selling so well I'm sure that all the customers who peek around the back at the garden would also be interested in these."

Hope sucked in a breath. Her first reaction was to argue—to tell Joy that she didn't need any more visitors than she already had. But as she thought about it, having all those people around was less of a bother than she thought. She also knew that if Emma enjoyed an apron like this others would too.

"That's a good idea, Joy. Let's talk to Lovina about that," Elizabeth grinned. "But that's not the only thing in this bag. I have something for Hope too."

Hope waved her hands. "Oh, you don't need to give me anything else."

"Nonsense." Elizabeth reached into the bag and pulled out a small wooden hoop. She handed it to Hope.

Hope turned it over, reading the needlepoint words. "Verily, verily, I say unto you, except a corn of wheat fall into the ground and die, it abideth alone: but if it die, it bringeth forth much fruit." Her brow furrowed and she guessed that Elizabeth thought this was a good quote for a gardener.

"I bet you've never seen that Scripture hanging on a kitchen wall, now, have you?" Elizabeth smiled. "It's a special verse for me. About a month after my wedding a new neighbor stopped by my house. She said she had a gift for me, but she'd been out of town. Her name was Miriam and she had twelve children, including two sets of twins. She said after the birth of her third child she was overwhelmed and weary. And that's when she came across this verse. In the Bible Jesus is talking about His death and return to life.

"A corn of wheat yields no increase unless it is cast to the ground," Elizabeth continued. "None of us could be called children of God now if Jesus had stayed in His heavenly glory, without becoming a man. And living the life of a family is following His example. A grain of wheat that stays in the granary has no life. There is a hidden germ of life inside, but it doesn't sprout unless it's sown. Once buried, what's inside grows and bears fruit, and what's outside falls away. Jesus's life was the greatest sacrifice. It saved our souls. And when we die to ourselves and are crucified with Christ, we too will get the newness of life. Our eternity counts on that. But there's a daily dying too—in our hearts. In our homes. As we die to our own desires we'll discover a new life, coming from the inside out, that's been just waiting for the time to grow."

Hope pressed it to her chest. "You've given me a lot to think about, Elizabeth."

"That's a good thing…just as long as you don't get your head into it all that much."

"What do you mean?"

"I mean, child, that we need to listen to our hearts, too, not just our logic. More than that, we need to listen to God's voice. The more time you spend with Him in the quiet, the more you learn to hear it. That's part of that new life that grows inside you when you give yourself to Him to die."

Elizabeth had just finished the last word when the door opened and two customers walked in. Joy rose. "I'd better get back to work."

"*Ja,* and I'd better start heading back to the garden. School is almost out and I'm sure I'll have some visitors, especially one who is going to love this apron."

Hope walked out of the fabric store, her heart full. It tugged on her and it expanded with hope and promise. She remembered picking raspberries with her sisters. With each berry added one at a time she couldn't feel the weight change. It wasn't until she filled one small metal pail and reached for the new empty one that she realized how heavy the pail had become.

Now her heart felt like that full pail, and she realized how empty it had been just months before. In Ohio she'd had her beautiful and perfect garden. But this new type of love—both for Jonas and Emma and for God—was too consuming.

And she could have missed it all. She could have stayed in Ohio. Or she could have found a position as a *maud* quickly and moved away. Or she could have built a fence around her garden behind Me, Myself, and Pie and never become the wiser.

Hope smiled as she sent up a silent prayer to God. *Thank You for all the prayers You didn't answer. Thank You for not allowing me to hide myself in a garden. Thank You for forcing me to crack open my heart by wrapping a wet little girl in my arms.*

Tears came to Hope's eyes then, and she paused and placed her hand on the metal pole holding up the crosswalk sign. As she waited, she thought about seeds being planted and being allowed to grow.

Seeds waited to germinate until three needs were met: water, a warm-enough temperature, and a good location, especially soil. But everything started with water.

Little did Hope know that wrapping up that wet little girl in her arms would start all of this—would water the seed. Tears filled her eyes as she imagined the brackish water from Emma's dress and the young girl's tears seeping through her own wet dress, penetrating her skin and going straight to her heart.

Hope's knees felt weak as she suddenly saw herself as part of God's plan in a different way than she ever had before. It was

God who'd brought her to Pinecraft—not her father's illness. It was God who'd put these gardening gifts inside her, but He was the One who also asked for them back. He didn't wrench them from her hand, but asked her to look at them in a different way. She didn't have a talent for gardening to build her own pride, or even to line her own pantry. God had made her a gardener so that she could bring the people of Pinecraft together. So that she could help Amish children understand gardens and life cycles, even though they were being raised away from a farm. But mostly so that she'd have a common place to spend time with Jonas.

Thinking about it, there would be no other place that they could have gotten to know each other quite as easily and quite as naturally. Working side by side for a common goal had connected them to the community, but mostly it had entwined their hearts.

But they needed time. More time. Hope, more than anyone, knew that seeds needed time to germinate, sprout, establish their roots, and grow.

May 16, 1943

Henry is home and it's harder than he thought adjusting to doing everything with one arm, one hand. My father welcomed us both into his home until Henry could get on his feet again. He dreams of finding us our own place soon. I hope it can happen—well, as long as it's not too far of a walk to the garden.

The war has been a horrible thing. So much missing. So much pain. So much loss. Yet I can't imagine where my life would be if it hadn't happened. I'm certain I wouldn't know my neighbors three doors down. I would have missed out on friendship. I would have missed out on so much love from Henry. Henry losing an arm doesn't mean much to me, especially since God returned the rest of him intact. There are so many women who aren't as lucky.

From the looks of it, the garden is going to do better than we thought this year—much better than last year. I smile at this. Somehow the little bit of knowledge that everyone brought together made the garden what it is. I knew a thing or two about tomatoes, but not enough to have lined my shelves or kept us satisfied for winter. Each neighbor knew enough of one thing to bring completeness to the whole. The garden is truly our *garden in so many ways.*

Even my parents have changed. Just a few days ago our cook was sick and Mother made a huge pot of sausage potato soup. That was surprising enough, but when it was clear that we had more than we could eat she invited the neighbors! Imagine that. It was a beautiful evening filled with good food and laughter.

I'll be enjoying every meal in the days to come with thanksgiving. Gratitude not only for a full belly, but for the friends and family with whom I will be sharing the meals. The war still rages, but we have each other. For now, that is enough.

Sausage Potato Soup

1 pound ground sausage

¼ cup onions, minced

1 stalk celery, minced

4-6 potatoes, peeled into ½-inch cubes

½ cup uncooked rice

2 tsp. salt

pinch ground black pepper (or more to taste)

pinch thyme

2 ham or beef bouillon cubes

1 cup frozen peas and carrots or mixed vegetables

Fry sausage in a kettle until browned. Add onions, celery, potatoes, and rice. Add enough water to cover potatoes plus 2 inches. Add salt, pepper, thyme, and bouillon cubes. Bring to boil and simmer for 10 minutes. Add peas and carrots (or mixed vegetables) and simmer for 5 minutes longer, or until potatoes are soft. Serve hot with crackers.

Chapter Thirty

Worry is interest paid on trouble before it is due.

AMISH PROVERB

〜◯〜

Jonas dressed early, taking time to smooth his hands over his shirt and remove the wrinkles. His hair fell over his ears, and he considered asking Ruth Ann to trim his hair. Amish men wore their hair shorter here in Pinecraft. Instead of buttoning his shirt at the cuffs he rolled up the sleeves in symmetrical folds. The thought of seeing Hope again—of saying what he wanted to say— wedged both expectation and anxiousness in his heart.

He paced in front of the dresser and then paused to look at his hand mirror. With slow movements he ran his hand down his beard. During his bachelor years he'd shaved it close, and from the day of his wedding to Sarah he let it grow. Once married, an Amish man would never consider shaving his beard, but it felt strange to start courting a young woman and still be wearing one. He could tell it bothered Hope too. All she had to do was look at his face to be reminded that he'd been married. To be reminded that he'd given away his heart once before.

He thought of Hope's greenish blue eyes. *Can you look past the beard, Hope? Can you look into my eyes and see my care for you?* He hoped she could.

⤳

Hope slowly dug a channel in the dark soil, keeping her eyes fixed on the corner of the building Jonas would walk around. She'd come early, hoping for quiet, and she'd found it. Well, except for the parrots that squawked in the tall tree just over the back fence.

A garden like this—and the quiet—was exactly what Hope had wanted. So why was there a pang of loneliness in her heart that she didn't expect? For the last two weeks Jonas had stopped by the garden every day on his way to school. Or rather, he'd gone out of his way to come to the garden since he had to walk right past the schoolhouse to get there. Yet today he was either running late or not coming at all. She hoped it wasn't the latter. She was getting used to seeing Jonas's smile. She enjoyed their morning talks.

Then she heard it, the sound of footsteps. She straightened her shoulders and her breath caught a little. His eyes met hers and her heart leaped. He looked different today, almost as if he was dressed up for church. Yet he still wore ordinary clothes. And then that's when she realized. It was his smile. There was something different about his smile.

His eyes stayed on her, and her throat felt tight, almost as if her kapp's strings were tied tight around it. He paused and tilted his head. Then he pointed to the tree behind her. "The way you're sitting there, there are a few beams of sunlight cutting through the branches and hitting your kapp."

"Oh, I meant to sit here. I was planning it. I wanted to glow when you saw me." She chuckled.

"So you were expecting me?"

She nodded, her heart in her throat. She swallowed hard.

"I—I was hoping." She touched her kapp. The sun's warming rays caused a few beads of sweat to touch her brow.

Jonas's hair was dark, but his beard seemed lighter. It had glints of blond and red, especially up close. The only man she'd been this close to was her dat, and she never knew what a jolt of excitement could come over her just to be near a handsome man. He smelled of nature, warm and distinctive.

"I came by this morning to talk to you, Hope. As you know, school will be over soon and Emma and I will be moving back to Kentucky—back home."

Emotion welled up in her throat and her heartbeat quickened as she waited for his words. "*Ja.*"

"I have something to ask you." He glanced at his shoes and then back to her again. "I've talked to my sister Judith—she lives right down the road from me—and she said you'd be welcome to move in with her. She only has one daughter left at home and plenty of room…"

Hope's brow furrowed. "But I don't understand. Why?"

"Well, so we could spend a lot of time together with the hopes of getting married. Then maybe by November's end…when harvest is done…"

"Marriage?" Hope's voice rose an octave. "Is that what you're asking me, to court you?"

"That's what I'm saying, Hope. I care about you. I'm hoping you feel the same."

Dozens of thoughts and emotions flashed through her mind. She wanted to say yes. She wanted to give Jonas all her heart, but seeing his beard—and remembering her mother's words—caused her to pause.

Hope reached up and rubbed her hand on his cheek. Then she moved her hand down to the roughness of his beard. "The first time I saw you—there at the creek—I thought you were married…I mean, still married. I didn't understand yet about your wife."

"*Ja*. I know what you're saying." He sighed. "It bothers you doesn't it? About Sarah?"

"It's just giving me time to get used to it," she said. She wanted to add *If we are going to be more than friends*, but she stopped. There was no if. They'd already moved past that point.

Jonas's hand covered hers. His teeth flashed—the largest smile she'd seen yet.

"What are you smiling about?"

"A simple thing really. We're having a real conversation, and you're not occupied with my daughter or the garden."

She flashed a smile. "They both are wonderfully distracting, you have to admit." She pulled back her hand.

He sighed and looked to the planter boxes. Green growth sprouted from every one of them. "It's hard to believe we'll be gone before most of this is harvested."

She stepped back just a few inches, as if putting more space between them would protect her heart. "I don't want to think about that. I can't imagine Pinecraft—this garden—without Emma. What a boring place it'll be."

Even as she said those words she realized she never responded to his offer of her going to Kentucky. She didn't know what to think of that. What if she moved there and things didn't work out? Besides, Eleanor had written yet again asking her to come.

"You'd just miss Emma?" Jonas's words interrupted her thoughts. His eyes held so much hope, so much love, she had to look away. It was almost too much to take in.

"I didn't say that." Hope's heart swelled with love, and it was a frightening feeling. When one dared to love, one opened themselves up to hurt, and to pain. Jonas—more than anyone else—knew that.

"It's *gut* that you care about my daughter, but I was wondering how you felt about me?"

Hope bit her lip. She knew what her heart felt, but how could she say it?

"You don't have to answer that now, but I'd like you to think about something. I'd like you to consider visiting Kentucky. Seeing my farm. And the garden."

Hope took another step back. "Can I think about that?"

"It seems that you have a lot to think about."

Jonas reached forward and grabbed her calloused hand, kissing it. He made her feel cherished, feel like more than just a gardener. So what was holding her back?

"Dare to hope…dare to believe in us," he whispered. Then he turned and walked away.

◦⊙

She was waiting for him outside the schoolhouse. He paused with his hand still on the doorknob. The children were gone, and the other teachers too. He's stayed late to grade papers. Jonas turned and locked the door and then hurried to her.

"How long have you been waiting there?"

"Long enough to meet a new couple who just bought a house here, talk with a few Englisch ladies who were taking photos, and help a little boy get his cat from the tree." She pointed to the tree in front of the school.

He approached her. "And how did you manage to do that?"

"I lifted the boy up, and he grabbed the scared thing." She squeezed her arm. "I'm stronger than I look."

TRICIA GOYER & SHERRY GORE

"I hope so...because there's a lot of work on a farm." He turned to wave at an older woman riding by on a bicycle, noticing she didn't answer that.

Jonas ran a hand down his beard and dared to look at her. Her eyes were blue-green and today they were the color of acceptance. She smiled, and with that smile the loneliness of Jonas's life faded like a chord from a guitar string. Until this moment he hadn't realized how strong the note had been, always ringing around the edges of his heart. His hand touched her arm and he smiled. *Of course her name is Hope...for that's what she's bringing me.*

"Would you like to get some ice cream at Big Olaf's?" She pointed down the road.

"*Ja*, I'd like that."

As they walked in silence side by side, Jonas sent up a silent prayer, thanking God for her. He didn't know what he'd done to deserve two women to love—two women who loved him—but he was thankful.

They each ordered two scoops. They considered sitting at the tables behind Big Olaf's, but instead kept walking and made their way back to the garden. They sat side by side, listening to the parrots chattering above and staring at the garden beds that held so much promise. Above all the things he'd missed, this had left the greatest void—just being with someone. Being side by side and knowing that you were wanted there.

They sat on the two chairs that they'd borrowed from Lovina's pie shop weeks ago and never returned. Hope ate her ice cream in silence and he knew she wanted to talk. He also knew not to rush her.

"I've been reading in the Victory Journal and Pauline—Janet's mother—remarried after her husband's death. She seems happy, but I've been wondering about that. Wondering if it's possible to fully love again when you've already given your heart away."

Jonas moved his fingers, sliding his between hers until they locked together. "I'm not sure about Pauline. I haven't read the journal. But if you're really asking about me, the answer is yes."

She turned to him and her eyes widened. "Oh…" was all she said.

"Yes, Hope. My love for you is full and complete. Please don't ever doubt that."

⁓

Hope's heart beat like the wings of a hummingbird, so fast and yet so fragile. She'd never felt this way about anyone before, and she didn't know if she liked feeling so vulnerable. She had a garden, but she couldn't hide away. She'd never be able to hide away again after hearing Jonas's words.

It was what she wanted to hear but was afraid of at the same time. And deep down she knew she felt the same. She'd opened herself up to love, which also meant opening herself up to heartbreak.

"Hope, is there something bothering you?"

The silence turned tense, but she couldn't answer. Not yet.

Jonas crossed his arms over his chest. She could see from his face that he was confused. The problem was, so was she. She wanted to confess her love in return, but the words wouldn't come. She wanted to be with him, yet she was fearful of that very thing. The fears were small, but there were many of them, and they joined forces to choke out all the hopes she had in her heart. She should have known better. She should have plucked each fear, like a weed, when it first planted itself in her mind. Hope could see that now, but that didn't make ridding herself of them any easier. Instead of telling him she loved him too, she knew she had another question. One she needed an answer to.

"Jonas, I've been wanting to ask. Did you ever get angry at God...for allowing that to happen to Sarah?"

"Angry, no. Confused, yes. I know God has a right to do as He chooses. I just didn't understand why it had to be her. And why Emma had to hurt so." He sighed. "It was harder seeing Emma's struggle than anything. One day she had a healthy mem who'd chase her around the yard and dance with her in the grass, and the next...well..." He shrugged.

"My Bible is what helped me most. And there was one verse that played over and over in my mind."

"What's that?"

"'They that sow in tears shall reap in joy.' It's in the Psalms."

"That seems fitting for a farmer, but how did it help?"

"The rest of the verse talks about going forth and weeping, carrying precious seed. Preparing soil takes work. The planting takes labor. But in the end we rejoice and bring sheaves. That verse helped me because even when we discovered Sarah was getting weaker, not stronger, I was encouraged that I couldn't give up on my family or my farm. I had to trust that there would be a good harvest in the future, even though I couldn't see it. For Sarah that meant stepping into her eternal life. For Emma and I—well, I'm just now starting to get a glimpse of what that could be."

She smiled at that, thinking that God had written this as part of her story—his story—even before they'd met. "I wish you didn't have to hurt so." She reached over and took his hand, feelings its warmth, its strength.

"In life there are times when we don't think there will ever be an end to our weeping, but that's not what we need to look at, Hope. Instead, because of our relationship with God, we'll have no end of joy. Joy wins in the end, and that's where I place my hope."

Hope looked into Jonas's face. A hint of tears touched the

corners of his eyes. She'd been worried about having this conversation with him. She'd expected it to be hard to listen to his love for Sarah. Instead, it showed her something else. He was a man capable of loving deeply. He was a man who cared about his family. He was also someone who turned to God during difficult times. Those were all things to be respected.

"Do you want to walk with me?" He stood. "I told Ruth Ann and Emma I'd meet them at the park for a picnic dinner."

"*Ja*, of course." She stood and followed him, and as they walked she realized there weren't very many people out. So many of the Amish had returned to their farms up north to prepare for spring.

As they walked, Hope stared up at the tall Royal Palms. Every time she saw the palm trees it reminded her she was far from home. To her it felt like she'd been on a very long vacation. But walking side by side with Jonas made her feel as if she was exactly where she should be. There was something familiar about him. Maybe *he* was the home she was looking for.

But with each passing day the clock ticked down. The school year would be over in just a few weeks' time. Should she move to Kentucky with the hopes there could be something more to come? She wanted to say yes, but something held her in check.

Why couldn't she just allow herself to love like Lovina? What was keeping her from the hope that her future was with Jonas, wherever that might be?

Chapter Thirty-One

Sometimes the simplest things are the very best.

AMISH PROVERB

Jonas held Hope's hand as they walked to the park, and with each step he sent up a prayer. He prayed God would take away all her fears. He prayed she would be willing to move to Kentucky. Reluctantly, he also prayed that if Hope wasn't God's will for him and Emma, that God would make that clear too.

They found Ruth Ann and Emma at the park, relaxing on a quilt with a picnic basket set between them. Every few seconds Emma's hand reached in for a grape, and Ruth Ann pretended not to notice. The oldest of the siblings, Ruth Ann was usually more firm and strict, but as they'd been in Pinecraft God had used Emma to soften his sister's heart—just in time for the twins to arrive, Jonas guessed.

Hope released his hand as they approached, and disappointment flooded his heart. But Jonas didn't have time to think about that now. His daughter's face brightened as she saw them.

"Dat, Hope! Come eat with us," Emma insisted.

Hope was easy to persuade, and together they enjoyed the sandwiches, potato salad, and homemade lemonade.

"Do you know what sounds good now?" Hope sat straighter. "Pie, my treat! I know Lovina is trying a new recipe today. We should go try it out."

"Oh, but I wanted to play with Sadie and Natalie." Emma pointed to the grassy areas where two little girls played with a jump rope. "Their mem said she'd watch me if I wanted to stay."

Jonas turned to Ruth Ann.

Ruth Ann nodded. "*Ja*, Mary Miller did offer to let Emma stay after the picnic. She said she'd walk her home later."

Jonas stood and patted his belly. "It's settled then. Emma stay and burn off calories, and we'll go add more on."

Hope chuckled, wiping grass from the hem of her dress. "Sounds like a plan to me."

The three of them made their way to Me, Myself, and Pie, and Hope moved to the door. "Jonas, I'll get the pie and bring it around the back. Why don't you show Ruth Ann the garden? I think she'll be surprised by how well everything is doing."

Ruth Ann smiled. "Not surprised, Hope, but I'm sure I'll be pleased. I never doubted you."

They walked toward the back of the pie shop, and as they neared the garden Jonas paused. "I need you to know, Ruth Ann, that when Emma and I return to Kentucky I'm hoping Hope will come too. Judith offered for her to stay there. I want her to see the farm, and for us to spend time together. Then, around November, we could have a wedding—either there or here."

Ruth Ann's mouth dropped open. "This November? I do like Hope, I do, but don't you think this is fast?" Her voice rose, and Jonas turned to make sure his sister's comment wasn't overheard.

On the street, two women rode by slowly on three-wheeled bicycles. An older couple strolled by with a picnic basket, most likely headed to the park. Jonah had always pictured himself and

Sarah like that, spending their golden years together. Now, in the recent weeks, a new face had replaced Sarah's in his mind. He smiled whenever he thought of Hope. He delighted that it appeared God had given him a second chance at finding love.

"Fast? Don't you think that Emma's been without a mother long enough? You've seen them together, Ruth Ann."

"Is that what this is about?" Ruth Ann's words were sharper than he expected.

"I don't know what you mean."

"A mother for Emma. Is that what matters most?"

He continued toward the garden and motioned for Ruth Ann to follow, knowing that his sister had no idea how her voice carried.

They rounded the corner, and Jonas lowered his voice. "I wouldn't say it matters most, but it's something that I do want. Do you know how hard it is to raise a young girl in an Amish community without a mother? Do you know how hard it is depending on everyone else for help? I can't sew her dresses, and I do a poor job with her hair and kapp. Emma doesn't know how to bake bread or even sew a button. What type of mother will she be some day? How will she care for her own home?"

"What about you, Jonas? What about your heart?"

"I care for Hope, I really do."

"Do you care enough to spend the rest of your life with her?"

Jonas nodded, but he didn't answer. Of course he loved Hope—his heart confirmed that—but a part of him felt guilty. It seemed wrong to love again. It seemed unfair to Sarah. He cringed when he thought how she would feel if she knew he was loving another.

"It's what I want, Ruth Ann. You have to trust me on this."

⁓

Hope balanced three plates of Luscious Lemonade pie in her hand, and she walked to the garden. Her footsteps slowed as voices carried. It was Jonas's voice and Ruth Ann's, and when Hope noticed the tone in the woman's voice she stopped short.

"When are you going to ask her, Jonas? And when do you want her to move to Kentucky?"

"I've already asked her."

"I just want to know why you're taking things so quickly."

"You're the one who set up this thing with the garden, aren't you? You started talking to Clyde about it because you thought Hope and I would make a good couple. Isn't this what you hoped would happen all along?"

"I *hoped* that you would find a friend. I *hoped* that maybe you'd be willing to love again, but Jonas, what if it doesn't work out?"

"Why do you think it won't work out?"

"Well, Hope is so different from Sarah. They're opposites almost. Hope's a good friend to Emma, but can she be a good mother? More than that, I just want you to know for certain that she's the one you want to spend your life with. There were many women back in Kentucky interested if you would have given them the time of day…"

"It's too late for that. We're already so close—"

The rumbling of a truck split the air, blocking out their words. Hope glanced over her shoulder, wishing it away. Jonas said something more, but Hope couldn't make out his words over the noise of the truck. Hope took another step closer—as close as she dared without being seen—and strained to listen.

"—I'm not going to do that to Emma. I'm not going to hurt her again. All she can talk about is Hope, and if we lose her it'll be just like losing Sarah again."

"I understand that…" Ruth Ann's voice trailed off. "I just don't want to see *your* heart broken. From what I hear she's a loner. She likes to keep to herself. Who says she'll even stick around?"

"Anytime you offer your heart there's a chance it'll get broken. You know that."

Footsteps sounded behind her, and Hope turned. Amish Henry approached with a bread bag in his hand. It looked as if it were full, and he wore a contented smile on his face.

"I been collecting popcorn and old bread to feed the ducks at the park. I was just coming by to see if Emma's around."

Hope turned and smiled. "Emma, uh, she's already at the park. I was just bringing pie to Jonas. I'm sure Emma and her friends would like to feed the birds with you. Jonas is in back; we can ask him."

Hope forced a smile, pretending her heart wasn't breaking into a million pieces. *He's doing this for Emma after all. He doesn't want to break her heart.* She'd been waiting for Jonas to tell his sister that he was in love. She'd been waiting for him to say that she *was* the person he wanted to spend his life with, but the words didn't come.

"You know what?" Hope thrust the three plates of pie in Amish Henry's direction. "I just had something come up. Why don't you take this pie to them and enjoy a piece yourself. Tell Jonas I'll talk to him later."

A large grin split Amish Henry's face. "Why, I've never said no to a piece of pie."

"*Gut.*" Hope thrust the plates into his hand. Her knees felt weak, and she knew she'd never make it home. Instead, she decided to go inside.

Her feet couldn't carry her to the door of Me, Myself, and Pie fast enough. The place was filled with customers enjoying their pie and chatting. For once she was thankful for the noise and commotion. Two small girls Emma's age stood at the picket fence barrier and peered over, watching Lovina with fascination. Hope's heart pinched seeing them, but she couldn't think of Emma now.

She spotted a small empty table in the back. Hope hurried that direction. She pushed the empty pie plate that had been left by the last customer to the side and leaned her elbows on the table. She lowered her head, staring intently at her hands folded on the table in front of her, but she didn't really see them. An ache filled her chest, and she chided herself for not taking Eleanor's offer for a job in Walnut Creek earlier. She'd dared to hope she'd found something special in Jonas. She'd also given her heart away too easily and she'd fallen in love with that little girl.

Of course he'd been thankful for someone who made his daughter smile again. What good father wouldn't want that for this little girl after she'd lost so much? But had he really been so intent on Emma's happiness that he'd been willing to marry someone he didn't love—even going so far as to lie about loving her? Apparently so.

Hope closed her eyes, feeling like such a fool.

"Hope, there you are!" Jonas said. He reached down and touched her shoulder. She glanced up, hoping he didn't notice the thin film of tears in her eyes.

"Oh, *ja*. I . . ." She couldn't think of a good excuse, and she didn't want to lie.

"Henry said you gave him your pie." Jonas smiled, but his gaze displayed worry as he studied her face.

"Yes, I—uh—was going to order another piece." She forced a smile. "There's always more where that came from."

"I'll get it for you then."

He strode away with determined steps, and Hope's stomach sank, as if it was filled with lead. She watched him as he approached the counter and asked one of Lovina's clerks for another piece. He smiled as he chatted and placed a few folded bills in the tip jar after he paid. Hope's heart broke watching the interaction. She was certain that she'd never met a more caring and thoughtful man. And up until fifteen minutes ago she'd even dared to dream that man could be her husband. But now...now she knew she'd never let him go through with marrying her. She cared for Jonas too much to let him settle for someone he didn't love with all his heart, no matter what he said.

He returned a moment later with a plate. He placed the pie before her and Hope said a quick thanks.

Hope looked down at her plate. The last thing she wanted to do was eat, but if she didn't Jonas would start asking questions, and how could she ever explain that she'd overheard him and Ruth Ann? How could she explain that after four months of appreciating every moment with him and Emma, she now wished she'd never even met them? Maybe then the ache inside wouldn't be so intense.

She picked up the fork, keeping her head adverted and her eyes on the plate. She took a bite of pie. It tasted good but she couldn't swallow.

Jonas sat across from her, but she didn't trust herself to catch his gaze. She didn't want to try to read more into Jonas's gaze than he was really wanting to give. And she didn't want him to see that her heart had just broken in two.

Jonas leaned over the table, and she dared to glance up at him. "Hope, I know I've only known you four months, but it seems like years. You're an answer to a prayer I had been too timid to pray. I never thought I'd find someone again. But from the first moment I saw you, when you were dripping wet and Emma was in your arms...well, it seemed so natural." He lowered his head. "It was hard losing Sarah. I'd known her since I was a child, and even before *rumspringa* I wanted her to be my wife. But what broke my heart most was knowing my little girl would be raised without a mother…" He paused as if trying to find the right words to say.

A cold chill traveled though her, and she knew what she had to do—where she had to go. Yes, it was true that some couples married because they were a good match and love came later, but that wasn't what she wanted. Hope wanted—needed—someone to know her and understand her quiet ways. She wanted to be an adored wife, not simply an adored mother. She couldn't think of anything worse than being lonely in marriage.

When Jonas returned to Kentucky he'd return to his farm, his community, his friends. And where would that leave her? Yes, he'd have someone to be a mother to his daughter, but was he ready to share every part of himself with her? His life and his heart? Hope questioned that.

Hope stood. She leaned down toward him so only he could hear. "Jonas, I've been thinking about the future, too, and I think we're rushing things. My moving to Kentucky is a big step. A big commitment. I've enjoyed spending time with you. Seeds of affection have been planted—in both of our hearts. Now, I think we need time to water them. We need time for them to grow."

Jonas's mouth gaped opened, and she could see that it was the last thing he expected to hear. "Hope, what are you saying?"

"Well, I'm saying, we don't need to rush things. You'd never want to dig up a carrot before it's time—"

"Hope—"

"I care about you, Jonas, I really do. And you know how I feel about Emma. That little girl means so much to me. I'm going to miss you."

"So you're not coming to Kentucky?"

"*Ne*, I'm going to move back to Ohio to help my cousin. We can keep in touch. There are always letters."

"Letters?"

"*Ja*." She straightened her shoulders. "We can spend some time writing letters. To really get to know each other better."

"Hope, we've spent nearly every day together for the last few months."

"I—It's—We…" She pressed her lips together.

"You're not ready for this. Not ready for marriage. Is that what you're saying?"

She nodded and tried to make herself sound convincing. "I'm not ready." She continued the thought in her mind. *I'm not ready to be loved as a mother more than a wife. I'm not ready to risk my heart.*

"I understand."

Jonas motioned for her to sit, and she did. Then he leaned forward and threaded his fingers through hers. "And I want you to know that seeds of love *are* growing in my heart. I'd love to start a life with you, and if it's later—rather than sooner—I'm willing to wait. If it's letters you want, then I can write letters."

Hope dared to look in Jonas's dark eyes, and for a moment her resolve nearly faded.

He pulled her hand close, kissing the top of it. "I just want you to know again that I want you as part of my life, of Emma's life."

Hope took his words in, but the worries filling her heart soon buried them. *Time will help us both know the truth,* she tried to convince herself. Time would bring out the true motive of Jonas's heart.

- -

Luscious Lemonade Pie

1 5-ounce can evaporated milk
1 package instant lemon pudding
1 8-ounce package cream cheese, softened
¾ cup lemonade concentrate
1 graham cracker crust

Combine milk and pudding; beat on low speed 2 minutes. Beat cream cheese until light and fluffy. Gradually beat in lemonade concentrate. Add to pudding mixture. Pour into crust. Cover and refrigerate.*

---

* Sherry Gore, *Simply Delicious Amish Cooking* (Grand Rapids, MI: Zondervan, 2013), 190.

Chapter Thirty-Two

〜

It was the day before school ended, and all the students and parents had come to Hope's garden.

"I know that many of you are full-time residents." Her eyes scanned the crowd. "Children, I know that so many of the things you planted haven't come up yet, but I'm afraid that I'm not going to be able to stick around to see that happen. I'm going to be moving up to Ohio soon, but I want you to know that you'll be in good hands. My dat is taking over the garden, and he'll have lots of helpers. There are a lot of people in Pinecraft who have found great joy seeing you learning so much about gardening. They'll be coming by to help you too."

The children looked at each other. Some of them contorted their faces in both sadness and disbelief. Two girls looked at each other lifting their eyebrows. One older girl bit her bottom lip. A boy peered at her with a look of dismay. Their surprise and sadness was displayed without words. Emma's head was down and her shoulders slumped. Her whole body seemed to melt forward, reminding Hope of the melting ice cream cone she'd held when Hope first saw her standing in front of the store.

Jonas had decided not to come. He used the excuse that he was finishing end-of-year reports at school, but Hope was happy for that. She didn't know how she'd hold up if she saw him.

"I have to say that spending time with all of you in this garden was the highlight of my year." Emotion caught in her throat. "I have to go see a friend, but there are many helpers here today to help you pick the vegetables you worked so hard to tend." She offered a quick wave. "I hope you enjoy them. And know these are here because of your hard work."

Without another word, she turned and left. She walked slowly, expecting Emma to come after her, but no one was following. With great sadness Hope walked to the car waiting for her. She had someone else to say goodbye to. Someone else she needed to thank.

∽

The driver waited outside while Hope went into Janet's new home. Gold Sun Senior Citizen's Home wasn't as large or as beautiful as Janet's home, but it had a flower garden out front. With everything in her Hope hoped that Janet had a view of those flowers from her room.

The air-conditioned building was refreshing as she entered. Hope paused just inside the doorway, looking around.

"Can I help you, miss?" A nurse eyed her kapp curiously.

"Yes, I've come to see Janet Walker."

"Oh, Janet is sleeping. I'm so sorry. She didn't have a good night."

"Oh no." Hope's hand covered her mouth. Then she lowered it. "Can I leave her a note and peek in? I'll be moving out of state soon. I'd like to see her." Hope refused to end the sentence with *one last time*.

The nurse nodded. "Yes, of course. Let me get you paper and pen."

Hope waited, and a minute later the nurse returned. She handed Hope a piece of notebook paper—nothing fancy, but it would have to do.

Dear Janet,

Words cannot express how much getting to know you has meant to me. I'll forever be thankful to you for offering your mother's Victory Journal for me to read. I don't have much left to read, and I was hoping that you'd let me borrow it a little longer. I promise to mail it back when I'm through. I have to mail it because I'll be going back to Walnut Creek, Ohio, where I was raised. My cousin needs help with her children and her garden. I'm thinking about inviting some of the local children to help me too.

I was also hoping to walk through Pauline's garden one last time, but I'll have to depend on my memories to take me back there again. It wouldn't seem right to go without you. Your friendship is forever dear to me, and I've learned so much about community, and friendships.

Hope was going to write, "and about love, too," but she stopped herself. Sometimes stories didn't end like Pauline and Henry's. Maybe hers would eventually, but only time would tell.

She finished the letter with *Forever your friend, Hope* and then the nurse let her peek into the room. Janet lay in a hospital bed. Her room was nearly bare except for one calendar with a garden scene. She looked so tiny in that bed, so thin. Tears filled Hope's eyes, and she backed up. She didn't want to see Janet like this. She wanted to remember her in the garden. Always the garden.

"Thank you," she whispered to the nurse. "Thank you."

She returned to the car, and as the driver took her home it seemed strange that she only had two things left to do. Since she was no longer in charge of the garden, she needed to pack and she needed to read. Maybe reading about Pauline's love story would carry her through.

>

January 1, 1944

There are days I wake up certain that this war will never end. It's hard to remember back to just a few short years ago when we didn't have to worry about rationing and blackout curtains, to hearing about another telegraph being delivered to a mother or a father in our town telling them their boy wouldn't be coming home.

This morning I woke to the sound of rain, and by the time we'd finished breakfast the sun had come out, and with it a beautiful rainbow. It was just what I needed. It was as if God was promising me that there would be an end, and that I could trust in that. It may not be this year or the next, but God is there.

It also reminded me to be thankful for all that we do have. We have a warm home. Because of the garden, we have a pantry filled with jars of food. I have Janet. I have friends. In fact, Mother and I have more friends than we ever had before, and for once in my life I feel part of a community. I've also had two men who have loved me.

So even though I woke up hopeless, I'm going to bed tonight filled with hope. And I have a new determination to live each day loving those I could well. I wish I would have lived with such a desire when Richard was still alive. It makes me sad to think how I wasted so many days. He'd want to ride to the beach, and I'd insist on finishing my chores. I would do anything to see him again. To let him see the love in my eyes.

I've learned my lesson, and I've learned to give myself wholly to Henry, and I'm thankful I did. I can look at our relationship with no regrets. I love him not because he always deserves it, but because I'm a better person when I pour out my love. I also realize a bit more God's unconditional love too.

Why would anyone choose to live alone rather than in love? Even worse, why would anyone hold back a part of one's heart instead of giving it away? Love is meant to be shared, and happy is the woman who's willing to risk all for that.

⌒

Jonas turned to his side. The splash of moonlight coming through the window turned the white blanket splayed over Emma into a soft shade of lavender. He'd always liked watching her sleep, even as a young baby. After Sarah's death he'd hired one of his nieces to tend to the house and care for Emma while he farmed and tended to the animals, but he'd always wanted to spend bedtimes with her—just the two of them. They'd read stories together and they'd pray, and then he'd sit in her room until her soft, even breaths told him she was asleep. He would do anything for his daughter, give her anything. And for the first time Ruth Ann's words gave him pause. Was he rushing things?

Hope had distanced herself over the last few days, and maybe it was for the better. It would be easier for things to cool off with Hope now than if she'd come to Kentucky.

Lord, is this Your way of protecting Emma's heart?

He leaned up on one arm and studied his daughter again. "Lord," he whispered, "I give You my heart. You can have all my plans too. I care for Hope deeply, Lord, but I want You to direct our steps. As hard as it may be to walk away, I trust You. I trust You…"

Chapter Thirty-Three

Too many people want to reach the Promised
Land without going through the wilderness.

AMISH PROVERB

～෧⁘

Emma had been crying in her room for the last hour, and Jonas felt his heart breaking in two. His daughter hadn't cried this hard when Sarah died. Maybe because Sarah's death had been expected. Maybe because she'd been younger. Maybe because Sarah had left them, and just the opposite was happening here. They were leaving Hope.

"The—the carrots are not ready yet. The beans…" A hiccupy sob interrupted her words.

"Sweetie. There is a garden back home. Our garden, remember? By the time we get back it'll be just the time to plant it."

"I don't want to plant it without Hope."

"Me either, sweetie. Me either. But Hope needs time. Hope needs space." He didn't know what else to say. "Hope knows how we feel—both of us. I just hope that it's enough."

Emma jutted out her chin. "How do you know that Hope knows how we feel?"

"You've told her. I've told her. I've done all I could." But even as he said the words Jonas knew it wasn't true. He hadn't gone to her again. He hadn't wanted to face that rejection.

"Can we go over to her house? I want to talk to her. I have something for her."

"Emma, it's late now. Everyone is already in bed."

"Not everyone! We're not sleeping. Maybe Hope's not sleeping too."

"But her family probably is. If we go over there we'll disturb them."

"But I have something for her!" Emma's voice rose.

Jonas balled his fist, trying to hide his frustration.

"What, Emma? What do you have?"

Emma moved to her shelf and pointed to an open box. Jonas looked inside and his heart nearly broke in two. His daughter loved Hope. He loved Hope. They couldn't force someone to love them in return…but they could do their best to win her heart.

Jonas turned back to Emma. He bent down on one knee and kneeled before her. "I'll tell you what. We have to leave in the morning. I've already paid for two seats on a van that's returning home." He brushed a strand of hair back from his daughter's cheek. "And I know it's hard to understand now, but Hope needs time to think. Pushing isn't going to help, but we can remind her how much we care."

Emma nodded and set her chin, looking older than her years.

"Do you want to know my idea?"

"*Ja.*" Emma sighed, and then she reached her arms to him. Jonas reached forward and pulled his daughter into his embrace. As much as she tried to be smart and strong and brave, she was just a little girl who needed to be reminded that he cared and would do his best to give her what she needed most. And in this case, it was what he needed most too.

⟳

Hope thought her heart would break as she stood by the curb in front of Ruth Ann's house watching Jonas packing the last of their things in the van.

She thought about going up to him. She considered saying goodbye, but she was afraid it would just make things harder for all of them. Instead she turned and walked to Elizabeth's shop, hoping the older woman would be able to give her some advice. But when she arrived Elizabeth wasn't there. Instead it was her sister Joy who sat behind the counter stitching.

"Have they left?" Joy asked, as soon as she entered.

"Almost." Hope sighed and sat next to her sister.

Joy paused her stitching and looked into Hope's face. "What are you afraid of, Hope?"

"What am I not afraid of? Over the last few days I've had the same worries, but new ones have arisen. I'm afraid that if I move to Kentucky I'm going to break his heart. He's already been through so much. I'm afraid I can't be everything he needs. I'm afraid I'm going to get upset if I know he's thinking about Sarah. I'm afraid we're going to disagree over disciplining Emma." Tears filled Hope's eyes. "I'm afraid I'll take his time away from her."

Hope paused, wondering where all those words had come from. She looked into Joy's eyes. Joy blew out a breath containing a trace of a laugh.

Hope's jaw dropped. "You—you think this is funny?"

"I'm sorry, but I have to say that I do. Don't you hear yourself, Hope? All your concerns aren't about yourself. They're about him. And isn't that the definition of love? Unselfish loyalty and care for another person? The fact that you're worried about all these things shows your love for Jonas and for Emma."

"I suppose I'd never really thought about it like that before." A warmth filled Hope's chest and she knew her love was real. Would she be this worried about Jonas if she didn't love him? And would he have invited her to Kentucky—knowing he could hurt his daughter if she didn't stay—if he didn't love her?

"And another thing I noticed. You're filled with fear over things that *could* happen. Maybe those will happen, and maybe they won't. And even if they don't, don't you believe that God will be there with you, giving you strength and wisdom? He's the one who brought Jonas into your life, isn't He?"

"*Ja,* I suppose so."

"There you go, Hope. You have a good man. Now it's all up to you."

Hope chuckled. "Joy, you surprise me. I've never known you to be so wise before." After all the worries, Joy's words were like a balm to her heart.

Joy chuckled. "I'm not sure whether that's a compliment or not! But what I do know is that working in the fabric shop with Elizabeth Bieler has made a difference in my life. She's been such a good mentor to me, and people come in all the time asking for advice. I can't help but pick up a bit of that wisdom."

"*Ja,* well, I'm not sure what to think about all of this. Everything you've said makes sense, but that doesn't mean those fears are gone." Hope sighed. "I can't help but think that things were easier in Ohio. My garden never asked for my heart. I couldn't hurt my garden's feelings. Life was so much easier when my closest companions were leafy green vegetables."

"Easier, but not better, right?"

"You know, three months ago I would have said things were both easier and better with my garden in Ohio, but now better means life with Jonas and Emma."

"Hope, I think you answered your own question. Go to them."

"What do you mean?"

"Didn't you say that Ruth Ann was going back to visit her other children? I'm sure the van isn't full. Pitch in some money for the driver and ask her if you can ride along."

"But Ruth Ann is supposed to be leaving tomorrow."

Joy winked. "Then I suppose you should hurry."

⁀◯

Hope opened the door to Me, Myself, and Pie and scanned the room. Lovina was sitting at the table next to Faith looking over the new spring menu. Hope rushed up to them. "Do you think I can borrow your bike?"

"*Ja*, I don't see why not."

"*Danke.*"

Hope rushed to the covered patio where the bike was kept, and she wasted no time. It only took five minutes to get to Ruth Ann's house, and she parked the bike, hurrying up to the front door.

She knocked twice, but no one answered. Hope's shoulders stooped. Had they left a day early? Was she too late?

She turned and slowly trudged down the sidewalk. She exited the front gate and placed her hands on the handlebars, feeling the tears come.

"Hope!" A voice called out to her. Hope turned and looked behind her. Ruth Ann approached with a large bag of oranges in her arms.

"Oh." Relief rushed out with her words. "I thought you'd left."

"*Ne.* Just had to get some oranges. I promised my son I'd bring some from Pinecraft. Do you need something? Did you need me to deliver something to Emma…or Jonas?"

There was compassion in Ruth Ann's face—compassion and concern. Was Ruth Ann second-guessing the words Hope had overheard?

Hope placed a hand over her heart. "How about me? Do you think you can deliver me?"

"You?" Ruth Ann readjusted her bag. The light in her eyes faded slightly. "I was planning to use that extra seat for some things I wanted to take to family. I'm sorry, Hope, I just don't have room."

Hope's jaw dropped. She didn't know what to say, what to do.

"I hope you have a *wunderbar* trip," she finally managed to say before getting back on Lovina's bike and riding away.

Chapter Thirty-Four

When you talk you only repeat what you already
know, but if you listen, you may learn something.

AMISH PROVERB

ᔍ

It had been hard for Hope getting used to going to a church
when she'd first moved to Pinecraft. It was one of the few places
in the country where the Amish had a church building instead
of holding services in people's homes. Long wooden benches ran
down two long aisles. The women sat on one side, the men the
other. The youngsters sat in the front and the older church members sat in the back. That, at least, was the same. Well, there was
one slight difference, the older Amish who had trouble hearing,
also sat in the front. Sometimes, depending on how close it was
to the height of the season, there were sometimes more older ones
than younger ones up front.

Hope greeted some of the ladies, answering their questions
about her new job in Walnut Creek.

"You'll be missed by the community," Vera said. "You did so
much work over the past few months."

"Work?" Hope forced a chuckle. "I was thankful when I got to
pull a weed once in a while. There were so many children coming

around in and out of school. And then there are all the retired farmers too. I'm sure they will do fine without me." A sad smile slipped over her lips. "It's nice to see those farmers spending time in the dirt, since they gave so much of their life to it."

"I bet it was hard for a time though, having to share," Vera said. "I'm sure you never thought it would end up like this when you started."

"No, I never imagined this. But the truth is I'm glad about it now." A lump filled her throat as she realized the truth in her words. "I didn't realize what I wanted all along."

The woman's eyes darted to the side as another friend stepped into the church house. "I'll let you go. I'm going to find my seat now."

Hope moved toward her normal bench, next to her mother and sisters. But as she approached, she stopped short. Pain shot from her heart into her chest when she realized that she'd be sitting alone today. Emma had been sitting with her for the last few months, but now she was gone. Hope pressed her hands to her chest, willing the ache to leave. She bit her lower lip and urged the tears not to come, but it did no good. "I—I'm going to use the restroom," she mumbled to her mem.

She turned and hurried to the back of the room where the bathroom was, but not before she caught Ruth Ann's gaze. The woman's brows were furrowed, and she wore a puzzled expression. Hope quickly glanced away and told herself not to be angry at the woman. A sister had every right to make sure her brother was making the right choice.

She quickened her pace and hurried to the bathroom. She'd barely made it into the bathroom stall before the tears came. If she was making the right choice for Jonas, then why did it hurt so bad? Worries again pressed down on her shoulders. Would he write her when he got back to Guthrie? Or would his attention turn to some of the other women there?

I wish I had an answer...

She wiped her eyes the best she could and then returned to the bench, keeping her head down. Her sisters had saved her spot, and she picked up the hymn book and the fan and placed them on her lap. The service started, and Hope smiled softly at the first song. She could still remember being Emma's age—just a child—and singing these words. Since the song was sung so slowly and the syllables drawn out, and all the words in German, she hadn't understood the words until she was a teenager, but it seemed with each passing year the words meant more and more.

> To be like Christ we love one another,
> through everything, here on this earth.
> We love one another,
> not just with words but in deeds...
> If we have of this world's goods
> (no matter how much or how little)
> and see that our brother has a need,
> but do not share with him
> what we have freely received –
> how can we say that we would be ready
> to give our lives for him if necessary?
> The one who is not faithful
> in the smallest thing,
> and who still seeks his own good
> which his heart desires –
> how can he be trusted
> with a charge over heavenly things?
> Let us keep our eyes on love!

As a gardener she understood what tending the small things was all about. If it weren't for the seeds there would be no garden.

Even though many could be blown away with a quick breath, they held so much promise. After the silent prayer one of the ministers strode to the front.

"Today I'm going to talk to you about a Scripture I've written on a notecard and kept in my pocket for many months. It's from the first book of Corinthians, chapter thirteen: 'And now abideth faith, hope, charity, these three; but the greatest of these *is* charity.'

"Christian brethren who read God's Word know there are three principles that can't be denied: faith, hope, and charity, which is love. These are things to pray for. These are things to offer thanksgiving for. And where do these things abide? Not only on earth, but in heaven.

"If a man lives rightly, then he fixes his hopes of reward on the other world—for the world beyond. We also do good with our earthly treasures, knowing there is nothing is this life worth clinging to for the sake of our souls. The more we fix our hope on the reward of heaven, the more free we are to do good with our earthly treasure. Because of faith in God, we have hope for our eternity. We have something to look forward to, but we should not forget the third gift, which is love.

"There is worldly love and there is appetite for pleasure. This is not the love I'm speaking of. I'm talking about love in a community, in a home, and in a marriage. For some, even when our faith is strong, and our hope is in heaven, we forget that we must love. We forget that love, too, requires faith and hope. As humans there are many things that keep us from loving completely. Fear is one of those things. Fear that the conditions won't be perfect to love. Fear that we cannot love enough. Fear that if we love completely it won't be returned."

Hope sucked in a breath at those words. *God, are You trying to tell me something?*

"That makes me think of a story that my grandmother told me. She told me that when she was a child she knew a woman who grew a type of flower that had every color of the rainbow. The colors were stitched together, almost like an Amish quilt, so perfectly were they designed. The woman loved her patch of flowers and everyone in the community would drive their buggies slowly by. At the end of the season she would collect the seeds and save them for the next year, but as the woman got older the seeds became more precious to her and she tried to protect them.

"When other neighbors asked if they could have some of the seeds, the woman rejected their request. What if her neighbors didn't care for the precious seeds correctly? What if they weren't tended well? Then there was the news that she heard in town one day. Some claimed that it would be a year of drought and that water would be hard to come by. So fearful that her plants would die in the drought the woman decided not to plant her seeds that year. The next year there were warnings of more storms than normal, and so the woman again refused to plant the seeds. Instead, she kept them in a small jar with a lid. And every so often she would take them out and look at them, remembering the promise of their beauty.

"Well, one day the woman was ill, and without knowing it she knocked the jar off the shelf and scattered the seeds to the ground. Since the woman could not tend to her house, a young neighbor girl came by to cook and clean. Not knowing what the seeds were, the young woman swept them up and tossed them into the barrel where the woman burned her trash. It wasn't until the woman was back on her feet again when she discovered the empty jar and knew what had happened. By then the trash had been burned and the seeds with it.

"The woman was heartbroken. She got on her hands and knees

and searched every crevice in her home, hoping the broom had somehow missed a few of the tiny seeds. To her delight it had, and three tiny seeds were discovered. The woman rejoiced, but fear once again sidled up to her and became her companion. She could plant the three seeds, but she needed to make sure the conditions were perfect.

"So she hid the seeds in a very special place. She waited one year, and then two. On the third year she awoke to a beautiful spring morning and decided that it was the perfect time to plant. She grasped them in her hands, but before she could make it to the garden the old woman collapsed from a heart attack. The last three seeds were never planted, and before that the seeds were never shared. Fear had caused the woman to try to protect the seeds, but in the end, keeping them to herself made them all become lost.

"Now I am certain that there were never really any seeds that grew flowers in every color of the rainbow, but even as a young child I understood my grandmother's point. Love that is kept hidden because of fear is love that dies. Only when we give love away can it grow and spread. Love requires releasing our grasp. When God's Word tells us to love our neighbor it doesn't say, 'under the right conditions' or 'only if you are certain your love will be returned.'

"Just like we have no part in making flower or garden seeds grow, we can't force love to grow either. Instead, we have to trust that both life and love are in God's hands. We have to trust that if we have faith and hope there will be a harvest."

Beside Hope Lovina's fan began to move in a slow arcing motion, and it was only then that Hope remembered where she was. She'd been so wrapped up in the speaker's words that her mind had taken her to another place. It had taken her to her garden, but in her mind's eye it wasn't the plants or the peace or the quiet that she sought out, but rather a memory of Jonas and Emma the last time she'd seen them there.

Even last night she prayed for an answer. She prayed that God would make His way known to her. It would take faith to give her heart completely to Jonas. But if she didn't she'd end up an old woman with a hard heart after putting up so many walls of protection.

It was safer hiding. It was safer keeping to herself. But it seemed this year God was prying that shell of protection away. Her goal for the year had been to find a simple job up north, but it seemed like God had different plans...better plans?

The tears came then, and her shoulders trembled. From the corner of her eye she saw Mem's head turn, but Hope continued looking straight ahead.

She'd never been one to cry easily, and she didn't understand why she'd been doing so much of it over the past week. Actually, she did know. Whether she wanted to admit it or not Jonas and Emma had wormed their ways into her heart. They'd found the cracks in her defenses, and they'd broken through. And God...He'd done the same. He hadn't given her what she wanted. God had given her what she *needed*. She didn't need a quiet garden. She didn't need to maintain those walls that she'd so carefully built around her heart. She needed Jonas and Emma. And she needed God.

The speaker shared more about how his grandmother influenced him, and he urged the older generation to spend time investing in the lives of their grandchildren. But as the minister scanned the crowd and paused thoughtfully, dramatically, Hope knew the words to come next would have special meaning.

"When we hide love inside us, protecting ourselves from other people, then we're no doubt hiding it from God too. Why are you holding back the love that was first given to you by God? Your heart is safe with Him. He will not abuse it. He has a better way. He is the Lord of the soil, water, wind, rain, and storms. And even if the hardship does come, He will see you through to the other side.

"A scripture I was reading this morning pricked my heart as I prepared in the back. And while I listened to this congregation lifting their voices in song I knew the words God was asking me to speak. They are words of faith, words of hope, and words of trust. The scripture is from Psalm 62: "Trust in him at all times; ye people, pour out your heart before him: God is a refuge for us.""

Listening to the speaker's words, a new reality hit Hope. *I haven't just been keeping others out. I've been keeping God out too.*

She'd spent all that time in her parents' garden growing up, enjoying God's creation and the world He created, but she had never let Him in—not really. And so He'd pushed Himself into the equation.

God had given her the opposite of what she asked for. She'd wanted quiet, and He'd given community. She'd wanted solitude, and He'd given her a chance to love and be loved. And even though community, and love of a man and a girl were things she needed, God knew that she needed Him even more.

God knew that she could not manage the responsibility of community, of a husband, and of a daughter without Him. God was there and she didn't have to try to face it all alone. Never alone.

᧬

The service ended, and Hope didn't turn to make eye contact with Lovina. She had no doubt there would be an "I hope you were listening to that" look in her sister's eyes.

Instead, she turned to Mem. "I'm going to help in the kitchen." Mem's eyebrows lifted slightly but she said nothing. The kitchen was usually the last place Hope liked to spend time, but today she needed the chatter to get her mind off her aching heart.

She rose and hurried back. She couldn't think of Jonas now. She couldn't think of Emma. Not yet. Hope was certain that if she did—if she really thought about how she'd hidden her seeds of love and refused to plant them—then she'd turn into a blubbering mess.

After washing her hands, Hope moved to the counter where fresh, homemade bread had been laid out, ready to be sliced. Hope took the knife and began to cut—maybe a little too hard and too uneven—for before she even got through a half a loaf an older woman placed a hand on her arm.

"Why don't you let me do that?" She offered a half-smile. "If you could open those jars of beets and pickles I'd be so grateful." She lifted her age-spotted hand and flexed her fingers. "I just don't have the grip I used to."

"*Ja*, of course."

Hope moved to the jars and quickly opened them. Then she set the lids to the side and placed a fork in each.

"Hope?"

The soft voice surprised her, and Hope turned. Ruth Ann stood there. Her face was blotchy and her eyes were red.

Hope hurried to her. "Ruth Ann, are you all right?"

"I—I'm fine, but what I've done isn't. Can I talk to you? Do you have a minute?"

"*Ja*, of course." Hope rinsed off her hands in the sink and then dried them on a dishtowel. She turned and followed Ruth Ann out.

Ruth Ann walked to the side of the church's shed, paused,

and then turned to face Hope. Hope swallowed hard. She'd been in that shed buying eggs long enough to know what was inside. Those who had chickens brought eggs for sale. Those who needed eggs opened the shed, took what they needed, and left their money in an ice cream bucket left solely for that purpose. Also kept in there were plain pine coffins. They were brought down from the north in case they were needed, and knowing that brought the story the minister just told to mind. *Don't die without risking love, without being willing to share your heart.*

"Hope, I've done you a disservice. I don't know if you know this, but I'm the one who first gave Jonas the idea about asking you to let the schoolchildren take part in the garden. I got the idea after seeing you with Emma. I could tell right away that the girl had taken a liking to you."

"Thank you for telling me." Hope crossed her arms over her chest. From the look on Ruth Ann's face the woman wanted to say more. Hope couldn't guess what that could be. So she just waited.

"At first I was pleased that you and Jonas seemed to get along so well. But then I started to get worried."

"Worried?"

"He seemed so smitten with you, so quickly. And then I saw how Emma started viewing you as her mother figure. I suppose there was a twinge of jealousy the first time she stopped sitting by me in the church service, instead going to sit with you. But what bothered me the most was how much Jonas was drawn to you. You're so different from Sarah, and I worried that he was moving too fast. I tried to talk to him, but he didn't listen."

"*Ja*, I know. I heard."

"You heard?"

"I was bringing Jonas pic, and I heard."

Ruth Ann reached out and touched her arm again. "You heard?"

Hope lowered her gaze. She didn't need to answer. The tears that filled her eyes answered for her.

"*Ach*, I'm so sorry, Hope. Do you forgive me?"

"Yes. I understood, and I started asking myself the same questions. Would I be the right mother for Emma. Would I be the right wife for Jonas—"

"Oh, I'm ashamed of myself for even putting those thoughts in your head. Is that why you decided not to go live with my sister? Why you decided to stay here instead of being close to Jonas?" She softly slapped her forehead with her palm. "It is, isn't it?"

Hope shrugged. "I told him we could write letters. I thought maybe we *should* take things slower, and…"

"But don't you think that message was for you, Hope?" Ruth Ann turned and pointed to the church house. "I mean, the whole time it was as if the minister was speaking to you and asking you to open your heart…and speaking to me, chiding me for having doubts."

"I had that feeling too. I've prayed for an answer…"

Ruth Ann's eyebrows lifted. "You can't get an answer clearer than that."

"But Jonas is gone. And Emma too. I told my cousin that I could come and help with her garden."

"Hope, this is love. Your cousin will understand. And what's the point of writing letters when you know you have to be together?" Ruth Ann grabbed both of Hope's arms.

Ruth Ann looked to the side, and Hope could tell she was thinking.

"It'll be fine, Ruth Ann. Maybe I will write my cousin and tell her that I can't come. Then I can save some money…"

Ruth Ann's head popped up. She jutted out her chin. "Tomorrow. We can leave tomorrow. I'll make space for you. It's just a short trip for me so I can come back for Hannah...but Hope, you can stay."

"Can you give me an hour to think about it?"

Ruth Ann tilted her head. "Thirty minutes. No more."

Hope nodded, and she headed to the one place she knew she could think well...to her garden.

Chapter Thirty-Five

It takes both rain and sunshine to make the garden grow.
AMISH PROVERB

⟨✦⟩

H ope walked between the long, raised beds. She smiled seeing the lettuce and the peas almost ready for the harvest to
come. She'd nearly gotten to the end of the aisle when she stopped
short. There, at the corner where two boards met, sat a little box.
Hope's mouth opened and then a hand covered it. She recognized
it immediately. It was Emma's keepsake box. Had it been sitting
there all through the night? She knew it had. She also knew that
it wasn't there by accident. Emma had left it for her. Emotion
swelled in her chest.

She rushed over to the box and sank down onto the grass, not
caring if dirt or grass stained her skirt. She opened it up. The first
thing she spotted was a white envelope. Her name was written on
the front. It was from Jonas. Hope lifted the envelope and placed
it to her chest. He'd been part of this too.

Under the envelope there was a collections of things, different
from what Hope had seen in there before. There was an empty
seed packet from the first seeds they'd planted together. There was

the recipe for Peanut Better Cookies. There was a drawing of the garden that Emma had made in art class. Hope had no idea that the young girl had been saving those things. She'd been collecting memories. Emma had been trying to fill the hole her mother had left behind, and for a time Hope had filled that place.

"Why didn't I go with them?"

You needed to hear today's story. You needed to be ready to plant your love deep.

The words came like a whisper to her soul, and she remembered a saying that she'd read on a wooden sign in Yoder's store.

"From deepest roots tallest branches grow," she whispered. If she was going to Kentucky she needed to commit with her full heart. She needed to plant all her seeds of love in those two people and never look back. No doubt her staying back had already caused them to question, and if she were to go again, Hope knew she could never leave.

As she returned the seed packet to the box, three small seeds rolled out. It was then Hope had her answer. She wasn't going to hide those seeds and tuck them away. She knew the exact spot where they needed to go. She opened Jonas's letter, hoping that it confirmed her decision.

Dear Hope,

You asked that we write letters. You want to make sure that we know each other well enough before marriage. I understand. It has only been four months since I saw you sitting at the boat ramp of Phillippi Creek cradling Emma in your arms. I never expected to find love again—not like this. And I never expected it to happen so soon. This is my first letter, and I'll write a hundred more if that's what's needed to have you in my life.

As you're reading this I'm somewhere on the highway between here and Kentucky. On the drive down Emma and I played the alphabet game more times than I could count, so if I were to guess we might be doing the same at this moment. Of course, even if I'm pointing out letters on the Interstate and making polite conversation with our driver, my thoughts are probably on you. Are you in the garden or in the kitchen cooking up recipes from 1942?

I like to picture you both places, but lately I've been trying to picture you at my farm in Kentucky. I think you'll like it there. It's a rural area with rolling hills, tall trees, and farms that dot the countryside, and I know I've told you this before, but I have a large garden plot right by the road. One of the first things I'm going to do when I return home is prepare it for planting, and I'll be thinking of you as I do.

The minutes are ticking by, and I know I should be getting some sleep. I keep stopping to read what I've written, and I realize that it's not very good. As a teacher I'd give myself a C, and I'd write at the top "Get to the point." So if there is a point to this letter (and there is) I want to make sure I tell you this: Hope, I know in my heart that I love you, I want to marry you someday, and I want you to be my daughter's mother.

Those are three things, and for a while I thought they conflicted with one another. Even my sister talked to me and made sure I didn't want to marry you just because of Emma. Everyone has seen how well you two get along. She wanted me to be certain that I loved you just as much for myself too. And I do.

The other day I was praying about this. I asked God, "Did You give me Hope for myself? Or did You give me Hope for Emma?" I shouldn't have been surprised by His answer, but I was. I didn't hear a voice, but I felt it in my spirit, and it was just one word: "Yes."

I don't have to be guilty for loving you and wanting you to be my future wife, and I don't have to wonder if my desire is simply for a mother to Emma. God has answered both prayers in one person. He's answered both prayers in you. That might be a lot to share in my first letter, but I don't want you to worry about where you stand. I will come back to Pinecraft as often as I can to see you. And I'd love you to come to Kentucky any time. You'll always have a place.

And know that when you finally get to Kentucky I'll turn the garden plot all over to you, as well as my heart. It's yours, Hope.

With you in my thoughts,
Jonas

Hope pressed the letter to her chest, and it was only as she felt a drop of wetness on her arm that she realized she was crying. How could one letter start so simply and end up so profound? How could all the worries, concerns, and questions she'd bottled up inside be answered in a few paragraphs? Jonas loved her for his daughter. Jonas loved her for himself. She'd hoped for that, but feared it wasn't the case. Now she had hope in the future too. She didn't have to worry or question. If she were to grade this letter she would have given him an A.

Hope also knew what she had to do.

⌒

Hope pulled her suitcase out from under her bed. She'd bought it when her family moved to Pinecraft, but she hadn't used it since. She'd planned on using it when she traveled up to Ohio to work as a *maud*, but that wouldn't be the case. Instead, she was packing for the future she hoped awaited—one she hoped she hadn't hindered due to her worries and fears.

She packed both her work and church dresses and her church shoes, and she placed her covering in the hat box. It was an old Schwann's ice cream bucket that Faith had covered with contact paper and decorated for her birthday. Looking at her bookshelf, Hope picked up the notebook she'd started in January. There were only a few lines written on the first page.

Find a job up north and a garden to tend.

Write to cousins and friends and inquire about work as a maud *and gardener.*

Hope pulled a pen from her desk drawer and sat. She skipped a few lines and then started again. Today she was starting a new list, and it had nothing to do with finding a job up north. Instead, she had a few ideas of what else she could find, and she wrote them down.

Find hope instead of fear.

Find love instead of loneliness.

Find community instead of solitude.

Find a man I want to spend my life with. (He's in Kentucky.)

Find a young girl to call daughter. (She's there too.)

Find a garden to tend in a home where I wish to spend the rest of my life. (It's at his place.)

Write my cousin and tell her I'm not coming. Also remind her not to give up on the dreams and gifts that God placed deep inside her heart.

Find ways to thank God every day for not giving us what we want, but rather giving us what we need.

Hope put the pen back in the drawer, and she tucked her notebook and her Bible in with her clothes. She was excited to share her story with Emma one day. Share about how she'd planned and prayed only to discover that her plans were pushed aside for something greater.

God had given her more than she ever hoped and dreamed in those two, and she wanted them to know that. She just hoped they'd forgive her and allow her into their hearts once again.

They'd been hurt so much already, and it caused her heart to ache that she'd hurt them again. But still she continued packing because she had hope. And hope was something that she was clinging to.

Chapter Thirty-Six

A friend is one who knows all about you and still loves you.

AMISH PROVERB

⤳

Spring came to Kentucky in quiet ways. It seemed strange to Jonas that they'd been basking in the sun for months in Florida, but here on his farm the last patches of snow had only recently surrendered to the warm rays. Emma had been quiet this morning, and he was thankful for the new litter of pups to distract her. Even now she romped with the three of them in the treed area just behind the house, last year's leaves clinging to her skirt.

Jonas stepped outside, standing on the top step of the back porch. One of the pups dug his teeth into the hem of Emma's dress and clung on. She struggled forward, her laughter filling the area. Hearing it caused Jonas to smile, but it did nothing to push away the ache in his heart. He was home. It was time for spring planting—his favorite time of the year—but he'd never felt so lonely.

After Sarah had died in January he'd spent a long winter mourning her, and by spring he'd been ready for sunshine, fresh air, seeds of promise, and tiny sprouts of life. But this time—losing

Hope—was different. He didn't want to plant alone, especially not after doing so with her by his side.

He closed his eyes, remembering her anxiety about the children digging in her soil, but also her joy over each day's growth. She had been the sunshine in Pinecraft—that was evident now. And even though the sun had come to Kentucky it seemed like nothing more than gloom without her here.

Footsteps sounded, and Jonas's eyes fluttered open. He nearly jumped to see his brother-in-law Matthew, and not Emma, standing there.

"It's barely eight. Napping already?"

"Not napping. Just thinking."

Matthew nodded. "Not thinking of planting, I guess?"

"*Ne.*"

"Or the garden."

"Not really."

"From the look on your face I'd say you were thinking about a woman."

Jonas swallowed hard. He wasn't ready to talk about Hope—about his missing her—and he scurried for an excuse. "That might be because it would have been Sarah's birthday in a few weeks. Maybe—"

Matthew held up a hand, interrupting Jonas's words. "Or maybe it has something to do with that pretty woman out front, digging through your garden."

"My garden?" Jonas jumped to his feet. "There's a woman in my garden?"

His heart pounded, but he told himself not to get his hopes up. He had no reason to believe Hope would be here. He'd last seen her standing in front of Me, Myself, and Pie three days ago when they'd pulled out. But from the twinkle in Matthew's eyes he still had to hope.

"It's probably just a neighbor woman who doesn't know we're home and is trying to help us out," Jonas said.

Matthew jutted out his chin. "It's no neighbor lady—at least none I've met. She's too pretty for me to miss otherwise, with hair that's both red and gold—like nothing I've ever seen."

"She calls it strawberry blonde…" Jonas quickened his steps toward the side of the house and then paused. As much as he wanted to run to Hope, to ask her what she was doing here, he'd never be forgiven if he did it alone.

Jonas hurried back to where Emma had been playing with the puppies. He didn't see her, but he heard her voice coming from the barn.

He bolted in the door and paused, letting his eyes adjust to the light. Emma was sitting down next to the mother dog and the pups, watching them eat.

Seeing him rush in, her eyes widened, and then she glanced around as if making sure she wasn't doing anything wrong.

"Emma, I need you to come with me."

"But the puppies…" She pointed. "I think they're almost done."

"You can come back to this. There's something…someone you need to see."

"Someone?" Instead of excitement, Emma's brows furrowed, causing Jonas to second-guess himself. What if it wasn't Hope after all? What if it was someone else—someone new to their community? His stomach sank, and more than anything he didn't want to break his daughter's heart.

"Well, Uncle Matthew said there's someone in the garden. We should go and see who it is. Then, while we're there, we can look around and make some plans for planting a garden."

Instead of the smiles he'd seen in Pinecraft, Emma's lower lip rose into a pout. She stood, but her shoulders sagged. And it seemed to take all her strength to slip her smaller hand into his larger one.

They walked together, and Jonas couldn't help but walk faster than normal. Thankfully, Emma kept up without asking any questions. She stared into the unplowed field with a far-off look, and he wondered if she was thinking of Hope and their garden back in Pinecraft. He had no doubt she was.

They stepped out of the barn and walked along the side of the house. Matthew was nowhere in sight, and Jonas guessed he'd gone inside to pour himself a cup of coffee and sit in the front room near the window to get a better view of the garden. Jonas knew his brother-in-law well.

They rounded the front of the house. In the garden there was one lone figure, bent down, sitting on her haunches. Her white *kapp* contrasted with the dark brown of the soil. He couldn't see her face or the color of her hair from this angle, but his heart leapt at the color of her dress. It was coral, a color that wasn't common around these parts, but a color he'd seen often in Pinecraft.

Jonas paused and then swept down and picked up Emma. She was heavier than he remembered—when was the last time he carried her like this? It had been too long, for Emma looked at him with wide-eyed surprise.

Jonas pointed to the garden. "Emma, look!"

Emma's eyes widened. Her small lips opened with a gasp. She stretched her arms in the direction in the garden, and her legs began moving as if she was already running. Jonas chuckled and then put her down. Emma ran full speed to the garden, and Jonas jogged along, not too far behind.

"Hope. Hope. Hope!" Emma's voice filled the air.

Hope stood and turned. She placed a hand on her *kapp* and smiled. Her eyes moved to Emma first and her smile grew. Then she looked to him, and uncertainty filled her gaze.

Jonas's steps slowed, and he gave the two of them space. He

watched as Hope bent down and opened her arms up to Emma. The small girl plowed into Hope's arms, nearly bowling her over.

Hope's laughter rang out. Emma was talking, but he couldn't make out her words. Then, with slow steps, he approached.

"My, my. That wasn't what I expected to find in my garden today."

"It's not really what I expected either." Hope stood and held up her hand. In it was a rotting carrot. "Jonas Sutter, you left and went to Pinecraft and you still had root vegetables in the ground. The least you could have done was alerted your neighbors. They could have dug them out instead of letting them go to waste."

"*Ja*, you're right. It was a split-second decision, you see. Ruth Ann needed my help in Pinecraft, and Emma and I needed some sunshine, but you're right. It's such a waste, but I'm not sure what I can do about it now."

"I'll tell you what you should do." Hope's voice softened. "You should get a gardener—someone who will dedicate her time to this space." She swept her arm toward the field beyond the garden. "This is too much for you to tend, especially when you have all that land to cultivate."

Jonas smiled, ready to play along. He shook his head and let out a heavy sigh. "I know. I tried, but there is really only one gardener who I trust with this space, but she told me plainly that she's not ready to make the move."

"First, she was a fool for saying that. Second, she changed her mind." Hope took a step forward and reached for his hand. "And that's why she caught a ride this direction and urged the driver to drive through the night. She wants to apologize."

"So is that a yes, Hope—"

"It's two yeses. First, the garden."

"And second?" He pulled her hand up and placed it on his heart.

"And second, I do want to be part of your family forever."

A small giggle erupted, and Jonas remembered then that they were not alone. Emma stood right behind him. Hearing the news, she grabbed his leg and then peeked around his side, as if suddenly shy.

Hope leaned forward and placed her elbows on her knees. Her face was even with Emma's. "That is, if you do want me as part of your family, Emma."

The girl's eyes grew wide. Then she lifted her arms up and wrapped them around Hope's neck. "Yes, Hope, yes!"

Tears came to Jonas's eyes, overflowing and unexpected. He quickly wiped them away, but not before Hope noticed them. Hope lifted Emma and placed her on her hip. Emma's long legs hung below Hope's knees, but he could tell from the grin on his daughter's face that she liked the idea of having a mother.

Hope put Emma back down and stepped closer to him.

"Are you okay?" Hope asked him. "I didn't mean to surprise you…I mean, I did, but I didn't think that it would be hard for you…for me to be here, that is."

"Oh, Hope." He sighed. "That's not it at all. These are happy tears. God has given me more than I hoped for. I never thought I'd have this…you…*us* like this."

"I'm glad they are happy tears, but I want you to know that sad ones are okay too." She looked down at the soil. "I can't think of anything more beautiful than tears watering a garden." She sighed. "Sometimes the most beautiful things come after the tears."

"I'd agree with that."

"So do you think we should wait for November for a wedding? It's the typical Amish way," she asked.

"I don't know about you, but I can't wait that long, Hope. How about next month? It'll be beautiful in Pinecraft, in your garden."

"It's not my garden any more. It's the school garden and the community's garden too. But I do think it'll be a beautiful place for a wedding. And when we return here—come home—I'd like to consider inviting some of the local children to garden with me." She turned to Emma. "Would you like that?"

Emma nodded, still clinging to Hope's skirt. "Ja." Then her smile brightened. "Want to see the puppies?" Emma asked next, as if the decisions that had just been made in the last two minutes were the most natural thing ever. In a way they were.

God had given Jonas a reason to hope again, and he'd done that through a beautiful woman by the same name. He'd also brought joy to his little girl, something he wanted more than anything.

They walked to the barn in one line. Hope held his hand on her right, and Emma's hand on her left. As they walked he noticed violets poking up near the front door steps and a cardinal hopping around on the dewy front lawn looking for worms. Together they walked under a dogwood tree toward the barn. Jonas allowed himself to look into the future and imagine the moments to come: newly washed clothes on the clothes line, two faces—and later more—looking through the eight-paned windows as he drove this buggy down the lane. He imagined Hope and Emma barefoot in the garden, leading the way for other barefoot children.

When Sarah was struggling to cling to life Jonas had found himself afraid to think of the future without her. And after her death he found himself looking back—thinking of all he'd had and lost. But Hope had come into his life, not only filling up his days, but giving him something to look *forward* to.

That was what hope was about, wasn't it? A promise of what was to come, and with these two by his side Jonas couldn't imagine anything more promising than that.

Epilogue

༄

Anna Miller knew what was in the small package. It had to be the Victory Journal. What else would Hope send Priority mail?

She opened the box. A letter sat on top. Before she even glanced at the journal, Anna excitedly tore open the letter from her daughter. Hope had left in such a hurry, and Anna wanted to know how she was doing. The fact that it had been a week, and Hope hadn't come back, proved that Hope had been welcomed by Jonas. And maybe this letter would include information about a wedding. Anna had warmed up to that idea. Jonas was a good man, even though he'd been married before. And Hope was happy…that was what mattered most.

Dear Mem,

I know you've been asking for a chance to look at the Victory Journal. I've sent it back and I ask you to return it for me. I've written to Janet to tell her again how much her mother's story influenced mine. I'm changed from reading it. I've discovered elements of myself I never realized. I've learned what it means to love.

But before you give it back, I've marked a page that I want you

to especially take note of. Jonas, Emma, and I plan to return in July.
When you see the page you'll understand.

Love,
Hope

Anna opened the journal to the page marked by a white ribbon. It was a recipe. She was confused until she saw what type of recipe. She closed the journal and hurried to the backyard where her husband sat. He had work to do. He had a community garden to ready for a most special event.

Wedding Cake

4½ cups (1 pound) sifted cake flour

1 tsp. baking powder

½ tsp. cloves

½ tsp. cinnamon

½ tsp. mace

1 pound shortening

1 pound brown sugar

10 eggs, well beaten

½ pound candied cherries, cut into halves

½ pound candied pineapple, diced

1 pound dates, seeded and sliced

1 pound raisins

1 pound currants

½ pound citron, thinly sliced

½ pound candied orange and lemon peel, sliced

½ pound nut meats, chopped

1 cup honey

1 cup molasses

½ cup cider

Sift flour, baking powder, and spices together 3 times. Cream shortening and sugar until fluffy. Add eggs, fruit, nuts, honey, molasses, and cider. Add flour in small amounts, mixing well after each addition. Turn into cake pans which have been greased, lined with heavy paper, and again greased. Bake in a very slow oven (250°). For large loaves, bake in 8x4x3 inch pans about 4 hours. For small loaves, bake in 6x3x2½-inch pans about 2½ to 3 hours. For 8½-inch tube pan, bake 4 to 5 hours. Test with toothpick or cake tester before removing from oven. Makes 10 pounds fruit cake. Spread Ornamental Icing on top and sides of cake and decorate with simple borders, festoons, and rosettes of Ornamental Icing. For a terraced cake, bake in pans of several sizes and use a pastry tube to decorate.

Ornamental Icing

2 cups powdered sugar
1 cup water
3 egg whites
¼ tsp. cream of tartar
½ tsp. vanilla

Boil sugar and water (without stirring) to 242° or until a small amount dropped from tip of spoon spins a thread. Beat egg whites until stiff but not dry and pour on hot syrup in a thin stream, while beating constantly. Add cream of tartar and vanilla and beat until thick enough to spread. Cover cake smoothly with part of the icing and beat remaining icing until cool and stiff enough to hold shape when forced through pastry tube. When coating on cake has hardened decorate as desired with remaining icing forced through pastry tube. If icing becomes too thick to spread smoothly, add a few drops of hot water.*

* Ruth Berolzheimer, *250 Superb Pies and Pastries* (Culinary Arts Institute, 1940), 41.

Tricia Goyer is a busy wife, mom of ten, and grandmother of two. A *USA Today* bestselling author, Tricia has published over 50 books and has written more than 500 articles. She's well-known for her Big Sky and Seven Brides for Seven Bachelors Amish series. For more information visit Tricia at www.TriciaGoyer.com.

Sherry Gore is the author of *Simply Delicious Amish Cooking* and *Me, Myself and Pie* and is a weekly scribe for the national edition of the Amish newspaper *The Budget*. Sherry's culinary adventures have been seen on NBC Daytime, Today.com, and Mr. Food Test Kitchen. Sherry is a resident of Sarasota, Florida, the vacation paradise of the Plain People. She has three children and is a member of a Beachy Amish Mennonite church.

To learn more about books by Tricia Goyer and Sherry Gore
or to read sample chapters, log on to our website:

www.harvesthousepublishers.com

HARVEST HOUSE PUBLISHERS
EUGENE, OREGON